THE LODGE

MIRANDA RIJKS

INKUBATOR
BOOKS

Published by Inkubator Books

www.inkubatorbooks.com

Copyright © 2023 by Miranda Rijks

ISBN (eBook): 978-1-83756-211-4

ISBN (Paperback): 978-1-83756-212-1

ISBN (Hardback): 978-1-83756-213-8

Miranda Rijks has asserted her right to be identified as the author of this work.

THE LODGE is a work of fiction. People, places, events, and situations are the product of the author's imagination. Any resemblance to actual persons, living or dead is entirely coincidental.

PROLOGUE

The night is surprisingly cold and I shiver, despite wearing a thick sweater. Flickers of excitement course through me. I am a survivor. As Darwin suggested, it is not the strongest of the species that survives, nor the most intelligent. It is the one that is the most adaptable to change. And that is me. I am just like the lions out there in the bush.

The moon is almost full although a few clouds are beginning to hide the awe-inspiring galaxies. They say that the African sky is some of the least light-polluted and most vivid in the world and I have to agree. I stare out into the distance, knowing that it's impossible to see what is lurking between those blades of grass, under the damp branches of the bushes. The dangers.

I turn around and smile. The candlelight is low, and it makes our eyes glisten. I reach under my blanket and wrap my fingers around the cold metal.

The time has come.

A shot rings out, deafeningly loud, reverberating for

miles. I don't feel it at first. Is it shock or is it because I wasn't expecting it? But then, when I try to move, the pain sears through me, making my stomach heave.

Bang.

I fall.

This was meant to be the beginning. The prologue to the greatest ever adventure. But I know now in this longest of seconds that it isn't a prologue at all. It's a finale.

1

ANNA

'You are not going to believe what I've got to tell you!' Joel shouts from the open back door. He'll be doing what he does every evening – shedding his filthy, muck-covered overalls and kicking off his muddy boots.

I roll my eyes. Probably not a fair reaction but my fiancé has a tendency to be over-exuberant and he's likely going to tell me that he's just delivered triplet calves or sewn up the wounds of a rampaging bull. Joel is a vet specialising in large animals, which means he spends most of his time visiting cattle and sheep farms in the south of England, with a highlight being a visit to the equine therapy centre.

He strides into the living room where I'm sitting with my laptop balanced on my knees.

'We're going on a safari!' he says with a big grin. His honey-blond hair stands up on end and his green eyes sparkle. He's wearing a T-shirt and jeans and he has a fleck of mud on his forehead. It's cute.

'What?'

'A safari in South Africa. Can you believe it?'

I frown. We certainly can't afford a holiday as expensive as an African safari, especially as we're meant to be saving up for our wedding. A wedding for which we still haven't set a date.

'It's all expenses paid.'

My laptop wobbles and I catch it just before it tumbles to the floor. Joel takes the laptop, places it on the glass coffee table and grabs my hands, pulling me up to standing. He kisses me hard on the lips.

'Okay, tell me all,' I say, wrapping my arms around him. I've got accustomed to his pre-shower scent of *eau de vache*, as I call it.

'I got head-hunted to go for an interview at a new safari lodge in South Africa. They want me there before it opens to the public. They're doing a kind of trial run and have said I can bring my partner too; in other words, you. This could totally change our lives, Anna.'

I stand stock-still for a moment as I absorb Joel's words. 'You mean we might have to move to South Africa?' I step away from him, shock reverberating through my limbs. This was most certainly not part of my life plan.

'It's a dream come true for me, Anna. If I get the job then we'd be living out there, accommodation thrown in, as well as two flights a year to return home. I can't believe it even might be a possibility.' He runs his fingers through his hair. I bite my lip and stare at the floor, my eyes resting on a big hole Joel has in his left sock.

I don't know what to say. I've known it was Joel's dream to work in the bush, but I assumed it was a pipe dream, a bit like my desire to visit the moon. I've never travelled to Africa and I know absolutely nothing about living on a safari reserve. 'Were you actively looking for the job?' I ask eventually, wondering with dismay whether this is something Joel has been planning behind my back.

'No. That's what's so amazing. I thought I'd stay in the current job for another year or so and then perhaps go freelance. I would never look for a post abroad without discussing it with you, darling.' He strokes the side of my face. 'I know it's a lot to take in, but would you be okay if we at least go and visit? I probably won't be offered the job anyway, but if I am and you hate it there, then obviously I'll say no. It's got to be something that works for both of us.' He looks pained at the possibility.

I push away any thoughts of a future a million miles away from what I have imagined and focus on the fact we're going to be having the trip of a lifetime. 'Of course I'll come with you. I'm not going to say no to a freebie holiday. Will we get to see the big five and have sundowners out in the bush and sleep in a luxury tent?'

'Yes to all of that. It looks absolutely amazing.' He takes his phone out of his jeans pocket and hands it to me.

'*Twivali Safari Reserve and Lodge.*' I read the blurb out aloud. '*Set in ten thousand hectares of unspoilt African bushland, Twivali Private Safari Reserve is home to Africa's Big Five as well as an extraordinary array of other wildlife and birds. The luxurious lodge is small and intimate, catering for just eight guests. Our guides are highly trained and will lead you on an unforgettable wildlife experience.*' I flick through the photos and I have to agree with Joel; it looks absolutely stunning.

'You said they're interviewing you for a job?'

'Yes. They're looking for a vet to assist in the rehabilitation of injured animals.' He pauses whilst we both assess what it means for me. 'You'd have to leave your job, and I don't know if there'd be any work for you out there.' He takes my hand and runs his fingers gently along my palm. 'On the plus side, the salary is huge and all accommodation is thrown in, so we'd be quids in. We could rent this cottage out as well and build up a nice nest egg even without your salary. Perhaps you could write that book you've been talking about.' Joel nudges me.

He really has given this a lot of thought, but it's too much for me to take in. Would I really want to quit work and be wholly reliant on Joel? We're not even married yet. And what about living so far away from my friends and family?

I'm also a scientist but nothing as exciting as what Joel does. I work as a food technician for a massive company, and have spent the last four years specialising in ice-cream. The job has changed over the past couple of years and whereas before I was part of a team developing new as-healthy-as-possible products, last year I was promoted and now I'm much more involved in compliance. It's far from my dream job. Perhaps this could be the catalyst for a change of career for me too. But quite what I'd do stuck out in the middle of nowhere, I don't know. And although I like animals, and when we're married we've talked about getting a dog, wild animals and creepy crawlies in the bush are another story altogether.

Joel is clearly feeling my trepidation. 'I'm getting ahead of myself here.' He throws me a wonky smile, but he's being typically self-deprecating. Of course he'll be offered the job. He's charming, capable, and calm in a crisis.

'When are we meant to be going?'

He looks sheepish. 'In a fortnight?' Joel asks it as a question, which of course it isn't.

'A fortnight!' I exclaim. 'I don't know if I'll be able to get time off work so quickly.'

'Will you try?'

I nod.

'Whatever happens we'll have an amazing time. Perhaps it can be an early honeymoon.'

'I'd like to get married before having a honeymoon,' I murmur, and then I feel a bit guilty because Joel has repeatedly told me that his three-month stay in Botswana as a student on a game reserve were the best three months of his life, and how he'd like nothing more than for me to experience it too. The chances of that happening were, until now, slim. We had decided to save money for our wedding and forgo a honeymoon so that we could save more money to buy a bigger house. Joel's cottage is cute but it has just one and a half bedrooms and a perilously steep staircase; not at all appropriate should we wish to start a family.

Joel and I have been together for a year. We met walking dogs in our local park. I was dog-sitting for my mum and stepdad, who had gone away on holiday. Stupidly, I had let Limonie, their badly behaved lemon beagle, off the lead and she was point-blank refusing to listen to my increasingly desperate calls. Limonie took a liking to a small mutt of indiscriminate breed, and they were tumbling over each other. I was relieved to see the other owner was also struggling to recall his hound.

'Sorry,' he said as he approached me. 'She's not mine and clearly needs to go to puppy school.'

'Limonie isn't mine either.' I felt a bit awkward in his company during those first few minutes because Joel is classically handsome. His hair is a little unruly but he has clear green eyes and a square jaw that is more often than not covered in stubble because he hasn't had time to shave. Unlike many good-looking men, Joel doesn't realise how attractive he is. I certainly thought he was out of my league at that first meeting.

'Beagles are notoriously hard to train,' he said. 'I'm Joel, by the way, and that rascal is Ditto.'

I laughed as I shook his warm hand. 'If he's not yours, then surely you're excused.'

'That's kind of you to say so but I'm a vet and it's kind of embarrassing that I don't have greater control over my charge.'

'You're right, that is unforgivable,' I joked.

When it became obvious that our dogs had no intention of parting company, Joel suggested that we continue our walk together. That walk merged into coffee, which merged into drinks, followed by supper the next evening. Within a week, we had fallen for each other, hard. But I was nervous. It had been a year since the end of my last disastrous relationship, and although Joel was absolutely nothing like my ex, I wanted to be careful. I had no desire to fall for a handsome charmer ever again. But Joel has proven to be different. For starters he is an open book and character-wise totally different to anyone else I have dated. There have been no games in our relationship. He told me he loved me after a month and asked me to marry him after three months. I kept him waiting for six months but I did move into his little cottage on the edge of a Sussex village. It's meant my commute to work has doubled but Joel's hours are so inconsistent that we really needed to live together. That's what we tell each other, anyway. And so far, it's been wonderful.

2

ANNA

I hate flying. I've never had a bad experience but fear is contagious, and I caught it from my mum. Some years ago she did a fearful flying course and we were all so hopeful that my stepdad might get the long-haul holiday he'd been dreaming of for years. Mum agreed to do a short trip as a trial and they settled on a week in Majorca. It should have been fine other than Nick, my stepdad, forgot about the hour change. When the plane started descending a full hour before Mum expected it to, she freaked. And that was despite the Valium. If she could have returned home by boat, she would have done. Honestly, I don't know how Nick got her back. I think it was a mixture of sleeping pills and Valium, but she's sworn she'll never fly again.

I'm lucky with Nick. He brought me up as if I was his own child and I have no doubt that he has been a better father than Dad would have been. Mum and Dad split up when I was three. He was a drinker and he died when I was eleven. I pretend I wasn't scarred by it, but I probably was. But Mum married Nick when I was nine, so he's really the only father I've known. When I was a kid I often called him Dad. Less so these days.

Of course, I've taken flights over the years, going on holiday to the Mediterranean and taking the occasional business trip to New York and Paris. But flying all the way to Durban is a big deal for me. Joel keeps on reminding me that we're going to have the trip of a lifetime and that statistically, flying is the safest mode of travel. But all the rationalising in the world doesn't detract from my emotional response. So here I am at Heathrow airport, a pathetic bag of nerves, and our flight is delayed by two hours. Joel has offered to give me a dose of something which I fear might be horse tranquilliser or something equally dodgy. I've kindly declined and have decided to self-medicate with gin. By the time we actually get on the airplane I am merry. Joel steers me down the long aisle and guides me to our seats, where I settle in the window seat. I'm not sure it's a good idea to be next to the window as I can see one of the wings but I'm feeling sufficiently woozy not to resist.

For the next twelve hours my wonderful fiancé makes sure that I drink lots of water, watch a film that I immediately forget, and sleep, thanks to a sleeping pill. When all the lights are switched on and breakfast is being cleared away, I feel groggy and everything aches from being cramped in my economy seat. I stretch as best I can and glance out of the window. A flicker of excitement spins through me. We're above Africa and the scenery is so different to the UK, even from this height. The earth is red, interspersed with vast fields in an array of pale gold and green with the occasional patches of dark olive trees. And then we're circling over a glittering azure sea and flying lower and lower. Joel squeezes my hand. I grip him so hard as we come in to land, but the pilot does a fine job and we barely bounce as the wheels hit the shimmering tarmac.

'Welcome to South Africa,' Joel says putting his arm around my shoulders and giving me a kiss on the cheek. I feel dirty and tired. It takes a while to get through passport control and more long minutes as we wait for our luggage to arrive. When it finally does, I'm impatient to get outside, to feel the warmth on my sun-starved face. We walk out into the arrivals hall. Joel looks up at the signs but starts steering our trolley in the opposite direction to the car rental sign.

'Where are we going? Aren't we renting a car?' I ask. It hadn't crossed my mind to question Joel how we'll be getting from Durban to the game reserve. Stupidly, I've been so focused on the international flight.

Joel brings the trolley to a standstill and shuffles his feet. He grimaces. 'Um, no. Not exactly.'

'What do you mean?'

'The only way to get to Twivali is via an airplane.'

My stomach clenches.

'What sort of airplane?' I ask, even though I know the answer.

'It's small but you'll be fine, Anna. They do these journeys several times every day. The pilots are experienced and the planes well looked after. No need to worry.'

'Why didn't you tell me this before?' I snap.

'Because I knew the reaction I'd get. You'd refuse to come.'

'You got me here on false pretences!' I exclaim. A couple of people turn to stare at me. I'm furious. I walk beside him in silence. How could he trick me like this? This is the sort of thing my ex might do, not Joel. He knows how terrified I am of flying, and that's in a jumbo jet. The very last thing I would want to do is fly in a small airplane.

'Can't we drive there?' I ask.

'No.'

'Why not? It doesn't matter if it's a long way.'

'Not only would it be a really long drive but the road isn't even tarmacked for a large portion of it. Twivali has organised and paid for everything for us, including our internal flights.' Joel points to a sign. 'We need to go that way.' He pushes the trolley and strides forwards. What am I meant to do? Stand my ground and find a car rental place, get on the next flight home, or follow my fiancé? The first two options will be expensive, requiring money I don't have. Besides, it's dangerous driving in remote parts of Africa, isn't it? I could stay the night at the airport and get on the next flight home but I know if I do that, the relationship with Joel might not last. I really love this man, even if I feel he's duped me. I grit my teeth, clench my fists and stomp after him.

The small lounge we're ushered into after checking in for our internal flight is a million miles away from a typical airport lounge. Dark wood floors are echoed with black ceiling beams stretching the length of the room. Wicker chairs are placed around glass coffee tables and on a large dark wood side table are plates of food underneath glass domes. Billowing green plants in pale straw baskets and a light floral scent add to the tropical feel.

We're the only guests in the lounge. We are helping ourselves to bottles of water and pastries when a woman smartly dressed in a beige belted dress strides towards us.

'Good morning. Your flight is ready now so if you'd like to follow me. You can bring your water and food with you.' She speaks with a strong South African accent, her a's sounding more like eh's. On her lapel is a name badge. She's called Precious. What a delightful name.

My heart sinks as we walk outside into the hot morning. I should be enjoying the bright blue sky and the warmth on my bare skin, but all I see is the small airplane standing on the tarmac in front of us. It's gleaming white, with two propellers and five windows down each side. It's small. Really small. The tiniest aircraft I've ever been in.

'I don't know if I can do it,' I whisper to Joel, coming to a halt.

'You'll be fine,' he says, taking my hand. He turns to Precious. 'My fiancée is a fearful flyer,' Joel says loudly, and I cringe.

'Ah, we have many of those,' she laughs. 'I'll introduce you to your pilot and he can put your minds at rest.'

I force one foot in front of the other until we're standing at the bottom of the steps leading up to the aircraft. The pilot stands at the top of the short flight of stairs, smartly dressed in uniform, his salt and pepper hair neatly combed back. At least he looks mature, so hopefully he'll have lots of experience.

'Hello and welcome!' he says, shaking both of our hands as we climb up. 'You are our only guests this morning so please take a seat wherever you wish.'

'I'm terrified,' I murmur, feeling like an idiot.

'No need.' The pilot laughs and pats the side of the aircraft. 'These planes are some of the most reliable in the world and I've done this trip thousands of times. You'll be quite safe. There might be a few bumps along the way, but that's perfectly normal. I'm not expecting any bad weather.'

Joel has the widest grin on his face and I just wish I could feel some of his excitement. We settle into comfortable cream leather seats and before I know it, the pilot has started up the noisy engine and we're hurtling down the runway. As the plane lifts up into the air, pushing me back into my seat, I squeeze Joel's hand and keep my eyes tightly closed. I concentrate on my breathing, slowly in and slowly out.

'Open your eyes now,' Joel says after what seems like a really long time. 'Look how beautiful the landscape is.'

The flight is bumpy and at times I grab the paper bag wedged into the seat back but I don't use it. The pilot keeps us informed as to where we are and then, after about an hour, we start the descent.

'Just need to warn you guys that we might have to circle for a bit. Looks like there could be giraffe on the runway.'

I peer out of the window and all I can see is bush. And then a dusty track comes into view and just when I think we're going to continue downwards, the pilot pulls the aircraft up again and I let out a yelp.

'I'm going to swing around, so if you look to your left you'll see the giraffe on the runway,' the pilot explains. And sure enough there are two giraffe standing at the far end of a landing strip that is simply a wide path cut out between trees and shrubs.

'We're going to land there?' I mutter, staring in horror at the reddish-brown earth.

'Look at the giraffe! Aren't they stunning?' Joel says, totally ignoring my fear.

'I've radioed ahead,' the pilot announces, 'so the ranger should be here any moment to shoo the giraffe away and to drive you to the lodge.'

My heart is thumping. What if the pilot overshoots the end of the makeshift runway? Or if there's a mechanical problem? There are no emergency services out here in the middle of nowhere. What then?

'Breathe, Anna,' Joel says, absent-mindedly stroking the back of my hand. 'This is one of the most exciting things you'll have ever done.'

I grunt. Terrifying, more like. And then there's the sound of the engine decelerating and the plane tilts forwards. We're going down. Is this it? The end of my life? Am I going to die crumpled up in this metal box?

Once again, I squeeze my eyes tightly shut, clenching every muscle in my body. We touch down with a couple of bumps, but only when the plane comes to a complete stop do I open my eyes again.

'Welcome to Twivali Safari Reserve,' the pilot says, as he switches the engine off, gets out of his seat and turns around to talk to us. 'It's been recently renovated so I'm sure you'll have a wonderful time.'

As we descend the steps, the air is hot and dusty but it's the cacophony of sound that really hits me. The noise of cicadas mingles with strange chirrups from birds, clicks and cackles that may come from birds or insects. And then there's the rumble of an engine and an open-topped 4 x 4 comes hurtling down the runway towards us.

'I love those vehicles,' Joel says.

I frown at him.

'They're called Classic Overlanders. They're specially converted Land Rover Defenders, fitted with three rows of seats and the tent-like canvas on top so that passengers can get views in every direction.'

I snigger at my geeky fiancé. To me it just looks like an extra-long, open-topped green Defender.

'Your carriage!' our pilot says as he heaves our bags out of the airplane.

The car comes to a rapid halt and a man jumps down from the driver's seat and races towards us, a wide, welcoming smile on his face. 'Hello, hello!' He's wearing a taupe polo shirt with the name Twivali Safari Reserve embroidered on the pocket, matched with taupe chinos. His eyes sparkle as he vigorously shakes our hands.

'Welcome to our little piece of heaven,' he says. 'My name is Ntando and I'm your ranger and guide. Did you have a good flight?'

'Excellent,' Joel says enthusiastically. All I can think about is that I'm going to have to do the same flight all over again in just a few days when we leave here.

'Good, good. You're very welcome.' He hauls our bags into the back of the open vehicle, then opens a door for us to climb into the row of seats directly behind the driver. We're high off the ground and I can see that this makes for good views, but how on earth are open sides and a canvas roof going to protect us from a lion jumping into the car?

'Enjoy your stay!' the pilot says waving at us, before striding back to his plane.

Ntando turns the Defender so we're facing away from the runway. I relax back into the seat and breathe deeply. The air is hot and mildly scented; it feels so very exotic here. Even the vegetation is foreign to me: lots of grasses and acacia trees and low-lying scrub interspersed by succulents and termite mounds.

We've driven barely fifty metres before the car comes to a sudden stop.

'Look, just ahead of us on the side of the road!' Ntando stands up and points excitedly. 'Just there, underneath that prickly bush. It's a snouted cobra, known as the Wipneuskobra in Afrikaans. What a beautiful specimen! Look at the black band around its neck. That shows it's a young snake.'

'Is it poisonous?' I ask.

'Yes, highly venomous, and they can grow up to two and a half metres. Impressive specimens.'

'Are there lots of dangerous snakes here?'

'Sure.' He chuckles. 'But they're not going to hurt you unless you approach them aggressively or tread on one accidentally. It's very special to see a snake like this.'

I shiver but neither Joel nor Ntando notice.

'Just remember that snakes are more scared of us than we are of them,' Joel says, giving me a gentle nudge in the ribs.

I very much doubt that.

All I can think of is why did my first close-up sighting of wildlife have to be a deadly snake? I just pray that it's not an ominous sign.

3

ANNA

We drive for about forty minutes, bouncing up and down along dirt tracks, not spotting any more animals. And then we see a big wrought iron sign saying:

Twivali Safari Lodge Private Game Reserve.

'Welcome!' Ntando says, throwing us a smile over his shoulder as he slows the Defender down, passing through the gates and coming to a full stop outside a building.

We jump out of the Land Rover and follow him inside.

The lodge is stunning. Truly the most beautiful building I've ever stood in. It's a circular construction with a thatched roof, and looking up to the underside of the ceiling, there are numerous pale wood struts that stretch upwards, gathering at a point like the interior of a tepee. The large open-plan room is full of natural materials. Sawn-off tree trunks for side tables, a massive wavy-edged wooden dining table with ten leather chairs. Pendant bulbs hang from ropes at varying heights and the floor is covered in hide rugs. To the left is the living area with plump cream sofas and stools covered in curly sheepskin. A big leather trunk features as a coffee table, and on it are piles of beautiful hardback books, candles in circular containers and three artfully arranged ostrich eggs. On the far wall is a bar, a shining dark wooden counter behind which are wall shelves with numerous bottles and gleaming glasses. A cool breeze sweeps through the building while a large old-fashioned fan hums from the ceiling. But the real star of the place doesn't lie inside. It's the huge windowless opening in front of us that displays a vast view that stretches from the wooden veranda that sweeps across the front of the building and out to the bush. Leaving Ntando and Joel behind, I stride through the room to the veranda and stand, leaning against the wooden fence, catching the faint scent of jasmine. There's a large watering hole about a hundred metres away and in every direction, as far as the eye can see, there are low trees and shrubs. I stand there for a few moments and then gasp. An elephant appears from behind a tree, its trunk curling as it pulls down branches.

'Joel! Look!' I exclaim, all fears of the flight forgotten. He steps forwards to stand next to me.

'Ah. I see you've already been captivated by our wildlife.' I turn around at the sound of a female voice. 'Welcome to Twivali Private Game Reserve,' she says, holding out her hand. 'I'm the owner, Nancy Theakston, and I'm delighted that you're here. You must be Anna.'

The woman is probably mid-thirties. She has blond hair swept back into a low pony tail and she's wearing a white, loose-fitting linen blouse over cream linen trousers. Her hair and clothes look expensive, without a crease despite being linen. A pair of over-sized designer sunglasses are perched on her head and her lips are pillar box red.

'It's glorious here,' I say.

'Indeed it is. I'm very lucky to have found this place.' She clicks her fingers out to her right side, murmuring, 'Bhutana, please.'

A young woman appears holding a silver tray. On it are two white flannels and two glasses filled with a pale orange juice.

'Please, help yourself,' Nancy says, wriggling her fingers.

I take a hot flannel and wipe it across my face, keen to remove the dirt from our international travels.

'The juice is freshly squeezed. A special recipe devised by our chef, Lulama. Enjoy.' She swivels around to face Joel. 'And you must be our vet. Welcome. I'm so glad that you were able to come.'

'Thank you for inviting us,' Joel says. She shakes his hand using both of hers.

After exchanging pleasantries about our long journey, Nancy offers to show us around. She leads us around the wooden deck but when I glance backwards to the watering hole, to my disappointment, the elephant has disappeared.

'Around here we have our fire pit.' Nancy shows us a wide circular area, where cushions have been placed on two sections of semi-circular raised brickwork surrounding a large iron fire pit. 'We have braais here at night.'

'Braais?' Joel asks.

'It's the Afrikaans word for barbecues.' She walks a few further steps around the corner and we come to a small but beautiful pool made from intricate blue and white mosaic also surrounded by a wooden deck. A couple lie on padded sun loungers, the woman wearing a navy bikini, the man in floral swim trunks.

'May I introduce you to some of our other guests, Zak and Katie.'

Zak makes to get up. 'Please don't get up for us,' I say hurriedly. Katie mouths hello.

'Zak and Katie arrived yesterday so they've already had their first game drive. Perhaps you'd like to join them here at the pool after you've freshened up.'

'Sure,' we both say a bit awkwardly.

We walk back into the main lodge. 'Help yourselves to drinks whenever you like. It's an honesty bar. All our guests eat together.' She points at the long dining table. 'If you have any dietary requirements please let one of us know, but now I'd like to show you to your tent.'

We walk away from the main lodge along a paved path. Either side of it are cacti and exotic bushes the likes of which I've never seen before.

'We have four guest tents but only three are occupied at the moment. As you'll see, they're not your typical tent.'

I'm relieved about that. I can't imagine canvas would be much of a deterrent for a raging buffalo. She gestures towards a large structure set discretely behind an acacia tree and other dense vegetation. 'I've put you in the tent the furthest away as it gives you the most privacy. There are a couple of things you need to be aware of. Firstly, under no circumstances can you walk back to your tent alone at night. We're surrounded by wild animals and although it's rare for lions or cheetah to come up to the main buildings, it's possible. You'll always be accompanied by Ntando or another member of staff who carries a gun. It's for your own safety. During the day time, please be on the lookout for animals. If you see any, stay in your tent and call reception. A member of staff will come to accompany you.'

I glance at Joel but he has a look of little-boy wonder on his face, as if this is the most exciting thing ever. The thought of being mauled by a wild animal and having to be accompanied by a man with a gun makes me extremely uneasy. We walk down several steps, around a corner and there in front of us is our tent. It's huge. Although the walls and ceiling are made from cream canvas, the structure is supported by wooden poles that look like thin tree trunks. Yet the floor is polished wood and the interior is decorated to the standards of a five star hotel. A super king-sized bed is made up with plump pillows and a duvet in the finest white linen, with a fawn cashmere throw covering the foot of the bed. It's surrounded by a billowing white mosquito net. On the banquette at the end of the bed are two elephant heads sculpted from white bathroom towels. Either side of the bed are dark wood butler tray tables on which stand oversized lamps made from porcupine spines. To the front of the tent is a huge, white freestanding bath with sublime views over the plain. Nancy gestures to behind the bed where there are hanging wardrobes and a separate WC and sink. Our luggage is already there.

'If you step this way, here is the shower,' she says. The shower, with its massive circular head, is outside. Totally invisible from prying eyes, it's carved out of rock and blends seamlessly into the scenery. I've never seen anything like it.

'This place is stunning,' I say.

'It's been designed to be as comfortable as possible.' She smiles warmly. If there's anything you need, please don't hesitate to ask me or one of the staff. Just a few more house rules, I'm afraid, because we are in the middle of nowhere and it's nearly a three-hour drive to the nearest decent-sized town. Please, no food of any sort in your tent. If you leave food around, it'll attract rodents and where there are rodents, there are snakes.'

I can't help but shiver.

'If you do happen to come across a snake, just back away.'

'Do you keep anti-venom just in case?' Joel asks.

'We stock all the basics for first aid but if God forbid there was a medical emergency, we'd have to call for helicopter evacuation. Fortunately we haven't had to put that to the test. Likewise, keep an eye out for venomous spiders and scorpions. When your room is made up, our staff check for insects, and they check again in the early evening, but it's good practice to shake your shoes out before putting them on. It's a matter of common sense.'

'Yes, of course,' Joel says, as if this is the most normal thing ever. It sure as hell isn't normal for me. I come from England where the most exotic things I've ever seen is a harmless grass snake and a large, totally benign spider in the bath.

'We do two game drives each day. The first is at 6 a.m. There'll be hot drinks and basic breakfast items for you to help yourselves to in the main lounge before you go. You'll return about 10 a.m. for a big breakfast. Lunch is a smaller affair at 2 p.m. and during the day you're welcome to doze, use the pool and just relax. The second game drive is at 5 p.m. You'll have drinks on your game drive and will return back here for supper at 8 p.m. Have you got any questions?'

'Do you have Wi-Fi?' I ask. 'I have to show Mum and Sasha around this amazing place.'

Nancy pulls a face. 'I'm sorry but we have very limited

reception out here. You won't get mobile reception but if you need to contact the outside world urgently, we have a satellite phone. We encourage our guests to totally switch off. There aren't many places in the world where you can have a complete digital detox.'

'Do you regularly see the big five?' Joel asks.

'Absolutely. Obviously this isn't a safari park, so we can't guarantee sightings of any animal, but Ntando is an excellent ranger and he has radio contact with rangers from the adjacent reserves, so it's likely you'll see many different species.'

Joel can't wipe the grin off his face.

'I'll leave you to freshen up. Lunch is in an hour, so if you feel like a dip in the pool beforehand, feel free. See you later.'

And then she's gone.

'Oh. My. God!' Joel exclaims. 'This place is amazing. I can't believe she's treating us like guests! I mean, I'm here for an interview. I thought we might be put up in staff accommodation or something. I never thought it'd be a room like this.'

'I'm glad you didn't tell me that,' I mutter. I might not have agreed to travel halfway across the world if I had thought we would have to slum it. But this. This is glorious. It's as if the interiors have been lifted from the glossy pages of a luxury travel brochure. 'Nancy talks as if this place has been running for a long time, not as if we're her first guests,' I say.

'I guess she's just practicing her spiel for when she opens to the public,' Joel replies. He starts pulling off his clothes. 'I want to use that shower.' He grabs a towel.

I glance around me, trying to take it all in. 'Are these

tents safe, with open sides like that? Can't the animals just get in?' I ask. Despite the beauty of this place I can't shrug off a sense of unease.

'They'll shut the sides at night, and don't worry, I'll look after you.' Joel throws his arms around me and we stand on the wooden veranda together, staring at the expansive landscape, listening to the cacophony of insects and birds.

4

ANNA

The outside shower is glorious. I smother myself in a deliciously scented shower gel and stand there for ages, with the water battering down on my aching limbs, drinking in the huge landscape. Eventually Joel pokes his head around the corner.

'Not sure you should use so much water, Anna,' he says. I turn the tap off and envelope myself in a cotton towel. 'They've got major water shortages in South Africa.'

'Why didn't you tell me before?' I ask.

'I thought you deserved a bit of a break but that was a long shower.'

He kisses me but as he leads me to the bed I glance at my watch. It's nearly 2 p.m. 'We need to get dressed,' I say, pointing at my watch. Joel groans. 'But we can have a nap after lunch and before the afternoon game drive.'

Although there is a proper wooden door leading into our tent, there is no lock. I suppose it's very safe out here – not exactly a place that attracts speculative burglars. Joel takes my hand as we saunter to the main lodge and it really does feel like we're on our honeymoon.

Zak and Katie are already seated at the long dining table.

'Sorry we didn't wait for you,' Katie says. 'We're starving despite having done absolutely nothing today except go out on an early game drive.'

Zak is piling a selection of salads onto his plate. Everything looks delicious and so fresh despite our remote location.

After we've stacked our plates full of food, we sit down opposite them.

'Are you here on holiday?' I ask.

'No. My wife Katie is a travel journalist and I'm a wildlife photographer. Nancy has invited us here in return for some press coverage.'

'I think you must have some of the best jobs in the world trying out new places such as this,' Joel muses.

'Yup, it's a tough life,' Katie laughs.

Joel explains that he's a vet but he doesn't say we're here as part of the interview process. Conversation drifts to the game drive they did this morning where they tell us they saw lions, hippos, zebra and impala. I feel a flicker of excitement in anticipation of our outing this afternoon.

We're just finishing off our meal when another woman hurries in.

'Sorry I'm late,' she says. She's wearing a white crocheted tunic over a pink bikini and her attractive face is caked with heavy makeup.

'Did you have a good snooze, Lois?' Zak asks.

'Yes, thanks. Nearly missed lunch.' She places a few lettuce leaves and sticks of carrot on her plate and walks away with it. It's strange.

Just before 5 p.m. we stroll back to the main lodge. I'm wearing a pair of chinos and I have a sweater with me because Nancy explained that the temperature drops dramatically once the sun goes down. Joel is armed with his camera and binoculars. We're the last to arrive. Ntando steps forwards to greet us. We nod and smile at Zak and Katie and I turn to say hello to Lois.

It's only then that I notice the man standing next to her.

I think I'm going to pass out.

My knees feel as if they're about to give way and the blood drains from my head. I grab the back of the sofa to steady myself.

It's Clayton.

My dead ex.

He is dressed in a khaki T-shirt and cargo trousers, his dark hair is a little longer than I remember it and his face is tanned. But otherwise he's the same. He's deep in conversation with Nancy and hasn't seen me.

'Are you alright?' Lois asks in an East London accent. Joel jumps to my side and puts his arm around my shoulders but even the reassuring touch of my fiancé fails to mitigate the shock.

'What's up, Anna?' he whispers. I can't speak.

Clayton is dead.

Yet Clayton is here.

Ntando is talking to us, telling us what we can expect to see this afternoon and where we're going but I only absorb the occasional word.

'Do you want a glass of water? Are you too exhausted to go out?' Joel persists.

'I'm fine,' I mutter. The others are walking forwards, following Ntando to the Land Rover. Still Clayton hasn't turned around, hasn't noticed me. Will he recognise me? My hair is different, cut short in a dark bob that sits above my jawline, and I've got sunglasses perched on my head, but otherwise I'm the same. A little chubbier, because I don't have a partner who criticises the size of my hips and tells me not to eat the last chocolate in the box. He strides forwards, puts his hand on Zak's shoulder, saying something that makes Zak smile. Clayton's hyena-like laugh cuts straight through me. It is him, isn't it? Yet, how can it be? Was Sasha wrong? And then he turns around and looks straight at me.

'Oh my God!' he exclaims, his eyes wide with recognition and his hand rushing up to cover his mouth. 'Anna? Anna, is that you?' He steps towards me, his arms outstretched. I step backwards onto Joel's foot.

'Yes,' I say simply, my stomach sinking.

'Oh my goodness, I can't believe it! It's so wonderful to see you,' he gushes. 'You look amazing. A little chubbier than before, and why did you cut off your gorgeous hair? But otherwise you look fantastic!'

'Do you know each other?' Joel asks.

'Yes. This is Clayton,' I say, my voice thick.

'We used to go out together,' Clayton says. 'In fact we were engaged. Good years, weren't they? And what are the chances of us meeting out here in the bush?'

The others are all staring at us now. Joel grips me tightly.

'Meet Lois, my girlfriend,' Clayton says reaching across to take Lois's hand. Her smile is tight. The atmosphere is awful.

'I thought you were dead,' I say.

There's a long pause before he breaks it with a laugh. 'I've been called many things, but I've never been described as dead.' He sniggers. 'How did I die? Rescuing a child from a burning building? A stoic passing after developing a rare illness?'

'It's not a laughing matter,' I say through gritted teeth. 'Sasha received a phone call from your sister about a year ago to say that you took your own life whilst you were travelling in Australia.'

'Well, that's ridiculous. I don't even have a sister. And me, taking my own life? That's nonsense. I expect it was Sasha playing stupid games with you. I never liked her.'

'Sasha wouldn't make up something like that,' I say with a clenched jaw.

'Are we ready to go?' Ntando interrupts us and I'm so relieved. Zak and Katie are already in the vehicle, seated on the rear row of seats. Clayton climbs up into the Defender and sits down next to Lois in the second row, leaving me and Joel to sit directly in front of them. I am so conscious of Clayton seated right behind me. His very presence sends chills through my bones.

'Everyone ready?' Ntando asks, glancing back at us.

The others all say an excited yes. I just keep my eyes straight ahead as Ntando starts up the Defender and we begin bumping up and down along the dusty track.

'Are you alright, darling?' Joel whispers, his hand gripping mine.

I nod, but I'm not alright. That sense of foreboding that I felt earlier enshrouds me. It's been nearly a year since I learned that Clayton was dead, and dreadful as it sounds, I was so relieved. I never confirmed his death, but why would I? He'd been gone from my life for well over a year. And yet here he is, sitting just inches behind me.

And I don't believe in coincidences.

Because what are the chances of running into my 'dead' ex on a safari in the middle of South Africa?

There's a tap on my shoulder. I swivel around and Clayton is learning forwards, his face practically level with mine. 'Did you check to see if the information was true? Did I have a funeral? Were there death notices?'

'No, I didn't check,' I say through gritted teeth. 'Why would I? We were out of each other's lives.' Politeness stops me from saying I was relieved he was dead.

He grins. 'Never mind that. We're back in contact again! What are the chances of that? Meeting on a glorious safari in the middle of South Africa.' He throws his arms open wide and then, as if he's remembering that his girlfriend is sitting right next to him, he puts an arm around her shoulders and pulls her towards him, placing a kiss on the side of her head.

I am rigid in my seat. Joel puts a protective arm around my shoulders and whispers, 'Is he who I think he is?'

'Yup. Will tell you all later.' My lovely fiancé hugs me tightly.

We drive in silence for long minutes until Ntando brings the vehicle to a sudden stop. Just ahead of us is a herd of zebra, their black and white stripes dazzling.

'Look! There's a baby,' Katie exclaims.

He's adorable, a miniature zebra standing in the middle of his herd. He lifts his head up to look at us, but the adult zebras graze totally unperturbed by our presence. I love zebra. They've always been my favourite animals, yet this is the first time I've seen any in real life. It's a magical moment, or at least it should be, if I could ignore the presence behind me.

'Do you want the binoculars?' Joel asks, handing them to

me. I stand up to get a better look and as I do so I feel Clayton's eyes on me, yet I refuse to turn to look at him. I can't believe he's here. What are the chances of him being another guest in the same safari lodge? It feels so wrong. But how could Clayton have engineered our meeting? I can't get my head around it.

'Zebra live in groups called harems,' Ntando explains. Sniggers come from behind me. 'These groups consist of one male, several mares and their offspring, and they stay together for long periods of time, creating stable family units.'

'Lucky bastards,' Clayton says. I cringe.

Ntando starts the vehicle up again and we continue on rugged tracks. During the next hour we see impala, ostriches and giraffe. It's a truly magical experience except it's tainted somehow, knowing that I'm sharing this experience with my dreadful ex. We pull up onto a flat patch of land. Below us is a lake.

'If you'd like to stretch your legs, it's safe here. Just stay where I can see you.'

When we get out of the vehicle, Clayton makes a beeline for me as I knew he would.

'It's so wonderful to see you again, Anna. How is Sasha? Are you still living with her?'

I don't want him talking about Sasha. In fact I don't want to talk to him at all. 'I'll catch up with you later,' I say, grabbing Joel's hand and tugging him towards Ntando.

Sasha is my best friend; almost like a sister. We met in sixth form at school and went to Durham University together where we shared a house in our second and third years. When we both moved to London, we shared again. The only rocky moment in our friendship was during the time I was in a relationship with Clayton. She never liked him. When I got engaged to Joel and he asked me to move in with him, I was terrified of telling Sasha, of letting her down. But my closest friend was magnanimous about it and said the time had come for her to stand on her own two feet. She's rented a one bedroom flat in Highgate but she's also in a serious relationship and I wouldn't be surprised if she doesn't end the tenancy and move in with her new man.

'Look, everyone! There are a couple of hippopotamus in the lake.' Ntando points to the centre of the watering hole. A hippo lifts its head out of the water and opens its jaw so wide we can see all its terrifying, enormous teeth. I'm not prone to violence and I shock myself with the thought, but right now I wish Clayton's head was in that hippo's jaw.

5

ANNA – THEN

'I don't want to go,' I moan, lying back on our sagging sofa.

'You're turning into an old spinster,' Sasha says. 'Besides, the parties we don't want to go to inevitably turn into the best ones.'

'That's easy for you to say because you know everyone there. I won't know a soul.'

'You know me and I'll stay by your side. Besides, that new dress needs an outing. It's gorgeous on you. Megan is loaded, and according to Fletcher she has the most stunning apartment.'

I have no idea who Megan or Fletcher are, but somehow my best friend and flatmate persuades me to attend a party thrown by one of her solicitor work colleagues. It's a cold November night when we hobble in our high heels into the entrance lobby of a riverside block of apartments. The building is shiny and new, and a million miles away from our grotty flat in Hackney. A concierge lets us in. Who in their twenties lives in an apartment block with a concierge, marble and glass entrance lobby with a massive flower arrangement on a central table? Certainly no one that I know. We are whizzed up to the eleventh floor in a glass lift that moves silently and speedily. I get the giggles despite only having had one glass of wine before we left home.

'Behave!' Sasha prods me. 'You never know whom you're going to meet.'

I adjust my black dress in the lift's mirror. I'm really pleased with the purchase, even though I couldn't afford it. It hugs my curves in all the right places and makes me look a lot more sophisticated than I feel.

The front door to the apartment is open and music is playing. It's loud but perhaps the neighbours have been invited too, or maybe these flats are so well soundproofed, it doesn't matter. There must be at least thirty people already in the stunning open-plan apartment, drinking from cocktail glasses and chatting away, yet it doesn't feel crowded.

'Wow!' I say out aloud. This place is gorgeous. There are double-height windows looking onto the River Thames with twinkling views of Westminster to the right. London looks spectacular from up here, brightly lit up at night. I tear my eyes away from the views to look at the interior of the duplex. There is a high-end open-plan kitchen and an island unit that's about the size of our whole flat. A metal spiral staircase winds upwards to a mezzanine area above us. The furniture is modern and sleek, mostly in hues of pale grey.

'Here,' Sasha says, handing me a cocktail glass filled with a clear liquid and a red glacé cherry floating on top. I don't bother asking what it is and just take a sip. It's delicious.

'Do you know anyone here?' I ask.

She glances around. 'Not many. Oooh. Don't look but

there's a gorgeous man over there who can't keep his eyes off you.'

The trouble is if we're told not to look, our instinct is to do the opposite. My eyes swing around. Sasha is right. He is looking directly at me and the second my eyes meet his he starts walking towards us. This man is quite possibly the best-looking male I've ever laid eyes upon outside of a magazine or social media. He has dark, almost black, slightly curly hair, bright blue eyes and a chiselled jaw, and looks as if he's walked straight out of a boardroom in his white shirt open at the neck, slim-fitting black suit trousers and a jacket artfully slung over one arm. A red tie pokes out of a pocket.

'Hello, ladies,' he says. 'I'm sorry to interrupt but...' He stops and shakes his head. 'Oh, damn it. All of my standard chat-up lines sound so smarmy.' He runs the fingers of his right hand through his hair and glances at me coyly through long lashes. My stomach flips. 'My name is Clayton and I just wanted to say hello.'

'Hello,' I say, giggling. 'I'm Anna.' I glance to my side, about to introduce my best friend, but she has scarpered to the other side of the room. Why has she done that? Although I suppose it isn't too bad being left alone with this Adonis.

'How do you know Megan?' he asks.

'Megan?'

'The person whose party this is,' he laughs.

'I don't. My flatmate works with her. And you?'

'I work with her boyfriend.'

'What do you do?'

'Boring, in the city. Investments and fund management.'

Which explains why he's wearing a designer suit.

He glances around and then bends his head towards

mine. 'I haven't eaten all day. Do you fancy sneaking out of here and getting a bite? There's a fabulous Japanese restaurant around the corner.'

Sasha and I ate burgers and chips before coming out for the evening, stodgy food to absorb the considerable alcohol we knew we were going to consume. I'm not hungry and I've never tasted Japanese food before, but just looking at Clayton makes my stomach flip. Why not? If I need to have another meal tonight, I can handle that. I catch Sasha's eyes and signal that I'm leaving. She grins at me lewdly. We've known each other long enough to have a shorthand and sign language for most social situations.

Clayton is the perfect gentleman. He holds doors open for me, pulls back my chair, makes sure I understand what I'm ordering and keeps my gaze throughout the meal, so much so it feels like I'm the only woman in the room. When we're the last people in the restaurant, I realise I've lost track of time. And how much I've drunk.

'Will you come home with me?' Clayton asks, holding both of my hands and gazing into my eyes as we stand outside in the cold night air. I know I shouldn't, but I've drunk a lot and this man makes me weak. And then he starts kissing me, right outside the restaurant, on the pavement, underneath a street lamp, and I never want this kiss to end. Clayton knows what he's doing and he's very accomplished. So the slut that I am, I do go home with him, and in the taxi we can't keep our hands off each other.

It isn't until the next morning when I wake up to the pale grey light and find myself in this stranger's home that I realise how irresponsibly I've behaved. But oh, it was so good. And now Clayton is propped up on one elbow gazing at me.

'You're beautiful, Anna,' he says, bringing his lips down on mine.

Much later, after we've made love again, taken a shower in his black and white bathroom and are sitting at his breakfast bar, I look around his apartment. It's big and very empty, as if he hasn't gotten around to buying enough furniture. And what there is has little character. This could be a show flat. I don't see any personal belongings, no photos, no pictures on the walls and none of the normal detritus one finds on kitchen counters. I wonder if he's just moved in.

'When can I see you again?' he asks.

'I haven't left yet,' I giggle.

'But you will and I know that I'll feel desolate immediately.'

This is new territory for me. I've never had a man be so vocal in his feelings and it's strange.

'I have to go to work today because we're in the middle of a big merger deal, but can I see you tonight?' he asks.

It's Sunday and I tend not to go out on a Sunday night. I hesitate.

He strokes the side of my face and gently holds my chin so I'm looking at him straight on. 'You've done something to me, Anna. I've never felt like this before.'

I gulp. Being wanted makes me feel good too, so I agree. I'll see him tonight.

Tonight turns into tomorrow night and the night after, and soon it's nearly a fortnight since Clayton and I met and we've spent every night together bar two. I've barely seen Sasha because I always stay at Clayton's. I can't imagine this grown-up man sleeping with me in my small double bed in our makeshift apartment. He doesn't offer to come to mine and I don't suggest it.

We start our evenings in some fancy wine bar of his choice and then either go out for supper or he orders meals in. Clayton doesn't cook and money seems to be no object. I offer to pay but he always insists on picking up the bill. At the end of the fortnight, Sasha sends me a sarky message and says she's missing me. I suggest to Clayton that we go to the pub so I can introduce him to some of my friends. I know they're going to love him and the girls and boys alike are going to be so jealous of my new, drop-dead gorgeous boyfriend.

The Wild Hen is an old-fashioned pub that smells of stale beer and has sticky tables. The wooden chairs and ragged banquettes are far from comfortable, but it's *our* pub and it has an authenticity that the more salubrious gastropubs discarded years ago. Clayton doesn't say anything when we walk in, but he tenses slightly and I'm sure I see a momentary turning up of his nose. I would be reluctant to come here too but my university friends and some additional friends we've picked up along the way have been coming here since we all moved to London. It's our regular.

Sasha and the gang are already here, gathered around three tables that they've wedged together. We walk towards them and Clayton puts his arm around my shoulders as I introduce him to everyone.

'It's a pleasure to meet you all,' he says. 'And since I'm the newcomer here, I'd like to buy you all a round of drinks. What would everyone like?'

We don't do that in my friendship group, largely because none of us can afford it. There are twelve of us and everyone is startled, but heck, no one declines. Clayton notes down what everyone wants on his phone and disappears to the bar. Sasha raises her eyebrows at me but doesn't say anything. A few minutes later, he returns accompanied by a barman carrying a large tray piled with full glasses. I chat to my friends and Clayton sits there with his arm protectively around me. He doesn't say much but I get it must be awkward when we all know each other and he only knows me.

'Right, everyone. Who's coming with me to the bar to get in another round?' Matt asks. He studied chemistry with me at uni.

'Not us,' Clayton says, standing up suddenly. 'Anna and I have to leave but it was a pleasure to meet you all.' I'm startled but quickly pretend that this was always the plan. It's not like I can argue with him in front of my friends. We say our goodbyes and with his hand in the centre of my back, Clayton steers me through the pub and out the door. The moment we're on the street, Clayton says, 'I've booked us a table at one of my favourite Italian restaurants near Covent Garden. I want to celebrate our two-week anniversary.'

I look at him with surprise. I hadn't appreciated it was two weeks to the day since we met. I mean, that's the kind of thing innocent teenagers celebrate, isn't it? It's sweet but slightly weird. He bends down to give me a kiss, so I don't have to think of anything to say.

Later, when we're back at Clayton's flat and he's in the bathroom, I text Sasha and ask her what she thinks of Clayton.

> He's gorge but it was a bit ostentatious to
> buy us all drinks.

That wasn't the response I was hoping for.

That night, just as I'm dozing off to sleep, Clayton turns to me in bed and whispers, 'I love you, Anna.' I'm shocked. I mean, we've only known each other a fortnight. Yes, it's been intense and the sex has been amazing, but to use the love word... I keep my eyes shut and my breath steady.

The next morning, Clayton announces that he's booked to take me to a five star spa hotel for the weekend. It's one of those super-fancy places that famous people go to and according to press reports is booked up for months in advance. I'm blown away. I can't believe how much Clayton is spoiling me. When we get there, it's as stunning as I imagined it would be. There are rose petals scattered on our enormous bed and in the freestanding copper bathtub standing in the corner of the room, and the big picture window has views over the extensive manicured gardens to the South Downs in the distance.

'I've booked us a package of couples' therapies,' Clayton says with a big grin. I'm surprised. I didn't think he'd be the type to go in for massages and facials. Everything is glorious and by late afternoon, we're back in our sumptuous suite and he makes slow and beautiful love to me. This time he tells me he loves me during and afterwards. I hold him tight because I've never had a boyfriend who has told me he loves me. At least not in the cold light of day, or in this instance at dusk as we're getting ready for dinner.

'You do something to me, Anna,' Clayton says, holding my hand as we walk towards the dining room. 'I've never fallen for someone like I've fallen for you. I know it's probably all a bit too quick for you, and I don't expect you to feel the same way, not yet at least, but I hope you will soon enough.'

'I do feel for you,' I say, and I mean it. It's just I'm not sure it's love yet. It's certainly lust and obsession, but love? Maybe.

6

ANNA

We all climb back into the vehicle and sit there in silence watching the hippos for a few minutes. They are extraordinary beasts, prehistoric, terrifying, yet appealing all at the same time. Zak and Joel take lots of photos but the rest of us just enjoy the moment. Or at least I would if Clayton wasn't seated right behind me. I admit that Clayton seemed as surprised to see me as I was to see him, but surely it's too much of a coincidence.

'Anna, are you okay?' Joel whispers as he sits down next to me. I try to unclench my jaw, and I lean into my fiancé, just grateful that he's here with me; here to protect me.

'Yes, just a bit of a shock,' I murmur as quietly as I can. I'm conscious of Clayton's eyes on my back but I refuse to let him know I'm rattled that he's here. Joel kisses my cheek and puts his arm around my shoulders again. I feel a rush of love for my fiancé, and for the first time allow myself to enjoy the warm breeze in my hair and that unique scent of dust and rich vegetation. I'm in the most exotic place I've ever visited and it's truly magical. I smile. This has got to be the best job interview ever.

After driving for another fifteen minutes or so, Ntando brings the Land Rover to a sudden stop.

'There are two elephants right behind those trees,' he whispers, standing up and looking through his binoculars. 'We're in luck. It's a mother and her calf. Stay very still, everyone.' He speaks in a low voice and stands there motion-less. As we sit quietly, there's the rustle of leaves and then a loud crack as a branch comes tumbling down just metres from the vehicle. Lois lets out a little whimper from behind me. But then the elephants appear and it is the most glorious sight I've ever seen.

'The calf is about four months old,' Ntando whispers. 'She won't reach full size until she's about twenty years old. Elephants can eat over three hundred pounds a day and calves drink around five gallons of milk a day. She'll be weaned off milk and start eating vegetation when she's two.'

Suddenly there's a loud ruckus, the sound of more cracking branches, followed by a deafening trumpeting sound. Ntando quickly sits down and puts the Defender into reverse. Lois squeals again and I can't help but turn around to look at her. Clayton has his arm around her but she looks terrified. I have to control my snigger.

Our vehicle is some distance from the elephants now, but to my delight there's quite a herd. I count at least six of these amazing beasts. We stay there silently for long minutes, watching the elephants destroy the bushes and trees in their path, and we even get to see the little calf gallivant around. It's joyous. Quite possibly one of the highlights of my life. As we pull away, I can't wipe the grin from my face. Even knowing Clayton is sitting behind me doesn't change the lightness in my heart.

After we leave the elephants, Ntando drives us out of the thickets onto a plain and we see zebra, giraffe and various types of antelope, including many impala. But now the sun is beginning to go down. Ntando stops the Land Rover on a hill where we have magnificent views of a winding river and untouched bush as far as the eye can see.

'Time for a drink, everyone?' he asks with his infectious grin. Ntando pulls out a collapsible table from the rear of the vehicle, and in moments there is an array of drinks and nibbles, sparkling crystal glasses and white linen napkins. It seems so incongruous to magically create a fully stocked bar out here in the middle of nowhere. I have a large gin and tonic and can't stop eating the biltong, the dried, cured meat that Ntando says is a speciality of South Africa.

'It's truly magical, isn't it?' Katie murmurs as we gaze at the rapidly sinking orange sun. And then I see Clayton making a beeline for Joel. They're standing too far away for me to hear their conversation but Clayton puts his hand on Joel's shoulder and says something that makes Joel smile. Tension creates knots in my stomach and I excuse myself from any further conversation with Katie and make my way over to the men.

'It's such an amazing coincidence that you're here,' Clayton says, beaming at me. I stand as close to Joel as I can, hoping somehow that he's going to protect me.

'What brings you to Twivali?' Joel asks.

'I'm an investor in leisure businesses and am diversifying into African safaris. Safari investment funds present highly lucrative investment opportunities. I mean we're talking of up to twenty-five percent return on investment per annum, which is very exciting for my clients and myself. In fact if you have any cash to invest, I'd be delighted to talk you through the proposal.' Clayton stares at Joel expectantly.

'Sadly, I don't have any spare cash lying around,' Joel says. 'We're saving up for our wedding.'

'We are too, aren't we, darling?' Lois says as she walks over to us. I notice that she's drinking champagne and she's already on her second glass. Clayton smiles tightly but doesn't say anything. I'm just relieved that Clayton has a serious girlfriend and seems to have moved on from the car crash of our relationship. I'm surprised he's involved in leisure businesses. I never really understood what he did but he certainly didn't mention hotels or safari lodges when we were together.

'Tell me about your work,' Clayton says to Joel, and I think for the moment at least, the conversation is safe.

'Seems we share a taste in men.' Lois chuckles. I try not to visibly cringe.

'How long have you been together?' I ask.

'Just over a year.' She changes the subject and I don't blame her because it must be even more awkward for her to be talking to her boyfriend's ex. 'I've never been on a safari before. Have you?'

'No. It's amazing, isn't it?'

'Except that car is so bloody uncomfortable. I'm going to have some butt fillers put in and wish I'd had surgery done before we came out here. My backside feels numb.' She rubs her neat derriere and then peers at my face. 'You haven't had any work done, have you?'

'No,' I reply, slightly startled.

'Haven't you considered Botox in your lips and a bit of a lift around the eyes?'

'Um, no. Maybe when I'm older.' I've got nothing against people who choose cosmetic surgery but it's not something I've ever considered and I doubt I ever will. I wonder why Lois thinks she needs it. She looks like she's in her late twenties and I'm sure she has attractive features without the enhancements.

The sun has sunk behind the horizon and the sky is lighting up with dramatic orange and pink stripes. It's beautiful but the air is turning colder by the minute and I shiver. Joel and Clayton have their heads close together now and I can't hear what they're saying, which makes me uncomfortable. The light is low but I can see that the others have faint rosy cheeks and their words and laughter is higher pitched than normal, likely an indication of how much they've drunk. I've stuck to the one glass only, despite wanting the numbing and warming effect of alcohol. But I can't risk getting tipsy; not with Clayton here. My senses are heightened and they need to stay that way.

Suddenly there's the most terrible scream followed by more deafening screeching just metres from where we're standing. I freeze, my heart thumping with terror.

'Everyone get into the vehicle,' Ntando says, his early jolliness instantly dissipating. I've never seen anyone move as quickly and awkwardly as Lois. She drops her glass onto the ground and throws herself into the Defender. Joel appears by my side and helps me up, followed swiftly by Clayton. Katie and Zak get in from the other side.

'What's happened?' I ask.

'A killing,' Joel says.

I shiver.

Ntando scoops up the bottles, empty glasses and our other detritus with impressive speed, suggesting he's done this many times before. He shoves everything into the rear of the Defender and hops into the driver's seat.

'The lions are closer to us than I thought. That was most likely a lion killing an impala.'

'Can we see it?' Zak asks.

I don't want to see it. My nerves are frayed enough as it is and that horrific noise of an animal's last seconds still rings in my ears.

'It's too dark and not safe enough. I need to get you guys back to the lodge because your supper will be ready soon. Hopefully tomorrow we can spot the lions.'

It's really cold now and I'm grateful for the scratchy woollen blankets that have been stored underneath our seats. I wrap mine around me tightly and lean into Joel for warmth.

'I'd love to see a kill,' Clayton says, speaking loudly over the noisy engine. 'It's nature at its rawest.'

'You're weird,' Lois says. And I have to agree with her.

By the time we reach the lodge, it's pitch black outside and the Land Rover's headlights just illuminate the track directly in front of us. It's an unnerving thought to know that the most dangerous of animals could be right next to us, but we wouldn't know. They can see us, but we can't see them. When the lights of the main building appear, I'm relieved. Exhaustion from our long journey has caught up with me and I just want to sleep. Ntando switches the engine off and we all climb down from the vehicle. The beautiful young black woman, Bhutana, who greeted us earlier, is standing in the doorway holding a silver tray laden with steaming hot flannels. I take one gratefully, enjoying the scent of lemon as I wipe the dust off my face. We follow her into the main building where Nancy stands, a welcoming smile on her face. She's changed into black trousers and a tightly fitted V-neck black sweater. A dramatic, hammered gold pendant sits at her collarbone.

'How was it?' she asks.

'Amazing,' Katie replies for all of us.

'I hope you're all hungry. Our cook, Lulama, has prepared a feast for you. Our food is all plant based but I'm fairly confident that the carnivores amongst you won't miss meat.'

'I'd murder a sirloin steak right now,' Clayton says. That's so typical Clayton – not only wanting the best of the best, but particularly something he can't have.

It's obvious that I'm not the only one who is tired because supper is a subdued affair. The food is delicious, and Nancy is right; I, for one, am not missing any fish or meat. I find it difficult to suppress my yawns, so when Nancy asks who would like to have a post-dinner drink and who would like to return to their tent, I find myself putting my hand up like a school child.

'I'm knackered,' I say. 'I need my bed.'

'You've had a long day.' Nancy smiles sympathetically. She produces a small walkie-talkie which I hadn't noticed was clipped to her belt, and speaks quietly into it. A mere thirty seconds later Ntando appears, holding a torch. To my shock, he has a rifle slung over his shoulder. I know Nancy said we would have to be accompanied back to our tent at night and she'd mentioned something about a gun, but actually seeing it is a surprise. I guess that's the Britishness in me. Guns are not part of our everyday life.

'Good night, everyone,' Joel says. Clayton ostentatiously chews on something and is the only person who doesn't wish us good night. No surprise there.

My heart is beating a little too fast as we follow Ntando to our tent. I know it's silly but the night is so dark yet so loud with the sound of strange chirrups and distant barking noises that sound like cackling. To think that just twenty-four hours ago we were in Joel's safe little cottage in the home counties and now we're thousands of miles away in a totally strange landscape that feels anything but safe.

'The hyaenas,' Ntando says. 'You'll hear lots of noises in the night but you'll be perfectly safe so long as you don't venture outside.'

I'm not sure that his words comfort me.

Ntando stands to one side to let us into our tent. 'Would you like an early morning call? I can wake you at 5 or 5.30 a.m. ready for our 6 a.m. game drive.'

'We've got alarm clocks so we should be fine,' Joel says.

'In which case, sleep well and I'll see you first thing tomorrow morning.'

'So what's the story with Clayton?' Joel asks, once we're lying in bed, cosseted by the smoothest cotton sheets, our heads on cloud-like pillows. 'I mean, I know he's your ex and he was controlling, but you really don't like him, do you?'

'No. And it's just weird that he's here. We were told he was dead.'

'Such a coincidence, and as you say, a bit weird. Someone clearly got their wires mixed up. But he seems alright; a bit full of himself perhaps.'

'He's not alright,' I say. 'Not at all.'

'Do you want to talk about it?' Joel asks, placing a gentle kiss on my lips.

'I'm exhausted.'

'Me too. I think we should try to sleep.'

I can't sleep. The noises outside startle me into wakefulness every time I'm just about to drop off, yet Joel snores lightly next to me, unperturbed by the alien sounds. But it's not just the strange animal sounds from outside; it's knowing that Clayton is here, just metres away from me. I've tried so hard to move on from him during the past two years, and although I've told Joel snippets about my relationship with Clayton, I haven't told him the truth. I can't because I barely allow myself to reminisce on the truth. It's just too horrible. Too humiliating.

7

ANNA – THEN

Clayton and I have been together for three months. It's been the most intense three months of my life. Every day he tells me how much he loves me, how grateful he is that I'm in his life, that he's the luckiest man in the world. I tell him I love him too, and I think I do. But the truth is I've never had a relationship like this; one where the emotion runs so high and is articulated. Mostly I am loving all the attention: the fancy restaurants and hotels, the beautiful bouquets of flowers, the silk lingerie and pearl earrings. But today, Clayton is in a foul mood.

It's Sasha's birthday and I told Clayton that tonight was going to be a girl's night. Five of us are meeting at ours for cocktails and then we're going to a dive in Soho for a boozy night dancing to nineties' music. I spent last night at Clayton's, as I do most nights, and this morning we went shopping at Borough Market. Despite Clayton not cooking, I love it and I wanted to make us lunch – a complicated Ottolenghi recipe that I tried once before. Cooking is a bit like my meditation and I lose myself in the process. Some of my food scientist colleagues no longer cook at home, considering it too similar to what we do at work. I disagree. At work every item is measured, documented and tested. It's a scientific process. Cooking at home is more of an art and I allow myself to be freer, never worrying about measuring to the last gram, and replacing ingredients on a whim. It's more of an experimentation process.

I have to admit that Clayton's kitchen looks like a bomb has hit it. I've used pretty much every pan and dish he owns (which isn't many) and I'm humming away listening to music through my earbuds. When he first walks in, I just blow him a kiss and assume he'll settle down to read the papers on his iPad. It takes me a few long moments to realise that he's standing there in front of me, his hands on his hips, a stony look on his face.

'What's up?' I ask, switching the music off.

'This,' he says, waving his hands at the open-plan kitchen. 'It's disgusting.'

I frown. 'I'm cooking. That's what happens. You use lots of cooking paraphernalia. It'll be worth it, I promise.'

'You need to clean up as you go along. I can't have the kitchen in this mess.'

'Chill, Clayton,' I say with a smile.

A nerve pings in his jaw. 'I don't like mess.'

'I realise that, but it's temporary. If you want, you can start on the washing up.'

I think he is going to explode now. His face reddens and his eyes narrow. 'You made this mess. You'll clean it up,' he says through gritted teeth. He then strides out of the room, slamming the door behind him.

Wow. That was quite the overreaction. I know that he's a neat freak. I mean, who else lines up tins in their cupboards and makes sure that every glass is spaced equally from the next one? And rehangs the towels in the bathroom if I don't put them back as tidily as he likes, or I hang the toilet paper the wrong way around. And I certainly don't know anyone else who has a cleaning lady come three times a week. I might begin to understand it if Clayton cooked but we're out every night, so the kitchen is spotless and the oven looks like it's never been used. There isn't even any ironing to do because his shirts and bedlinen get picked up by the local dry cleaners and dropped back again. I suppose he has some sort of obsessive compulsive disorder, but I haven't noticed the telltale signs that we all know – the hand washing, rechecking of locked doors and the like. And he isn't squeamish when it comes to sex and bodily fluids. It's strange, yet I don't feel that I'm at the stage in our relationship that I can question him about it.

I'm unsure whether to continue cooking lunch. I half-heartedly rinse some dishes under the tap and decide to carry on. Just because Clayton is in a bad mood doesn't mean I should have to deprive myself of a tasty lunch. Half an hour later and the meal is ready. I put as many dirty pots and pans in the dishwasher as I can fit in and pile up the rest in the sink. I walk next door and knock on the closed bedroom door.

'Lunch is ready, Clayton.'

There's no answer. I open the door gingerly but he's not in there. I knock on the spare bedroom door and immediately open it. He's sitting at a desk, his back to me, shoulders hunched up.

'Food's ready,' I say, trying to keep my voice light.

'I'm not hungry. Thanks,' he adds begrudgingly, as if it's an afterthought.

'Come on, babe,' I say, throwing my arms around his neck and nuzzling into him. His laptop is open in front of him and he clicks away a spreadsheet.

'Please just leave me alone, Anna. I'm not in the mood.'

'That's the problem. You are in a mood. And I want to know why.'

He bristles.

'I thought it was okay me cooking here. I'll leave your kitchen as spotless as I found it.'

'That's not the issue.'

'So what is?'

'I'd booked something for tonight, for both of us.'

I move away from him and perch on the edge of the desk.

'But I told you a week ago that I'm going out with Sasha tonight. It's her birthday.'

'I got us tickets to see Elton John.'

'You what?' I exclaim. 'But those sold out within minutes ages ago.' I can't believe it. I only told Clayton a week ago how much I'd like to see Elton John in concert before he retires forever.

'I pulled some strings,' he says, tonelessly.

'Maybe if I explain to Sasha –'

'It's too late. I've sold them.'

I'm speechless. It's like he proffered me a fabulous gift and then immediately snatched it away. 'I'm sorry,' I say, although I'm not really sure what it is I'm apologising for. 'Are you sure you don't want any lunch?'

He sighs loudly. 'I suppose I could eat something.'

Lunch is a quiet affair, although Clayton does have the good grace to compliment my cooking.

'Is it because you don't want me to go out with my girlfriends tonight?' I ask him eventually.

'Of course!' he says, as if I'm really dim and have only just caught onto the truth. 'I can't bear the thought of you around other people, without me being there to look after you, to make sure you get home safely.'

I open and close my mouth. I managed perfectly well prior to three months ago when Clayton came into my life. I suppose my face is a picture of dismay.

'Look, Anna,' he says, putting down his cutlery and grabbing my hand. 'It's just because I love you so much and want to be there with you all the time. You understand that, don't you?'

I nod, because it is rather sweet, but when I've completely cleared up from lunch (Clayton doesn't offer to help) and I kiss him goodbye, he's still tense.

'Please message me when you get home, whatever time of the night it is,' he says. 'Otherwise I'll worry about you and won't sleep. I love you so much, Anna.'

Two weeks later and it's my twenty-seventh birthday. I spend the night before at Clayton's flat, as I do pretty much every night.

'Happy birthday, darling,' he says, placing a light kiss on my lips. He reaches across to his bedside table and produces a small gift bag in that recognisable Tiffany blue. 'You shouldn't have,' I say as I pull myself up in bed. The bag alone suggests it's going to be valuable. I remove the small turquoise box tied in white ribbon. Nestled inside is a key made out of little diamonds hanging from a discrete platinum chain. 'It's beautiful,' I say, lifting it up. I'm not sure I'm the type of girl who wants to wear a key around her neck, but I can tell immediately that it's valuable. Very valuable, I suspect. And it's sparkly – just not the sort of thing I would choose for myself.

'Let me put it on you,' Clayton says.

When he's fastened it, he leans in and kisses me on the neck. 'You hold the key to my heart,' he murmurs. He's so soppy, I have to restrain a giggle.

'I've booked a car to collect you from work at 5 p.m. It'll bring you back here where you can get changed and then we're going out.' He glances at the bedside clock. 'I've got to get a move on but have a wonderful day, darling.'

'I don't have any clothes to change into here,' I say.

'I meant to say it'll take you to your flat,' he replies, although the edges of his lips flicker and I'm pretty sure he's got something planned he's not telling me about.

On the dot of 5 p.m., I hurry down to the foyer of my work's building. I'm feeling rather full as my colleagues bought a big box of cupcakes which we've spent the last hour working our way through. And it wasn't cake produced by our company either, which made it extra special.

'There's a taxi out front,' Jim, the building's concierge says. 'A black Mercedes.'

'Thanks, Jim,' I say as I hurry out. He's right. It's big and black and shiny and the driver is dressed in a dark uniform.

'Miss Evans?' he asks.

'Yes.' He holds the rear passenger door open and I slip in. The interior smells of leather and vanilla air freshener.

It's such a luxury to be driven rather than having to take an overland train followed by the tube, which is my normal commute. It isn't until he pulls up outside Clayton's apartment block that I realise he hasn't taken me home. But there's no point in me questioning the driver. Clayton will have his reasons. I thank him and use the key Clayton has given me to let myself in.

As soon as I open the door to his apartment, I see a trail

of rose petals on the floor. I can't help giggling. Clayton is such a crazy romantic. I follow the petals, which lead into his bedroom. Lying on the bed is a pale blue dress, cream stiletto heels and a cream cashmere coat. On the pillow is a set of cream lace underwear, and a single white rose lies on top of it. There's a little card.

I chose these for you to wear tonight. I hope you like the clothes. See you soon. Cx

I lift the dress up and see the designer label. I've never owned clothes like these before: formal, beautiful fabric, costing the earth. I slip them on and to my surprise, everything fits like a glove. Clayton must have checked out the sizing on clothing I've left here, but even so, it's as if it's made to measure. The dress is more formal than what I'd normally wear, with a high neck and long sleeves, but as I slip my feet into the shoes, I feel so glamorous. Much older too.

Clayton sneaks in so quietly he makes me jump.

'Happy birthday, gorgeous,' he says. He leans in to kiss me on the lips and then produces a massive bouquet of cream roses. There must be at least fifty flowers.

'We're going to the theatre and then out for dinner.'

'Oh,' I say, because I've never been much of a theatre goer. But it'll do me good to do something cultural. 'What are we seeing?' I ask.

'Romeo and Juliet at the London Palladium.'

'Wow!' I say, although if I'm honest, I'd rather have gone to a comedy than see Shakespeare.

An hour later, we're in the Royal Circle, in great seats, with Clayton next to the aisle so he can stretch his long legs, watching the performance. I surprise myself and thoroughly enjoy it, helped considerably by two glasses of champagne during the interval. By the final curtain call, my stomach is rumbling and I'm looking forward to a decent dinner.

'Stay here,' Clayton says as the auditorium is plunged into darkness. The audience is clapping wildly, although some people are getting up and grabbing their coats, no doubt eager to get out before the main rush.

'Ladies and gentlemen,' a male voice comes over the theatre's loudspeakers. 'Please remain in your seats for just a moment longer.'

The clapping wanes slightly as we expect another curtain call. But this time, when the lights go on, the curtain remains down. Standing right in the middle of the stage is one man. He blinks slightly as if he's struggling with the bright lights.

My heart starts thumping.

What the hell is Clayton doing up on the London Palladium's stage?

He coughs awkwardly and I realise that he's holding a microphone.

'I have a very important question to ask,' he says, blinking rapidly. The auditorium falls silent now. And then to my utter dismay, he gets down on one knee, placing the microphone on the floor in front of him. He fumbles slightly and removes a small red box from his jacket pocket.

'Anna Veronica Louise Evans. Will you marry me?' He holds the box out in front of him.

There are a few gasps and some feeble clapping. Then the male voice comes out over the loudspeakers again.

'Anna Evans, please make yourself known.'

My cheeks are aflame as some auditorium lights come on

and everyone is peering around to see who this person is. I stand up, because what else can I do?

'Anna, please make your way to the stage,' the voice booms.

The people sitting next to me pat my arm and my back but I'm frozen to the spot. Do they really expect me to walk up on that stage in the presence of all of these thousands of people? I'm a scientist, an introvert. This is my idea of utter hell. Suddenly an usher appears holding a microphone, thrusting it in front of my face. Spotlights converge on me and I realise to my utter dismay that everyone, literally everyone is waiting for me. Waiting for my answer. I look at Clayton up on the stage. It's difficult to see him properly because of the bright lights honing in on me, but he's standing up now, still holding the little box in front of him. I realise there's a collective holding of breath.

'Yes,' I say eventually, in a very small voice. 'Yes, I'll marry you.'

And then the audience erupts. There are shouts of congratulations and clapping, and all I want to do is disappear. The humiliation. The embarrassment. What the hell was Clayton thinking? And do I really want to marry him? We've only known each other for three and a half months. That's no time. And if he knew me well, he'd know that I hate grand gestures like that. My cheeks feel as if they're on fire and I don't know where to look or what to say, so I sit back down in my chair, trying to ignore all the congratulations. Eventually, Clayton appears.

'You were meant to join me on stage.'

'Sorry,' I say, my eyes downcast, looking at the trampled crisps on the carpet in the aisle.

'But at least you said yes.' Clayton beams at me, clearly

oblivious to my discomfort. 'The future Mrs Clayton Klerk.' He holds out the little box and lifts up the lid. The ring is a sapphire surrounded by diamonds, reminiscent of Princess Diana's and now Catherine, Princess of Wales's engagement ring. It's classic, formal and nothing like what I would have chosen for myself. For a brief moment, I wonder if I can trade it in for a simple square cut diamond. And then I wonder. Do I really want to get married?

'Congratulations.' An American stranger wallops me on the back.

'Come on, darling. We've got a table booked for dinner.' Clayton slips the ring on my finger and it fits perfectly. 'I love you so much,' he says, putting his arms around me, and hugging me so tightly it feels as if I'm going to be suffocated by his thick coat.

I try very hard to be upbeat during dinner. I mean, this should be the happiest night of my life and yet I can't rid myself of the embarrassment from that grand gesture of Clayton's. What was he thinking? What strings did he pull and how much did he have to pay to be given the stage? Clayton is wittering on about which hotel we should have our wedding in – The Savoy or The Grosvenor.

'I haven't met any of your family or friends yet,' I say.

'Because I haven't got any,' he states with a smile.

'Friends or family?'

'Family. I'm the only child of deceased parents, both of whom were only children themselves. No cousins, no hangers-on. Everything I have will be yours, Anna.'

'So at least introduce me to your friends.'

'Of course I will, all in good time. But for now I just want to keep you all to myself. I love you so much, Anna. I've got another couple of surprises for you, darling.'

I tense. I really hope they're nothing like the previous surprise.

He puts his hand back into his jacket pocket and removes two keys, placing them on the table between us.

'What are these?' I ask.

He holds up the first one. 'A car for you. Nothing too grand because you'll be driving it around London. It's the new Volkswagen e-Golf. Obviously, when we have more than one child, we'll need to upgrade.'

Before I can utter another word, he holds the other key up.

'This is the key to our new home.' His smile is so wide it's as if his handsome face is being split into two.

'What?' I ask.

'We can't live in my apartment, can we? It's not suitable as a family home. I've bought us a house. Four bedrooms, three bathrooms, a lovely little garden on a good residential street in Fulham. You'll be able to make friends with the other mums around there, or if you decide to go back to work, then there are some great nurseries and pre-prep schools, or of course, we can find a nanny.'

'Whoa! Slow down, Clayton. We haven't talked about any of this!'

His face falls.

'I mean, it's all amazing. The ring, the car, a house!' I exclaim, but despite the generosity, it feels off. So rushed. 'I think we need to slow down, just a little. We barely know each other.'

'But I love you, Anna. I knew the moment I met you that we were destined to be together. And you love me too, don't you? You've just accepted my hand in marriage.'

'Yes, yes, I do.' I splutter slightly because right now I am totally confused. I think I love Clayton but all of this is so unexpected. And claustrophobic. It's like I've gone from a single, independent, career woman about town to a married mother in the space of an hour. And then there's the matter of money. I've no idea how much my engagement ring cost but I know for sure a decent house in Fulham could be upwards of three million. Where has all the money come from? And I'm not sure if I want someone choosing a new house and a new car for me. The car is fair enough. I probably would have selected something similar if I had the money, but the house? I have never seen myself as a yummy mummy living in Fulham. I'm a country girl at heart and I'd always imagined living in a little cottage with hollyhocks growing around my front door and views of hills in the distance.

A waiter walks over and asks us if we'd like a dessert. Clayton bats him away, quite rudely. 'Not now,' he says, flicking his hand at the man.

'We can go to the house in the morning. It's empty, so you can put your own mark on it. If you want me to get the decorators in before we move in, then that's fine. Take a bit of time. Create some Pinterest boards, or we can employ an interior designer to help you, if you prefer. I want it to be the perfect home for us both.'

I don't know what to say. This is too overwhelming. So I just sit there gawping. Clayton takes that as acquiescence. 'Oh, my darling,' he says, reaching across the table and squeezing my left hand so hard that the new engagement ring digs into the adjacent fingers. 'You're utterly adorable and we're going to be blissfully happy together for the rest of our lives.'

'I just need to go to the ladies,' I say, wriggling my fingers so he lets go of my hand. I push the chair back and feel quite dizzy when I stand up. It's not from alcohol because I've barely drunk since we got here, and my two glasses of champagne during the interval were ages ago. I think it's the surprise. Or shock. All I know is that I feel like I've been boxed into a little prison and I need to battle to get out. Yet with every step I take towards the toilets, I am conflicted. My gorgeous, rich fiancé has bought me a house, a car and a massive engagement ring. I glance down at my ring finger and the sapphire looks as black as the night. I pause. I could go to the toilets or I could walk straight out of here.

8

ANNA

I wake up with a racing heart, my torso covered in a film of perspiration.

'Are you alright?' Joel asks, propped up on one elbow.

'I didn't sleep well,' I say, rubbing my eyes. The light is still low outside, a dark grey that isn't ready to signal what weather the day might bring. 'Every time I was about to drop off, the screeching of an animal woke me.'

'Oh, poor you,' Joel says. 'You're perfectly safe in here, though; you do realise that.'

'Yes, of course,' I say. But in truth, it's not the animals that kept me awake. It was the thoughts of Clayton and how weird it is that I spent the last year thinking he was dead. And how disconcerting that he's right here in this remote place.

After a cursory wash in the bath, because I don't fancy an outside shower in this low light, we both dress hurriedly. Joel presses a walkie-talkie-type device that rings through to reception, and a couple of minutes later there's a rapping on our door.

'Good morning!' Ntando says, much too cheerfully for the early hour. His rifle is still slung casually over his shoulder. 'I trust you slept well and are ready for the morning game drive.'

Joel chats to Ntando as we walk, while I hang back slightly, trying to wake up. The sun is beginning to emerge from the horizon and it's going to be another clear blue sky. The others are already there, drinking hot drinks, nibbling at pastries. I help myself to a coffee and eat a shortbread-type biscuit. I purposefully avoid looking at Clayton, who is deep in conversation with Zak.

'Alright, folk, are we ready for our next adventure?'

As we approach the vehicle, Ntando suggests that Joel sits next to him in the front passenger seat. I wonder if this is somehow part of Joel's interview, but either way, the look of excitement on his face makes me smile too. Joel is such a kid at heart, his passion for animals shining through. It isn't until I've shuffled in that I realise Clayton is positioning himself right next to me. Short of coming across extremely rude, there's nothing I can do about it. I shift as far over to the door as I can. Clayton sits in the middle while Lois is on his left. Why is he doing that when there's a whole row of empty seats in front of us? I suppose it's on purpose, to make me feel uncomfortable. If so, it's working.

When Clayton puts his arm around Lois's shoulders, I relax a little. At least he has a new girlfriend and he appears to have moved on. He seems a lot more relaxed these days and I wonder if he's genuinely changed. Perhaps he's truly happy with Lois and she's bringing the best out in him. If so, I'm thrilled for both of them; relieved too. He doesn't talk to me at all during the next ninety minutes but then we're all totally absorbed in watching the animals. This morning we don't just hear the roar of the lions, we actually see them. There are two females, a male and a youngster just lounging underneath a large tree. They look so deceptively docile, except when the male yawns widely and exposes those monstrous teeth. Lois gasps and Clayton pokes her in the stomach and tells her she's a Silly Billy. I can't imagine him saying such a thing to me. He would have ribbed me mercilessly. Zak reckons he has got some amazing photos. He mentions he's hoping to place them in travel magazines and if he's really lucky, in wildlife magazines too.

Our second treat of the morning is coming across a herd of giraffe. Ntando mentions that they're often called a tower of giraffes rather than a herd, and the name seems appropriate for the gangly necked, extraordinary creatures. I can't decide whether giraffe or zebra are my favourite animals. I find their markings so intriguing.

By the time we head back for the lodge, my stomach is growling. The sun is quite high in the sky now and the day is going to be hot. My limbs feel heavy and the tiredness is definitely catching up.

Breakfast is a feast. We have waffles and pastries, glorious fruit salads, yoghurts, savoury and sweet pancakes. Conversation between us is subdued and I get the feeling I'm not the only one who is tired. Even Clayton barely says a word.

Nancy comes in and says good morning to us and then she asks Joel if she can have a quick word. Joel jumps up and joins her on the other side of the room. I can't make out what they're talking about.

When we've finished breakfast, Joel pulls me to one side.

'Nancy has asked if I'll join her for a chat.'

'Does that mean an interview?' I ask.

'She said she wants to explain more about the job vacancy and to work out whether we'll be a good fit.'

'We?' I say. 'Am I meant to be there too?'

'No. I think the first step is to find out if I'm right for the job and then I guess she'll look at us as a package.' He reddens slightly. 'Sorry, that sounded a bit offensive.'

I kiss him on the lips. 'Not in the slightest bit offended. I'm going back to sleep. Good luck with the interview.'

I return to our tent and the walk doesn't seem nearly as scary in broad daylight. Nevertheless, I'm still on high alert. A lion could jump out of nowhere or a snake might weave its way across the path. I'm constantly glancing all around me, looking behind me and scouring the bushes, but I hear and see nothing.

Our tent has been cleaned up: the bed made, the clothes that we dumped on the back of chairs neatly hung up in the wardrobe, and today the towels on the end of the bed have been crafted into two swan heads. I strip off my dusty clothes and take a hot shower in the outside shower. It's glorious. And then I climb into bed, and despite the bright light, I fall asleep almost instantly.

When I awake, my head feels muffled and it takes some long moments to realise where I am and that the time is now 1.30 p.m. and lunch is served at 2 p.m. I realise that the huge window at the front of the tent is totally open, the see-through canvas rolled up and secured by simple ties. Hot midday air is wafting inside, the sounds of insects and birds creating a cacophony. Was the window open when I went to sleep? I don't remember. Yet surely I wouldn't have felt relaxed knowing that an animal, bird or snake could come straight in? I swing my legs out of bed and lift up the white waffle slippers, checking they're insect free, and then I walk over to the window opening. The day is totally still, the sun beating down and creating a haze in the distance. I wonder how Joel got on. Well, I hope, as he hasn't returned here. I'm not hungry, having had such a big breakfast, but I'd like to know how he is and I could do with a drink. I put on a bikini with a fine cotton summery dress over the top, grab my sunhat and sunglasses and open the door.

I scream.

Lying on the doorstep is a dead animal. I don't know what it is. Some kind of rodent; a rat possibly, because it's much bigger than a mouse and there's blood. Lots of it. I step backwards into the tent but then realise I'm being pathetic. Dead animals are likely to be everywhere here. This is a game reserve after all. I take another look. It's too big for me to pick up with tissue paper and I whimper, 'Oh God.' I'm not sure I'm suited to live somewhere like this. How did it get here? What animal deposited it and why right on my doorstep?

'Is everything alright?' Clayton appears at the top of the path. 'What's happened, Anna? You look like you've seen a ghost.'

I almost quip, 'Yes, it's you,' but instead I just point to the corpse at my feet, trying to avoid looking at it too much. I think the head has been partly severed and if I look again properly, I think I might be sick. Clayton strides towards me and stands over the animal. I've retreated into the tent, standing in the open doorway.

'It's just a dead rat, Anna. It's not going to harm you.'

'I thought where there are rodents there are snakes.'

He makes a show of looking all around, peering under

bushes and then stands up straight, brushing his hands down his cargo trousers. 'Nope. No snakes here.'

'I'll ring Ntando to ask him to remove it,' I suggest. I want to walk inside the tent but I don't want to give Clayton the chance to come in with me.

'No need,' he says, removing a handkerchief from his pocket. He squats down and lifts the dead rodent up by its tail. I have to bite my lower lip to stop bile from rising up into my throat. Perhaps I am a lightweight but the mauled animal sickens me. Clayton steps towards me.

'Look,' he says.

'Take that thing away,' I retort.

'Isn't Joel a vet? Can't *he* deal with this?' Clayton asks, the dead rat dangling in front of him. A drop of blood lands next to his foot.

'Joel's up at the main lodge,' I mutter.

'In which case, I'll pop up there myself and dispose of this. You really don't need to look so worried, Anna,' Clayton says. 'It was never going to hurt you.'

I thank Clayton and retreat inside the tent, sitting on the wooden veranda for a few minutes wondering what the future might bring. About five minutes later, much to my relief, Joel appears.

'Hey, love,' he says. He hands me a tall glass of juice. 'Nancy thought you might like this.'

'That's kind,' I say, taking a sip.

'I gather you had an incident with a dead rat!' He laughs. I don't think it's funny.

'Clayton appeared all full of himself saying that he'd rescued you from the clutches of Ratatouille.'

'Hardly. I found it dead on the doorstep. Do you think it was put there on purpose?'

Joel guffaws. 'Oh darling, you're such a city girl. Although there are plenty of rats in London – everywhere in the UK, in fact – it's just you rarely see them. This is the bush and things get killed here all the time.'

He clocks the annoyance on my face. 'Sorry, Anna. I realise you're on edge. Clayton being here is really getting to you, isn't it?'

'Mmm,' I mutter, still irked.

'I'll do my best to make sure you're never alone with him. I know you have history but honestly, Clayton just comes across as a swaggering buffoon.'

I snort because Joel is right about that, at least. 'How did the interview go?'

'Really well.' Joel jumps up from his chair. 'Nancy is great and I think we hit it off. I reckon the chances are high that the job is mine.'

I smile but it feels forced. And I don't say anything because Joel's answer to my question isn't really the one that I want to hear.

9

ANNA - NOW

Joel accompanies me back to the main lodge where there is another amazing spread of food; salads mainly, ranging from sweet potato curry to rice with aubergine and sultanas. The choice is amazing and even though I didn't think I was hungry, I manage to devour a substantial plateful. As we're eating homemade sorbet, Nancy appears. She's wearing beige cotton trousers and a polo shirt with Twivali's logo embroidered on the chest.

'I was wondering if you'd all like to visit our sanctuary for sick animals this afternoon.'

'That sounds great,' Katie says enthusiastically.

'Not sure I'll be joining you,' Lois says, yawning without putting her hand in front of her mouth. Clayton frowns at her and I wonder if I see a little bit of the old Clayton there.

'Come on, love,' he says, squeezing her hand. 'This is a once-in-a-lifetime opportunity.'

She narrows her eyes and sighs but doesn't say anything further. When we all congregate outside to get into the vehicles, despite saying she didn't feel like it, Lois is right there,

Clayton's arm around her waist, gripping her as if she's his and he doesn't intend to let her go. I wonder how Lois feels. I wonder if she feels as claustrophobic as I did or whether she likes Clayton's controlling manner.

We go out in two Land Rovers. Ntando takes Katie, Zak, Joel and me, and I'm relieved when Clayton and Lois go with Nancy. For the first time since I realised Clayton was here, I feel like I can completely relax and fully take in how magical the landscape and wildlife is out here.

'The rehabilitation centre is very new,' Ntando explains. 'And right now we only have two rhino and some monkeys.'

After driving maybe fifteen minutes along unmade tracks, we arrive at a ramshackle shed. The roof is constructed from metal panels and the area around it is enclosed by a tall wire fence. When we're all standing in a huddle, me as far away from Clayton as I can politely manage, Nancy starts talking.

'We are small today,' she explains, 'but we have big plans, and that's one of the reasons I've invited Joel here. As you likely know, rhinoceros are an endangered species, so my intention is to create this into a purpose-built holding facility where we will care for any hurt rhino, raise orphans, and ultimately release them back into the wild. We have one little baby in our care at the moment who was orphaned a few months ago. The care is very intensive and requires a lot of staff. Our baby, whom we've named Aza, gets fed every two hours and can consume sixteen litres of milk a day. As you will appreciate, this is expensive work and I'm hoping to raise considerable funds to expand this facility.' She glances at Clayton, who nods his head. I wonder if that's why Clayton is here: to raise money. 'It's important we have as many rhino here as possible so they can create crashes.'

'Crashes?' Katie interrupts.

'That's a group of rhino. Together they learn how to socialise, learning rhino body language and how to interact with other rhino. Our aim is to treat all sick animals and rehabilitate not just on our reserve but on other reserves throughout South Africa. Katie, I can give you more information on this for your articles, if you wish.'

'Yes, thanks. That would be great,' she says.

And then a man appears carrying a huge bottle, and trotting alongside him is a little rhino. She isn't much larger than an Alsatian dog and she bounces excitedly. My heart melts.

'Lethabo is going to feed little Aza.'

We watch as the rhino sucks milk from the enormous plastic bottle, hungrily finishing her meal in record time. Zak is constantly taking photos; crouching down to capture the baby rhino from all angles, taking photos of us as we look adoringly at this cute sight. Lois is loving the attention from the camera, flicking her hair, softening her gaze at she watches the cute rhinoceros. And then I notice that Clayton is stepping to one side, out of shot, every time Zak points the camera anywhere near us. It's strange. Why is it that Clayton is avoiding having his photo taken? I don't remember him being camera shy in the past, but on the other hand, I don't have any photos of him either. If I did, I would have deleted them.

Nancy walks over to stand next to Joel. 'Can you shoot?' she asks.

'Yes.'

I recoil with surprise.

'You know how to use a gun?' I ask.

Joel laughs. 'Yes.'

'I thought you just used injections to put animals down.'

'Sorry, Nancy. I haven't explained the minutiae of my work to Anna. I don't shoot as part of my veterinary practice but I grew up on a farm, so yes, I do know how to shoot. And occasionally it's the kindest way to put a large animal down.'

I feel wrong-footed somehow.

'It's what I would have expected,' Nancy says. 'So you have a gun licence?'

'Yes, but I don't own any guns and I don't shoot game.'

'Not part of the trophy-hunting brigade, then?' Zak quips.

'Certainly not,' Joel replies. 'What are your views on it?' he asks Nancy.

'I'm sorry but I find it abhorrent. I don't understand how anyone could want to kill one of our majestic beasts and then stuff its head to display on a wall. It's a highly controversial topic. Some reserve owners are happy to use trophy hunting as a supposed method of conservation and charge tourists huge sums of money for the privilege. They claim that this money is used to preserve animals and enhance conservation efforts. I'm afraid that I just see it as another way to exacerbate the decline of an already threatened species. As I said, it's a very controversial topic and I'm perfectly aware that many disagree with my view.'

'I agree with you,' I murmur.

Nancy smiles and nods at me. 'But being able to shoot is a vital skill for a vet here. We dart animals to sedate them. Joel, we need to dart a white rhino to ear notch it for identification and to collect its DNA for research. I was wondering if you'd like to assist the team when we do that?'

Joel's eyes widen. 'I'd love that.'

'Fantastic. I'll let you know when it's happening. Right.

I'll take this Defender back to the lodge and the rest of you can join Ntando for a game drive. I hope you see some wonderful animals.' She waves us goodbye and hops into her Land Rover, driving away at speed. I'm so impressed by Nancy. It looks as if she's building up this game reserve all by herself. If she has a partner, we certainly haven't seen him or her. I decide to question Katie. If she's writing articles about Twivali, perhaps she'll know more of the background.

'How much do you know about Nancy?' I ask. 'She's such an impressive woman.'

'Yes, she is,' Katie agrees. 'I interviewed her a couple of days ago. She was brought up in South Africa, in Johannesburg I think, and she came into some money more latterly. It's been her dream to own a game reserve.'

'Does she have any experience in it?'

'No, but she's got very experienced staff. Ntando is excellent, isn't he?'

I nod in agreement. 'Does she have any family?'

'Not that I know about. She's doing this all by herself, which makes it even more remarkable. I think she's very brave.'

'It's obvious that she's passionate about animals. I can see how this would be the dream for someone like her,' I say. And the dream for Joel, I think, but is it the dream for me? I really don't know if I could live somewhere like this so far away from the nearest town, having to always be on the lookout for danger. Perhaps one gets used to it and it's no different to us looking both ways when we cross a busy road.

Back in the vehicle, it's Clayton's turn to sit in the front seat next to Ntando. I'm glad, as I can be as far away from him as possible. He chats to Ntando as we weave along the dirt tracks, bouncing up and down. Lois looks fed up and I get the impression she'd rather be in a luxury spa hotel than out here in the hot, dusty African bush. And then Ntando brings the vehicle to a gentle stop. There's static on his radio and a voice comes through. He talks for a moment in a language I don't understand.

'Good news, folk,' he says, without turning around to look at us. 'There's a family of cheetah nearby.' He stands up and peers through his binoculars. 'There's fresh cheetah dung just down there. They have satellite tracker collars and they're to the left of us in those trees.' He points to some dense shrubs with acacia trees behind them. 'I'm going to go and have a look. I want you all to stay here and under no circumstances get out of the vehicle. I won't be long.' Ntando jumps down from the Defender and I'm surprised that he leaves his rifle in the vehicle. He takes long strides and in seconds he has disappeared from sight.

'Is this normal?' I murmur to Joel.

'Perfectly. Trackers like Ntando know exactly what they're doing. They would never put us or themselves at risk. He can't drive the vehicle through that dense bush so he'll be working out how we can get to view the cheetah, from the other side probably.'

We wait for five minutes and I feel perfectly at ease with Joel by my side, anticipation rising at the thought of seeing magnificent cats.

'Don't move!'

I screech, as do some of the others. Out of nowhere, two men have appeared, one holding a rifle, the other a shotgun. They're wearing military fatigues. Both weapons are pointed at us.

Joel swears under his breath.

Oh my God. Have they got Ntando? Is that why he hasn't come back? Are we going to be kidnapped, or worse?

'Take off your jewellery and your watches,' the taller of the two says. I fumble trying to remove my watch. I attempt to tug off my engagement ring, the beautiful, simple small diamond that Joel and I chose together, but my fingers have swollen in the heat. Perhaps if I sit on my hand, they won't notice.

'You! Get down here now.' The taller man points at Lois. She screams.

'Shut up!' Clayton says in a harsh whisper.

The smaller man shakes his head and mutters something in a local dialect to the taller man before striding towards my door and beckoning his middle finger at me. 'Get down now!' he says, as he takes a step closer to the vehicle and wrenches my door open.

'What do you want with her?' Joel's voice quivers.

'For you to shut your face and me to have her.'

I'm trembling so much I can barely move. What should I do? Joel holds my hand but I tug away from him.

The stranger's dark eyes are fixed on mine and my throat constricts. 'Get down now. If you're not down by the count of three, I'm shooting you. Do you understand?'

'Yes,' I whisper. I try to stand up but I'm shaking. My legs feel like jelly.

'One. Two.'

'I'm coming,' I say as I tumble out of the Defender, my knees giving way as I land on the ground. Am I going to be the sacrificial lamb or am I going to be kidnapped? My heart constricts in my body and I think I might throw up.

'You're pretty,' he says, in a low, menacing voice. I stumble again, pushing myself up from the grassy soil with my hands. He grabs my hand and pulls me closer to him. 'Get up.' He's rough as he puts an arm under mine and when I'm standing there, just centimetres from him, he runs his finger down my cheek. 'Very pretty,' he says as he thrusts his groin towards me. I let out a whimper.

I glance up at Joel but he's as frozen as I am. Where is Ntando? Have they hurt him, or worse?

The shorter guy says something in a local dialect that I don't understand. The taller one sniggers. The shorter man is standing so close to me now his shotgun is practically touching my temple. His breath smells of garlic and his eyes are slightly bloodshot. There is total silence. I'm holding my breath and I think everyone in the vehicle is too. It's almost as if the birds have stopped singing and the insects chirruping. Am I going to die?

'I'll take her behind the bushes,' the smaller man says, looking pointedly at me as his face contorts into a lascivious grin. He puts an arm around my shoulders. I'm going to be raped. There I was, terrified about being attacked by a lion or an elephant. Yet it's another human being who is going to destroy me.

The ring of a shot makes me yelp. I glance back at the Defender and Clayton is standing up in the passenger seat, a rifle aimed at the head of the man holding me.

'Piss off and let her go,' he says. Clayton's voice is low and controlled. Terrifying. Suddenly he moves the gun, so quickly, and fires another shot. This time the bullet fires into the ground, just centimetres from the feet of the taller man. There's a collective inhale of breath and the man holding me lets go of my arm. All eyes are on Clayton. Slowly he aims the gun so it's pointing to the head of the short man, who is now standing next to me.

'If you don't let her get back in the vehicle, the next shot will be to your head. I'm a good shot.' He swings the gun towards the taller man. 'And the second one will be to your head.'

What is Clayton playing at? Is he really a good enough shot to save me?

'Just fuck off out of here! You've got three seconds, otherwise you're dead!' Clayton yells.

And to my utter relief, the men run. Clutching their guns, they race through the bushes, disappearing quickly out of sight. As if just to prove the point, Clayton points the gun in the air and fires again.

My legs give way and I collapse onto the ground, tears pouring down my face. Joel jumps down and flings his arms around me. 'Oh my God,' he says repeatedly, squeezing me so tightly I can barely breathe.

'What the hell were you playing at!' Zak yells at Clayton. 'You could have got us all killed.'

'But I didn't, did I? I saved Anna. Are you alright?' he asks me.

'Yes, I think so,' I say, holding onto a door handle of the Defender. Joel helps me back up inside but I'm trembling so much I feel dizzy. 'Thank you, Clayton,' I say.

Zak glares, stony faced. 'You shouldn't have done that. You got lucky, you know. Those bastards could have shot all of us.'

'That's bullshit,' Clayton says. 'I know how these guys think. It's just basic psychology. Any resistance and they panic, which is exactly what happened. I didn't see any of you reaching for the gun,' he says, eyeing Zak and Joel. 'No responsible ranger is going to leave his guests in a vehicle without a gun. But that's not the point, is it? You need to stand up to bullies. It's the same anywhere; stand up to them and they'll back off.'

'I don't know, Clayton,' Joel says. I squeeze his knee. There's no point in arguing with Clayton. Whatever we all think of Clayton's actions, he saved me. Saved us all probably.

'My ploy worked, though, didn't it? It's not like I had any choice. They'd have raped Anna and the rest of you would have just stood by and let it happen. Then most likely they'd have killed her and come back for Lois and Katie. You don't get it, though, do you, Joel? It's the law of the jungle out here, but of course, you're just a cosseted little vet from the home counties who doesn't know how to protect his woman.'

'What!' Joel stands up. His jaw is clenched in fury, but he doesn't know Clayton and how Clayton goads people.

'Just sit down,' I murmur, tugging at his hand.

There's rustling from the bushes and we all freeze. Again. We let out a collective breath when Ntando emerges.

'You should never have left us,' Clayton says angrily.

'I found the cheetah but then I heard gunshots.'

'I had to use the rifle to chase off some guys who wanted to rape Anna.'

Ntando's face turns grey. He looks as terrified as we felt. I wonder if he'll lose his job for this – leaving us alone in the vehicle. I hope not. He's such a nice guy.

'Are you alright?' he asks, his voice a whisper, as he looks at each of us in turn.

'I need a stiff drink,' Lois says.

'I think we all do,' Clayton echoes.

Ntando jumps into the driver's seat. 'I'll take you straight back to the lodge. I'm so terribly sorry, everyone. Nothing like that has ever happened before out here. Never.'

He speaks into his walkie-talkie and I notice that his hand is trembling. 'There's been an ambush,' he says. 'We're coming home.'

Back at the lodge, Nancy is there to greet us, her lips set in a rigid line, her face pale.

'I'm so sorry, guys,' she says. 'Nothing like that has ever happened before,' she repeats Ntando's earlier words.

But I wonder how she knows. She's only recently taken over the lodge, so perhaps this is a regular thing. Perhaps the previous owners 'forgot' to mention it. Perhaps the doors to the tents should have locks on them and maybe we need more than one ranger to accompany us on our game drives. I remember that snake we saw when we first got here and I think it really was an omen. I wish I could go home.

10

ANNA

'I want to leave.' Joel and I are back in our tent and I'm not sure which one of us is more anxious. He doesn't say anything but he does sit on the edge of the bed, hunched over, his face in his hands.

'It's too dangerous here. I don't want to be on holiday in this place, let alone live here. You do understand, don't you?'

He looks up at me with bloodshot eyes. 'What happened today is extremely rare. Nancy explained that to us.'

'Why should we put ourselves at unnecessary risk? It's happened so it could happen again.' It reminds me of a car accident I had when I was twenty. I was driving a bit too fast but there was oil on the road and it caused me to skid, spinning the car and hitting a tree. I was very, very lucky, sustaining minor injuries. I remember the policeman saying how unusual it was. Ever since, my view is, it could happen again. Just the very fact that something has occurred once demonstrates another occurrence is a possibility. As I think back over those couple of minutes this afternoon, my stomach clenches painfully. It was bad enough that they threatened to rape me, to steal our belongings, to possibly kill me, but the horror has been compounded by the fact that Clayton became my saviour. Yes, of course I'm grateful to him. But why did *he* have to be my rescuer? And how he gloated, rubbing Joel's nose in it. I expect he'll be insufferable now. He's another reason I want to get out of here.

'I'm sorry,' Joel murmurs. 'I'm sorry I'm just a middle-class vet from the home counties who doesn't know how to protect her fiancée from an ambush in the South African bush.'

'Don't be silly,' I say, walking around the bed and sitting next to him. 'It was just luck that Clayton had the gun within easy reach. If you'd been sitting in the front passenger seat, you'd have done the same.'

Joel shakes his head. 'You're wrong. I would never have pulled a gun like that. He was right, he did save us and I failed you. I'm sorry, Anna.'

I knock my knee against his. 'You're being ridiculous. Clayton always puts on a show of bravado and as Zak says, what he did was extremely dangerous. He could have got us all killed.'

'Except he didn't, and he rescued you.'

'I don't want you to feel bad about that. I love you, Joel.' I squeeze his hand.

'Do you think it'll get back to Nancy, how Clayton saved us all and I sat there like a frozen idiot? She's hardly going to want to employ me now, is she?'

I sigh. I know it's unfair to Joel but I hope she doesn't offer him the job. I know now that I couldn't live here, not with the threat that something terrible might happen to us. It's one thing worrying that burglars might break down the door to the garden shed at Joel's house and steal a chainsaw.

It's quite another thing to be terrified of the dangerous animals and armed men.

'I really want to go home,' I say again. 'I know you want to stay, and I don't want to get in your way. So you stay and I'll go home alone.' In truth, I know I can't leave. Our return flights have been paid for us and I hate to think how much it would cost to change my flights. I have no doubt it will be much too expensive.

'Please don't go,' Joel says. 'Look, if I'm offered the job, I'll turn it down. You are more important than any job.'

I shake my head. I don't know if I can destroy Joel's dream. I think of how many long years Joel trained to become a vet, how hard he's worked just to get to this point, how his childhood dream has been to work on a game reserve. How can I ruin that for him? Won't he come to resent me, and what will that do to our marriage? But the thought of not being with Joel is too much to bear. Perhaps we'll have to have a long-distance relationship. If he stays here for let's say three years, we could manage that, couldn't we? We trust each other.

'I'm sure that Nancy will tighten up the security around us,' Joel says. 'Stay with me. It's only another three days, and perhaps we'll see the cheetah. I know you don't like being around Clayton, but we can stay away from him. This mess is all my fault. If I hadn't let you down...'

I sigh. 'It's not your fault, Joel. None of us have the training as to what we should do in the face of armed robbers.'

'Except Clayton did.'

'Forget Clayton. It's you I love.'

'Please stay, darling,' he says putting his arms around me.

'Okay,' I say reluctantly, because I know I don't really

have any choice.

The late afternoon sun is beginning to set and the sky is turning shades of purple and orange.

'Come outside,' Joel says. We sit next to each other on the deck chairs on our veranda and watch the sun go down. I think back over the ambush and wonder why the attackers honed in on me. Lois is much more attractive, and they started off with her but quickly changed to me. Was it because I was sitting nearest to the men with guns? Is that why I was chosen? I wonder if I'll ever feel safe here. I think back over the years, the times when I've felt anxious or in fear of my life. The time I was in a car accident, thanks to an ex-boyfriend taking a corner too fast and then again, when I had the accident skidding on oil; when I had an appendicitis and was rushed to hospital; when I was walking home after a late night out at uni and stupidly decided to go home alone. There were footsteps behind me and I was positive I was going to get attacked. When eventually I plucked up the courage to look over my shoulder, it was another girl from my halls of residence. And then that other time, when I was walking home from Mum's place. I've been lucky, I suppose, to have experienced so few truly fearful moments.

When there's a knock on the door, we both jump. No doubt it's going to take a while for our nerves to settle. Joel hops up and goes to open the door.

'Could I have a quick word with your both?' I hear Nancy say.

She follows Joel out to veranda and leans her back against the simple wires that create a barrier.

'I just wanted to reiterate how sorry I am about this afternoon. Are you alright?' She peers at me.

'It was quite the shock,' I say.

'But we'll get over it,' Joel interrupts.

I bite my tongue. I can see what Joel's doing; downplaying the incident so it doesn't ruin his job chances. I cross my arms over my chest in annoyance.

'Joel,' Nancy says, turning her gaze to him. 'I've just received notice that they want to dart the white rhino in an hour's time. I know it's short notice and you might not feel up to it after what's happened, but it would be great if you could join Ntando and the crew. There'll be a number of rangers from adjacent reserves and I think it'll be quite the experience for you.'

Joel perks up as my heart sinks. 'I'd love that,' he says, excitement visible in his face.

'Really?' I say.

'It's a once-in-a-lifetime opportunity, Anna,' Joel says, his eyes pleading with me.

But if Joel is going to do that, I want to go too. I can't have Clayton acting as some bullish idiot and setting Joel up for failure. Horrific images of the rhino charging at Joel play out in my mind's eye.

'Can I go as well?' I ask.

Nancy's face falls. 'I'm so sorry, Anna, but it's too dangerous for someone with no animal experience. The only people there will be rangers and veterinary staff.'

I hope that means that Clayton won't be there.

Nancy continues. 'I've arranged wonderful massages for you, Katie and Lois. I promise you, it'll be a great experience and just what you need to relax. If you could both make your way to the main lodge in twenty minutes, that would be perfect. Once again, I'm so sorry about the terror you must have felt.'

'It's not your fault,' Joel says. 'But at least I know what to do if I'm ever in that situation again.'

'If you take the job, we'll make sure that you're given training should you come across poachers, but as I said earlier, facing an ambush like that never happens. You were just terribly unlucky.'

I'm quiet when Nancy leaves. And annoyed. Why can't I join Joel? I don't have to get close to the rhino. I could just stay in the vehicle to watch. I feel like I've been sidelined just at the time I need Joel to be with me, to help calm my jittery nervous system. Or am I being unreasonable? After all, it's him, not me, who is here for a job interview.

Joel latches onto my silence. 'There'll be another occasion when you can watch the rhino darting, I'm sure,' he says. 'Better to be safe than sorry.'

'But what about you? How safe is it for you? And will Clayton be going?'

'I doubt it. Nancy's just said it was for people with animal experience. And of course I'll be safe. There'll be lots of other experienced people around, and it's not as if I'm going to be firing the dart. I get that you're on edge, darling, but please don't worry.'

Easier said than done.

Twenty minutes later and we're back in the main lodge. Zak is talking to Ntando and when Joel joins them, the three of them leave.

'Is Clayton not going?' I ask Nancy, as casually as I can manage.

'No, he doesn't have animal experience. Zak is going so he can photograph everything.' She starts walking. 'Come with me, and I'll take you to where we've organised the massages.'

I'm relieved that Joel won't have to face any bravado and

one-upmanship from Clayton this afternoon but I don't like the thought that he's hanging around the lodge, especially as we're all about to have massages.

Nancy leads me to the small swimming pool. Three massage tables have been erected with bamboo screens around each. They have hung cotton gauze, which lightly flaps in the wind, and rose petals are scattered on the wooden terrace. It looks beautiful. Scented candles send wafts of bergamot and geranium into the hot air. Katie and Lois are already there, chatting, each holding a glass of champagne.

'Wow,' I say.

'It's beautiful, isn't it?' Lois comments. Unlike me, I reckon she's quite high maintenance and is probably used to having massages like this.

'Would you like a glass of champagne?' Bhutana appears holding a champagne flute and a bottle in a cooler basket.

'Thank you, Bhutana.' I take a seat between Lois and Katie and Bhutana grins at me widely. I wonder what it's like for her and her colleagues to be working out here in the middle of nowhere. There's something about this whole setup that makes me feel uneasy and I just hope that the staff are treated well.

'This is the life,' Katie says with a sigh, leaning back against her chair. 'How are you doing after the drama this afternoon?'

'Surprisingly alright. Or at least I hope I will be after a massage,' I say, although I'm not exactly being truthful. 'How about you, Lois?' I ask.

'Intending to get drunk. I sure as hell didn't expect to be shot dead when I signed up for this trip.'

'Signed up?' I ask.

She waves her hand. 'A manner of speaking. Clayton persuaded me to join him, said it would be fun. But as you know, Clayton's idea of fun isn't necessarily what our, girls' idea of fun is.' Her laugh is harsh. I wonder if all is not well in paradise.

'He saved us though,' Katie says.

'Are you aware of the history, you know, between Clayton and Anna?' Lois asks Katie as she winks at me.

'No.' Katie frowns.

'Clayton and Anna used to go out together.'

'Really?' Katie's eyes widen.

'Yup. What are the chances of that?' Lois says. 'Ending up in an exclusive safari with your ex.' The sarcasm in Lois's voice adds to my certainty that Clayton being here at the same time as me is no coincidence.

'I gather Clayton didn't join the other men,' I say.

'No. He's doing some work in our tent.'

'Do you live together?' I ask.

'No, although he wants us to.' Lois grins and throws her head backwards. 'I think there'll be a ring on my finger by the end of this holiday. Don't tell him, but I found a little jewellery box in his luggage with a great big ring in it.'

'Congratulations,' Katie says. 'And don't worry, our lips are sealed.'

I wonder if it's the sapphire surrounded by little diamonds that he gave me; the ring I returned to him. But it's not fair of me to ask Lois. All in all, I'm relieved. Good luck to Lois. It makes me feel more relaxed knowing that Clayton is in another serious relationship. Perhaps he has changed. Perhaps we can all be friends, or at least not friends, but cordial. That would make life so much easier. Perhaps I should believe in coincidences after all.

11

ANNA – THEN

The morning after Clayton proposes to me, he takes me to see our new house. It's on a smart street and has a single parking space at the front which, according to Clayton, is quite the selling point, because otherwise both of us would be battling to find somewhere to park. London and parking are two words that don't belong together. I wonder whether it'll be my car or more likely his Porsche that gets our single allocated space. The house looks like it's been modernised quite recently, similar to next door, except that one has a double buggy parked out the front, for twins perhaps.

The front door is shiny and black, with a brass knocker, and there's a lighter patch on the stone outside where a planter might once have stood. Clayton inserts a key, steps inside to input a code in the alarm panel and then stands back to let me in.

'Actually, no. Wait!' he says, blocking my way. He leans forwards and tries to pick me up in an awkward manoeuvre because I'm not expecting it. I bash the side of my head on the doorway and let out a yelp.

'Shit, I'm so sorry, darling,' he says. 'But I need to carry you over the threshold for good luck.'

'Isn't that for brides when they're married?'

'We're almost married.'

I let him lift me but I'm obviously heavier than he anticipated because he drops me to the floor the moment we're inside. I put my fingers to my head and can feel a small bump emerging. I'll have to ignore it.

The hallway is long and narrow, with faux panelling on the lower half of the walls. It's all been tastefully painted in one of those fancy paint brands with a name like Mules' Hoof or something, and the place smells of lavender, but a synthetic type of lavender, as if someone has emptied an aerosol into the place in anticipation of our arrival.

'It's a great-sized living room, isn't it?' Clayton says as he steps back for me to inspect it. There is a fireplace with a faux fire and built-in bookshelves either side, but plantation shutters over the bowed window make the room quite dark. Yes, it is a good-sized room but it feels very formal and grown up, and I don't consider myself to be either of those things. I try but fail to envisage what it might look like with furniture in it. The kitchen is even more impressive. It has sleek, white units and a long island unit, as well as enough space at the end for a sizeable kitchen table. An extension has been built at the back with extra-wide sliding doors that lead out to a neatly manicured garden. Upstairs, Clayton leads me straight to what he describes as the 'baby room'. It was obviously used as a nursery by the previous owners because the walls are covered with a naive animal-design wallpaper, and there's a matching fabric blind at the window.

'We won't need to change a thing in here; just get some suitable furniture,' Clayton says with a big grin on his face. I suppress a shiver. He shows me two more empty bedrooms and well-appointed bathrooms but saves the master bedroom until last. Inside there is a large double bed, and to my surprise it's made up, covered in a duvet with a white duvet cover and matching pillows.

I frown.

'I asked the previous owners to leave their bed and I made it up with my own linen. I didn't want to wait to christen the house until after we've moved in and I thought you might not appreciate making love on the carpet.' Clayton steps towards me, his arms outstretched.

'Oh,' I say, because this all feels so weird. Wrong some-how, not least that I'm expected to have sex with Clayton on someone else's bed as part of a carefully curated plan. I try to shake away the unease and remind myself that we all sleep on strangers' beds whenever we stay in a hotel so perhaps it's not that bizarre after all.

'So what do you think of the house? Do you love it?'

'Yes,' I say, because it's impressive, but does it feel as if it could be my home one day? No. I dream of living in a little cottage in the countryside, with hollyhocks in the garden and roses growing up the front. A townhouse in Fulham has never been on my radar. Yet I can't bring myself to say anything because I know how hurt Clayton will be.

'I sense a reluctance,' he says as he removes his sweater and folds it neatly, placing it on the floor next to the bed.

'I don't think we should move in together until after we're married,' I say.

Clayton stares at me. 'I don't understand. We're engaged and I bought us a beautiful new home.'

'I know, and I'm really grateful,' I say. 'But everything has gone so fast. I think we should take a bit of time before we get married, and move into this house then. I mean, you could live in it now, or perhaps rent it out for a year.'

'A year!' Clayton exclaims. 'This house is for you.' His red face is a mixture of perplexed and anger.

'Look, I love it and I love you. I just want to go a little slower. It doesn't mean I'm walking away.'

Clayton exhales loudly. 'It's your commitment issues, isn't it? It's because your parents got divorced and now you're worried about committing and leaving yourself vulnerable. That makes total sense, Anna, but I'm not your dad. I'll never let you down and I'll never leave you.' He puts his arms around me and squeezes me tightly. He then starts kissing me, and because I'm weak and my body craves his even though my mind is flashing big amber lights, I succumb and let him tug me onto the bed.

'I love you so much,' Clayton says, as he stares into my eyes half an hour later. 'I didn't know it was possible to love someone like this. You're my everything, Anna.'

I smile sleepily at him.

'Will you change your mind about moving in here with me? This is a proper home, not like the nasty little pad you share with Sasha. You'll be saving money too, not tipping your earnings down the drain renting somewhere. It won't cost you a penny to live here.'

I freeze. 'When we live together, I'll pay my share, contribute to the mortgage and bills.'

'That won't be necessary, darling,' he says.

I'm not going to fight Clayton now, but there is no way that I'm going to be a kept woman, married or not.

Over the next few days, Clayton tries repeatedly to get me to change my mind, but I'm resolute. I won't be moving in with him yet. We negotiate on the time-scales and I agree to rethink in three months' time. That seems to appease him slightly. But I know I won't be ready in three months, and I wonder if I'll ever be ready.

I return home, without Clayton, just in time to catch Sasha before she leaves for the airport. Her suitcase is packed and she's treating herself to an Uber to the airport, celebrating the first holiday she's taken in over a year. Sasha asked me to join her on a yoga and meditation retreat in Ibiza followed by a week on the beach, but I said no. I knew that Clayton wants me to go on holiday with him and he is mooting the Maldives or the Seychelles. Instead, Sasha is going with a friend of hers from work.

I hold out my left hand.

'Is that an engagement ring?' she asks, her eyes widening.

'Yup.'

'But you always said you wanted a simple solitaire diamond.'

'Yes,' I say, annoyed that I'd shared that wish with Sasha. Then again, we both know pretty much everything about each other. 'But this is lovely too, isn't it?'

'Mmm,' she says non-committedly. 'So you said yes to Clayton?' She knots her eyebrows together.

'Yes. Aren't you going to congratulate me?'

She shakes her head slightly as if she's reminding herself of her manners. Then she throws her arms around me. 'Congratulations, babe. It's just happened really quickly. I'm surprised, that's all.'

'I know and I'm trying to slow things down.'

'Will I still have a roof over my head when I get back from holiday?'

'Absolutely. I'm not going anywhere for the foreseeable.'

And then the doorbell rings and it's Sasha's Uber and she blows me a kiss before hurrying away.

I know I should be feeling elated but for some reason I don't. Instead it's as if I've been railroaded into getting engaged, yet at the same time I *think* this is what I want. Clayton adores me and his generosity is overwhelming. That's it. I feel overwhelmed. Rather smothered. I know Clayton would be devastated if I told him that so I'm going to have to slow things down without telling him the truth. It's the ideal period to do it as Sasha is away for a fortnight and I'll have my own space.

'I'm going to have to sleep at my place during the next fortnight because Sasha is away,' I tell Clayton when he calls me, just one of many calls he makes to me during the days we're not together.

'Why?'

'The landlord has asked us not to leave the place empty. There was a flood during the previous tenancy and I think it's something to do with that.'

There's silence on the other end of the line and I suspect that Clayton doesn't believe my lie.

'In which case I'll stay with you,' he says.

'Not tonight,' I say. 'I'm really tired and I'm going to Mum's for supper. Nick's away on business so she's alone and I want to tell her the wonderful news.'

'Do you want me to come with you?'

'You know what Mum is like. She'll smother you, then she'll interrogate you. It'll be a nightmare.' I feel bad for making Mum out to be overpowering because really she's not. It's just I know she'll think I'm rushing into things with Clayton and I don't want him to pick up on the negative vibes.

'Alright. But let's go out for supper tomorrow night.'

Mum lives in Islington, not too far from us in Hackney. It's one of the reasons I was happy to rent the flat I share with Sasha – I could easily hop to Mum's if I was after a home-made meal. She inherited her parents' house and back then, it was far from a desirable area. Now the house prices are exorbitant and it's one of London's chi chi districts. I guess it's another reason why I'm not thrilled about living in Fulham. It's the other side of town from Mum.

Mum's reaction is exactly as I anticipated. She's happy for me – because what parent wouldn't be happy for their daughter to be marrying a wealthy, handsome, attentive man? But she reminds me that I barely know him. I reassure her I won't be marrying Clayton imminently. We have a relaxed supper chatting about nothing much, and about 9 p.m. I set off for the walk home.

I always walk, despite it taking forty-five minutes. I'm about five minutes from home when I become aware of footsteps behind me. I slow down. The footsteps slow down. I speed up and they do the same. I swivel around but I can't see anyone in the dark shadows. There are no passing cars and I'm on a quiet residential street. There aren't many lights on in windows, either. So I start running. I race as fast as I can until I'm outside my building, my breath ragged, my heart racing. I shove the key in the lock to the main door and glance all around me. There's no one there.

After pushing the door open, I nip in and close it behind me. I run up the stairs, unlock our apartment door and when I'm inside, I bolt it top and bottom. I must have been imagining things. It takes a while to get my breath back. After drinking nearly a litre of water, I sink onto the sofa and channel-hop on the television. Then my mobile rings and it's a withheld number.

'Hello?' I say.

There's silence. 'Who's there?'

Still silence. I wait for a few moments then hang up.

Twenty minutes later, the phone rings again. This time I can hear someone's breath and it freaks me. 'Piss off and leave me alone,' I say before ending the call.

I ring Clayton.

'Have I woken you?' I ask, glancing at the clock. It's 11.15 p.m. but he's rarely asleep by now.

'Yes, but I don't mind being woken by your voice,' he says huskily. 'What's up?'

'I've had some silent calls from a withheld number. It's creeped me out.'

He suddenly sounds more alert. 'Would you like me to come over?'

'It's sweet of you but no. I need to sleep.'

'But you called me for a reason, Anna. You must be scared. I'll come over.'

I kick myself for calling him because I really don't want Clayton here.

'It's so kind of you but honestly, I'm fine. I just wanted to hear your voice. If it happens again, then I'll call you.'

'Alright,' he says reluctantly. 'If you're sure.'

He murmurs some smut to me, which I find embarrassing, and eventually we say goodnight.

The silent calls happen on my mobile phone with increasing regularity at all hours of the day and night, even when I'm at work. It's always from a withheld number, so there's no way that I can trace it. Any thought that it might have been a wrong number quickly dissipates and I wonder if I should notify the police. It's a tricky one, because I haven't been threatened with anything. All I can do is not answer the phone if it's a call from an unknown or withheld number. I discuss it with Clayton and he suggests I do nothing for the moment.

But then more weird things start happening. This evening, Clayton insisted on coming over and we're deciding what food to order in when the doorbell goes. I stride over to the intercom.

'Pizza delivery for Anna Evans.'

I pause. I haven't ordered anything yet and it certainly wouldn't be pizza because Clayton only eats 'proper' food, as he describes it.

'It's not for me,' I say.

'Flat 2, Anna Evans? A Hawaiian and a Margherita, both on thin crust.'

'I'm sorry, but I don't know what's happened. I didn't order anything. You'll have to take it away.'

'It's been paid for so you might as well have it. Leaving it on the doorstep.'

'Who paid for it?' I ask, but the delivery driver has gone.

I go downstairs and collect the two boxes. They're from a leading pizza company.

'I'm not eating those,' Clayton says, eyeing them with distaste. 'They might be poisoned.'

That had never crossed my mind, and even though I hate

the waste, I throw both pizzas away. Clayton orders us Japanese food from an upmarket restaurant.

The next day, I receive a bouquet of flowers. They're cheap flowers, not the fancy ones Clayton buys me, and there's no note. I try calling the company's customer service team but I'm told they can't give me the name of the sender due to data protection. I'm a little freaked out now, and when Clayton suggests that I go and stay with him tonight, I accept readily. What I hadn't expected was my fiancé's reaction to the unwanted attention I'm getting.

He is livid.

I've never seen him so angry. 'Whoever the bastard is who's following you, I'm going to murder him.'

'Hey,' I say, trying to appease him. 'I haven't even been threatened. It's just an annoyance.'

'It's my job to protect you, Anna. I'd give my life for yours. I'll do anything to make sure you're safe.'

'I appreciate that but I don't feel unsafe.' It's true, I don't. Not really.

'I've bought an alarm system for you, along with some security cameras. They're for your flat and your car. We can't take any risks.'

I know Clayton means well but I do think this is overkill. The car that he bought me is still sitting in the garage to his apartment block because I'm sure it'll get vandalised if I park it near our flat, so I'm still driving my twenty-year-old Fiat that is battered and worthless. I'm wondering if I should suggest he gives the car back, because I can't see myself driving it around London any time soon, but I don't want to seem ungrateful.

'Let's drive over to your place,' he says. 'And I'll install everything.'

And so he does. I let him install the cameras and he links them up to my phone. I let him install a dash cam in my car and the Golf that I haven't yet driven, and that night I sleep in Clayton's apartment. I wake up in the middle of the night and I'm wondering if I'm having a panic attack. It feels as if my chest is being compressed, while my heart is racing so fast I can't keep up with it. My breathing is shallow and rapid and uncontrollable. I swing my legs out of bed. Clayton is fast asleep, and as I look at it him in the low light I realise what is wrong. I don't know if I love him. I don't know if I want to marry him. He's making me feel utterly suffocated and it's not his fault, it's all mine. Clayton is simply doing his best to care for me, to love me. And it hits me then that I will have to leave him. It's not fair on Clayton for me to stay engaged when I'm not sure whether our relationship has a future. If I care for him – which I do – I need to let him go.

I don't sleep. I lie there in bed working out how I'm going to let Clayton down. How I can end things without shattering his heart. Deep down, I know that I can't.

I'm exhausted by the morning, and as we sit opposite each other at his table, him drinking mint tea and eating runny eggs, me drinking black coffee, I know I have to do it now.

'Clayton, I'm so sorry but this isn't working for me.'

He jumps up. 'I'm sorry, darling. Is it too strong?'

It takes me a moment to realise that he's talking about my coffee while I'm talking about our relationship.

'I can't stay engaged to you. I'm just not sure that this is what I want. I'm so, so sorry.'

His face goes very pale and as my words sink in, his jaw tightens and his eyes narrow. 'You don't mean it. You're just saying that because you got freaked out about whoever is stalking you.'

'I do mean it, Clayton. You've been so kind to me but I don't want to get married. Not to you. Not to anyone.'

He jumps up from the table and my coffee slurps over the side. 'So we won't get married. It's only a bit of paper. We'll just be together as we are now. No pressure.'

'No,' I say, gently shaking my head. 'We need to split up. I'm not feeling it. It's hard to explain but I don't think I want to be in a relationship.'

There's a long pause. 'The problem with you, Anna, is you don't know what you want. You need me, a strong person in your life to support you, to guide you even. I can give you everything and I know you better than you know yourself. It's obvious that all of this insecurity comes from your parents' failed relationship but as I said before, I'm not your father.'

'You can't get me to change my mind,' I say as I stand up. I slip off my engagement ring and put it on the table, then I walk out of the room towards the bedroom.

'You don't get to make this decision by yourself!' Clayton shouts after me. 'Anna! Come back here now!'

But I don't. I shove my belongings in my tote bag, double-checking I have everything from the bathroom. Clayton stands in the doorway from the bedroom.

'I'm sorry I've hurt you so much,' I murmur. 'You've been so kind to me.'

'You're not leaving,' he says, menace in his voice.

'Please let me get past,' I say. I'm shocked that there are tears in Clayton's eyes.

'I love you, Anna. I can't let you go.'

'Let's not be silly,' I say. Nerves flutter in my stomach. I have never seen Clayton behave like this before and he's making me feel uncomfortable.

'Give me another chance. I can't live without you.'

I wonder then if he's going to hurt me. Or is this some emotional blackmail?

'I need a break,' I say. 'I'm really sorry. Please let me go.'

'I don't think I'll ever let you go,' Clayton says. 'You have stolen my heart.'

I wonder for one horrible moment if he intends to keep me captive or perhaps he'll kill me to prevent me from leaving. But no. It's as if he crumbles in on himself, because he sinks into his knees and starts sobbing. It's shocking for someone as outwardly strong as Clayton to break down.

'I'm sorry,' I whisper again and squeeze past him. I race to the front door, fling it open and run. Clayton doesn't follow me.

The next afternoon, Mum sends me a text message.

> Can you pop in on your way home from work? I'll make supper. Love, Mum x.

Mum doesn't tell me why she's asked me over until we're sitting down eating a chicken casserole.

'Clayton came to see me today.'

'What!' I exclaim. 'How does he even know where you live?'

Mum shrugs her shoulders. The only time Clayton met Mum was when he took us both out for supper to a fancy restaurant in Soho. Mum was impressed.

'What did he say?'

'In a nutshell, that he can't live without you. He'd put together a full PowerPoint presentation as to why I should persuade you that the two of you are perfect for each other.'

I snort because I've never heard of anything so ridiculous, and then I start laughing, but my laughter has an edge of hysteria to it. Mum throws me a concerned glance.

'Did he leave you a copy?' I ask, still sniggering.

'No, and it didn't cross my mind to ask.'

'Seriously? A full presentation?'

'Yup, and it was very compelling.'

'Come on, Mum. It's just weird. It's not compelling, it's controlling.'

'So long as you're sure you're doing the right thing by ending the relationship,' she says.

I shake my head with dismay. I can't believe that Mum might have been taken in by Clayton, but then again, I thought he was the perfect man for a while until I understood what he is really like.

'I'm one hundred percent sure,' I say. 'I don't want anything to do with him.'

12

ANNA

The back massage was glorious. I was so relaxed afterwards, it felt like I floated back to our tent. I wasn't even concerned about snakes or any other venomous creature as I walked along the path, and when I sank onto our bed, I fell into a deep, dreamless sleep.

I awake to find Joel buttoning up a clean shirt.

'Sorry, did I wake you?' he asks.

'What's the time?' I glance at the clock. I've been asleep for nearly two hours.

'Time for supper.'

'No game drive this evening?' I ask.

'No. Nancy says the next one will be in the morning.'

I stretch and sit up in bed. It's dark outside now. 'How was your rhino darting?'

'Absolutely amazing. It was such a privilege to be part of something like that. Honestly, Anna, it was a dream-come-true experience for me. I remember watching something similar on the TV when I was a kid, and it's something that

I've always wanted to do but never thought I'd have the opportunity.'

'I'm glad,' I say, as I wriggle to the end of the bed and give him a kiss.

'I know it was terrifying when we were ambushed and you were freaked out by the dead animal, but do you think you could give this place a chance?'

I sigh. *Not that again.* He sits down next to me and takes my hand.

'I don't know.' And that's the truth. I don't view myself as feeble or someone whose life is ruled by fear, but there is so much danger out here, and the ambush was utterly terrifying. I love this man so much but could I live here? Would I be compromising too much?

'No point in worrying about it yet,' Joel says, hugging me. He's right. Suffice unto the day and all that.

We join Katie and Zak in the main lodge and I'm relieved that Clayton and Lois aren't here. Zak is buzzing as much as Joel was about the rhino darting. Bhutana offers us drinks and I ask for a gin and tonic, while Joel accepts a beer.

'I'm confident I've got some really good photos. It was extraordinary getting so close to a fully grown rhino, being able to touch it,' Zak says.

'I'm going to write an article about rhino poaching,' Katie adds. 'Hopefully I can place it with a mainstream consumer magazine.'

'I have to admit I don't know much about it,' I say. 'What's so special about a rhino horn anyway?'

'It's used in traditional Chinese medicine treating all sorts of conditions from food poisoning to typhoid. It's also considered to be an aphrodisiac,' Katie explains. 'The horn is either shaved into slivers or ground into a fine powder. It's dissolved into boiling water and then drunk.'

'Sounds disgusting,' I mutter.

'There's absolutely no scientific proof that it has medicinal properties,' Joel says. 'That's what makes it all so sad.'

'Rhino horn is just keratin, essentially, isn't it?' I ask, recalling snippets from my biology A Level.

'Yes. There is no scientific proof that it does anything at all, but it's nigh on impossible to change deep-rooted beliefs,' Katie explains. 'That's why it's up to us journalists to tell the world that rhinos are close to extinction for a vile and cruel practice that has no benefit to humans.'

Nancy wanders over to join us. 'The problem with rhino poaching is the rhino horn is considered a status symbol in certain Asian countries. The animals die a terrible death. Many of the poachers are supported by international gangs and supplied with tracking equipment and tranquilliser guns. When they've found a rhino, they tranquillise it and then hack off the horn, leaving the poor animal to bleed to death. It's truly wicked.'

'It's horrible,' I mutter.

'And the problem is, the more extinct the animals become, the higher the price of the horn, and because so many people living here are well below the poverty line, the chance to make money like this is just too hard to resist,' Katie explains.

'Over nine thousand African rhinos were killed in the past decade,' Nancy adds. We're all quiet for a moment, reflecting on these sobering numbers. 'However, things are improving in South Africa. Some of the larger reserves dehorn their rhino humanely and there is increased vigilance everywhere. Nevertheless, they're still an endangered species. We're lucky on this reserve. We share security with our neighbours and we have our own militia to keep things under control. That's why the ambush you experienced was such a shock. Our guys are normally on top of things like that.'

Lulama comes out of the kitchen, wiping her hands on a dishcloth. 'Supper is ready,' she announces.

Afterwards, Katie comes up to me. 'It was great meeting you,' she says. 'I gather Joel is here for a veterinary job.'

'Yes,' I say, wondering whether it was Nancy or Joel who mentioned it.

'We're leaving at the crack of dawn tomorrow, so I just wanted to say goodbye.'

'Will you let me know where you place your article? I'd love to read it.'

'Yes, of course.' We swap telephone numbers and email addresses.

'You will take care out here, won't you?' she says.

I would like to ask her what she means, but Zak is beckoning for her, and Ntando is waiting to accompany them back to their tent. I watch them leave and she throws me a concerned glance. It's unsettling. Did she just mean beware of the animals or was she referring to something or someone else? I consider messaging her but then recall I have no access to the internet. No way of contacting anyone in fact. I know my nerves are on edge, and whose wouldn't be after the horrific ambush, but it felt like Katie's message had an undertone to it, a secret warning somehow, as if she knows something that I don't. I'm quiet back in our tent but I don't say anything to Joel. He is so happy to be here and I want him to enjoy the fulfilment of his dream. But despite the astonishing beauty of this place, I know I won't feel at ease, properly relaxed, until we touch back down on English soil.

13

ANNA – THEN

I'm at work in the laboratory when reception calls up and tells me I have a visitor.

'Who is it?'

There's a smile in the receptionist's voice. 'It's a surprise.'

'I don't like surprises,' I say.

She hesitates and then laughs nervously. 'I'll bring it up if you like.'

So it's an 'it' not a 'he'. 'Don't worry. I'll be down in five minutes.'

I saunter into reception wearing my white coat. I remember when I was first given it. It made me feel so important, as if my job really mattered when I knew deep down that testing ice-cream was hardly going to change people's lives. As I walk towards the reception desk, I don't notice anything, not even a bouquet of flowers. I stride towards the receptionist, who glances up at me.

'I'm Anna Evans. You called me a few minutes ago.' She grins widely. There are over a thousand people working on this site and there's no reason for her to know who I am, so why is she smiling as if we're best friends?

'Anna!' she says too loudly. And then, to my dismay, Clayton pops up from behind a sofa to the right of the reception desk holding a huge bunch of red roses.

'Your fiancé is here. You're so lucky,' she whispers conspiratorially.

I sigh. I should have expected this. Clayton was never going to walk away quietly.

'Anna,' he says again, holding the bouquet out towards me. 'I've booked dinner for us at The Savoy.'

'The Savoy?' I gasp, looking down at my ordinary black trousers and cotton blouse underneath my white coat and then I remember that I'm not going to be going anywhere with Clayton. We're finished. He steps really close to me and whispers, 'You look so sexy in your white coat.'

'I'm at work, Clayton. You need to leave.'

'You finish in fifteen minutes, don't you? I'll wait for you.'

'No!' I say, but he doesn't hang around to continue the conversation and I find that I'm holding the bunch of roses and watching his back retreat out of the building.

'You've got such a good-looking and charming fiancé,' the receptionist says. I scowl at her and then, when I'm in the lift going up to the laboratory floor, I feel bad about it. Perhaps I'll give her the flowers on my way out.

The downside of this building is there is no back door. I have to exit the main entrance and consequently have no way of avoiding Clayton. I decide to work late and I switch my mobile phone off. I know it's petty and silly and not very fair on him, but I'm hopeful he'll give up waiting if he thinks I'm not coming out. It's nearly 8 p.m. by the time I leave the building, by which point it's dark outside and I'm one of the last people to leave our floor. I put the flowers in a sink in the ladies' loos, stick a post-it note on it saying, 'Help yourself' and leave them there. Perhaps one of the cleaners will take the bouquet.

As I stride out of the building towards the tube station I'm hopeful that Clayton has gone. I don't hear any footsteps behind me and as I glance around, I can't see him. Unfortunately the relief is short lived because Clayton is sitting on the steps to my house and there's nothing I can do to avoid him.

'I cancelled dinner,' he says tonelessly, getting to his feet.

'I'm sorry,' I say, although I'm not. 'I didn't want to hurt you. It's just I'm really not in the right place for a relationship at the moment and I should have realised that earlier.'

He doesn't say anything, just stands there with his hands in his coat pockets. I need him to move to one side so I can put my key in the lock and open the door. We're at an impasse and I don't know what to do. His silence is scaring me.

'Please, Clayton. Let me into my home. I'm sure we can be friends in the future.'

'Friends!' he scoffs. 'You're my soulmate, Anna. I don't know what's happened to you for you not to see that. I'm wondering if you're going down with something. The flu, maybe?"

'I'm perfectly well,' I say. He's getting ridiculous now and my frustration is growing. 'Please, can you move so I can get into my house. I don't want to have to shout for the neighbours.'

He makes a hissing sound but stands to one side.

'I'd like you to leave.'

'Oh Anna,' he says, putting a hand on my shoulder.

'There's no need for you to be aggressive with me. I'd never hurt you. I love you. I just want to care for you. Let me come in, just for one drink. I won't try anything on, I promise.'

'It's not a good idea,' I say, fumbling in my handbag to find my keys.

'I need to tell you what's going to happen,' he says. I frown as my fingers curl around the front door key.

'Nothing's going to happen because we won't be seeing each other anymore,' I say. My hand is trembling slightly as I try to get the key in.

'Let me,' Clayton says and before I can protest he's nudged me out of the way and is opening the front door.

'I don't want you to come in,' I say, but I'm too late. Clayton has pushed past me and is holding the door back for me to enter.

'Thanks,' I mutter, 'But please leave now.'

He steps forwards and lets the door slam behind him. We're standing together in the narrow corridor, wedged between the front door and my neighbour's bike that is really too big to be kept in the hallway. I'm nervous now because I'm the only one in the house. Like Sasha, the couple in the ground floor flat are away on holiday, and I've never spoken a word with the man in the basement because he has his own below-street entrance.

'You can't make me want to go out with you,' I say. I'm scared he's going to hit me as he clenches and unclenches his fists. I shrink backwards.

'Anna, you can't leave me! Why don't you understand that we're meant to be together, that it's destiny? I love you so much I can't exist without you.' His voice is higher than normal.

'I'm sorry, but I don't feel the same way.'

'This doesn't make any sense, Anna. We're a couple. I've bought us a house. We're going to have a family. I'll give you a few days alone if that's what you need, but you have to come to your senses.'

'Clayton, you're not listening to me! I don't love you. I don't want to be in a relationship with you.'

He stares at me uncomprehending for a long moment and then he lets out a wail. It's horrible. Scary. As if he's an out-of-control toddler, not a successful grown man. 'My life is over if you reject me, Anna.' He sobs. I don't know what to do as I watch the tears flow down his cheeks. It's embarrassing, uncomfortable. He swipes at his eyes with a white cotton handkerchief. 'You've done this to me,' he says in a hissed whisper. 'If you reject me, I'm going to take my own life. I can't live without you.'

'Come on, Clayton,' I say, patting his arm because I'm not sure what else I should do. 'This might hurt now but in a few days you'll have moved on. You're a handsome, successful man. You won't have a problem finding someone else.'

He stares at me then, his blue eyes surprisingly dark, the tears dried up. 'I don't want anyone else. You are the only woman for me, Anna. And I always get my way. Always.'

He then grabs the door handle, pulls it open and strides out, slamming it so hard that the whole building shakes.

I TRY to unpick what Clayton said and I can't work out whether he really believes that I'm the only woman for him or whether it's just his anger talking. Clayton is the kind of man who always gets his way. I'd like to know more about him, to find out whether he's a possible threat to me, or whether I should take his warning of suicide seriously, but not for the first time, I realise he didn't introduce me to anyone in his life. I haven't met any friends or family; not even work colleagues. I've let myself be bulldozed by him over the past few weeks, and all of those things that should have raised alarm bells, I've let slip. Clayton knows everything about me; I know next to nothing about him. All I can do is hope that he realises I'm serious and I don't want to be in a relationship with him.

I go to bed early but my phone rings at 2 a.m. and it's another of those silent calls with a heavy breather.

'I'm reporting this number to the police,' I yell down the line. But of course I can't, because it's a withheld number. I turn my phone off.

The silent calls return, happening every couple of hours during the day. At one point I say, 'I know this is you, Clayton, and it's really pathetic.' I get no response. On another occasion I scream loudly down the phone, hoping to blast the eardrums of the caller. That doesn't seem to do much either. And my service provider can't help. If this is still going on by the end of the week, I resolve to go to the police.

This morning, I'm going off site to visit our packaging manufacturer. I take my old Fiat as the factory is located near Guildford and it'll be easier to drive. The day goes well but when I'm on the A3 heading back to London I become aware of a car tailing me. It looks distinctly like Clayton's black Porsche, yet it stays just far enough behind me so I can't make out the face of the driver. When I speed up, it does the same. When I slow down, it hangs back. I try to lose the car as I drive through central London, taking back roads and even doubling back on myself a couple of times. Still the black Porsche trails me. At one point I let it get close enough to see the numberplate, but although I think it's Clayton's, now I can't recall what his numberplate is. It's the last thing I want to do, but I call him.

'Anna!' he says brightly. 'How are you?'

'Are you following me?'

'What?'

'Where are you right now?'

'Would you like to meet up, because I could be at yours within the hour?'

'No, I certainly don't want to meet up!' I exclaim. 'Where are you?' I repeat.

'Driving down the A1 having just returned from seeing a client. Why?'

I shouldn't have rung him. Of course he's going to deny following me, but it is rather a coincidence that he's also in his car. I turn into my road and look in my rear mirror. The black Porsche carries straight on. For a crazy moment I consider giving chase, but then realise how stupid that would be. My little Fiat would never keep up with his Porsche and it's not like I can speed along the streets of London. I find a parking space at the far end of the road and reverse into it cautiously, all the while looking out for the black car. It doesn't appear. No one follows me as I walk along the pavement and no one is watching as I put my key in the lock.

An hour or so later, the doorbell rings. 'Delivery for Anna Evans,' the young man says.

'I haven't ordered anything. What is it?'

'Takeaway from China Garden.'

'And what's in the order?'

'Um, Peking Duck and spring rolls. Can you come down, please.'

I lean against the wall and groan. It's my favourite meal

from my favourite takeaway restaurant and the only person who knows that, other than Sasha, is Clayton.

'Sorry, but I didn't order it. You can take it back.'

'It's been paid for!' he exclaims.

'Thanks for coming but you can eat it yourself.'

I'm not going to give Clayton the satisfaction of eating food that he's chosen for me. The delivery guy swears under his breath. I watch out of the window as he takes his bag and hops back onto his motorbike.

A few minutes later I get a text message from Clayton.

Hope you enjoyed your supper. Cx.

I don't respond.

The following night a couple of work colleagues have asked me to join them for drinks in a bar near Hammersmith. It's been a while since I've been out with them – well, four months to be exact. Ever since I started dating Clayton. It isn't until we're on our second drink that I remember how much I've missed this easy camaraderie.

'Are you going to start dating again?' Steve asks me.

'I'm done with dating,' I mutter. 'Only just finished with Clayton.'

'Oh, come on. You need to sign up to Bumble.'

'No. I'm not in the right space. I need some time alone.'

By our fourth round of drinks, Mandy, a friend and fellow food technician, has created a new profile for me and I'm already getting likes. We joke about it for a bit but then tiredness hits me and I call an Uber to take me home. It's as I'm walking out to the car that I see him. Clayton is standing on the opposite side of the road, his hands in his pockets, staring at me.

What the hell? How did he know where I was? Did he follow me from work?

I pretend not to see Clayton and hurry into the Uber.

'I'm being stalked. Can you drive away as quickly as possible?' I ask the driver.

I can't help but glance across to the other side of the road, where I see Clayton running towards us, waving his hands at me. The Uber driver puts his foot on the accelerator and we're away.

I send Clayton a text message.

> Please stay away from me. This is getting weird and stalkerish. If you carry on like this I'm going to the police and will take out a restraining order.

He replies immediately.

> I can't stop loving you, Anna. Please let me back into your life.

I don't reply but I do block his number.

And surprise, surprise. The silent calls start again as soon as I'm home. Once more, I switch my phone off.

The next day, during our lunch hour, Mandy insists on checking out my Bumble profile. To my utter dismay, I see that Clayton has also set up a profile and he's liked mine. How did he know? I can't imagine dating apps are his thing, but has he been checking them all to find out if I'm using them? To Mandy's disappointment, I delete my profile. I send Mum a message and tell her I'll be coming over for supper. I feel like a good home-cooked meal in the safe company of Mum. As normal, I take the tube, but when I'm coming out of the tube at Islington, Clayton appears.

'Stay away from me!' I yell.

A young man fixing his bicycle to a lamppost asks if I'm all right.

'I'm being stalked!' I say, glaring at Clayton. 'If you don't stay away from me, I'm going to the police,' I say. 'No more chances.'

Clayton looks furious but I don't care. I walk straight past him.

'Anna,' he says, running after me. 'I can't live without you. My life is worth nothing now.'

'I'm sorry you feel that way but if you carry on hassling me, I'm going to take out a restraining order. I've already told you that and this is your final warning.' I take my phone out and hover my fingers over the first nine.

Clayton's features darken and he clenches and unclenches his fists. I'm glad we're outside in a busy, public place because he scares me with that look. 'Just stay away,' I mutter. I carry on walking and when I've turned the street corner, I glance backwards. He isn't following me.

I'm shaking by the time I arrive at Mum and Nick's.

'Clayton's everywhere,' I explain to them over supper. 'It's like he knows where I'm going to be all the time and it's totally freaking me out.'

Nick, my lovely stepdad, puts his cutlery down on his plate. 'Have you considered that he might be tracking you, Anna? He could have put a tracker on your phone or in your car. It's easy enough to do.'

'Oh my God, you're right.' Yes, he must be tracking me. He knew where I was meeting my friends for drinks. He knew when I was at home. He knew that I was coming to Mum's tonight.

'Do you mind if I sleep over here?' I ask.

'Of course not, darling,' Mum says.

The next day I go to our IT department and talk to Karim, who is a computer software wiz. He's the person who monitors whether there are any corporate spies, other entities trying to access our secret recipes. Industrial espionage, they call it, which I used to think was hilarious. I mean, who would use spies to acquire the recipe of ice-cream? But it's a big thing, apparently.

'I've got a huge favour, not work related,' I say, perching on the edge of his desk.

'Go on.'

'I think my ex might have put spyware on my phone,' I say. 'Would you be able to take a look?' I wonder whether he'll be able to help me considering this is a personal issue.

'Sure. If he's tracking you at home, he's tracking you at work, and we can't have that.'

I hand over my phone and give him my password. He says he'll give me a call on the office phone when he's checked it over.

An hour later, Karim rings. 'You're right, you've got spyware on your phone. I'm going to delete it, okay?'

'Yes, please.' I feel a surge of anger. How dare Clayton spy on me! It's illegal, isn't it? When I go downstairs to the IT department to collect my phone, Karim has a concerned look on his kindly face. 'Have you checked for hidden cameras in your home and car?' he asks. 'Because if someone has put this on your phone, it might be elsewhere too.

'You're joking,' I say.

'You should check. This is a sophisticated spyware. There might be bugs elsewhere. I could come over after work and have a look, if you want?'

'Yes, please. I'd be really grateful.'

By early evening, we're at my flat and I've opened a couple of beers. Karim is doing a sweep of the flat. He finds two hidden cameras. One is in the living room, hidden in a smoke detector on the ceiling. The other is a tiny camera wedged inside a lattice candlestick holder on the mantle-piece, opposite my bed. I'm shaking with rage. How dare Clayton spy on me in my own bedroom! That's abhorrent.

'You'd best get your locks changed too,' Karim suggests. He doesn't find anything in my car, but as Karim explains, Clayton will have been able to find out where I was through the spyware on my mobile.

'You should go to the police,' he says. 'This guy is a creep.'

I agree with that description but I'm not sure that going to the police is the answer. If I report him, Clayton will defi-nitely go ballistic and I think I'll be less safe than I am now. It's not like the police can give me twenty-four hour protec-tion, and Clayton hasn't threatened to hurt me in any way; he just wants to be in my life. But he's unpredictable, and while I don't think he's going to get physical, that might change if I report him. But things can't stay as they are. He's controlling and verging on a psycho. There's only one solu-tion. It's dramatic, but I need to get away.

The next day I make an appointment with the head of human resources, Simonetta Gardiner. She has my personnel file on her desk when I settle down in the chair opposite her.

'I would like a transfer to another office,' I say. 'Some-where abroad. I speak good French. Is that possible?'

She frowns at me. 'I'm not sure that there are any vacan-cies,' she says.

'In which case I'll have to look for a job with a competitor.' I feel strangely bullish. Just a few weeks ago, I could never have imagined threatening to leave my job, but somehow, Clayton has made me stronger, more resolute.

'Right,' she says, her eyebrows knotted together. 'Leave it with me and I'll see what's available.' I'm surprised she's being this calm about my threat, but I remember Nick's wise words: other people value you in the way that you value yourself. I guess we'll soon find out if my company values me. But then I decide to tell her the truth.

'I'm being stalked by my ex and I need to get out of the country.'

'Goodness, Anna. That's rather dramatic. Have you been to the police?'

'Not yet, but I will.' I'm still hoping it won't come to that.

Three days later, Simonetta says she has an opening in Paris. Would I like to take it? I don't hesitate and say yes, immediately.

When Sasha returns from her holiday, I explain how I've broken up with Clayton and that he's been tracking and spying on me. After all, this is her flat too and the camera in the living room wasn't discriminate as to whether it was spying on me or her. My best friend is horrified and although she's sad that I'm going away for a few months, she agrees it's the right thing to do.

'I never liked him,' she says.

'I'm going to change phone numbers, get a PO Box for my post and leave no forwarding address, except with you. He can't find out where I've gone. You promise you won't tell him?'

'Of course,' she says, throwing her arms around me. 'If he comes anywhere near this place, I'll be calling the police.'

She pauses for a moment and it's obvious she's trying to decide whether to tell me something or not. Eventually she does. 'I heard a rumour about Clayton.'

I stiffen.

'Apparently he hit a previous girlfriend.'

'Why didn't you tell me?' I ask, recoiling.

'Because you wouldn't have believed me. You were too in love with him. Did he hurt you?'

'No!' I say. 'He's freaking me out but he didn't lay a finger on me. He was controlling though.' His dominating behaviour was insidious, cloaked in loving words. But now I reflect on our weeks together, I can see that he was isolating me from my friends, controlling what we did, where we went. And I'm sure it would only have gotten worse.

'He will never find out where you are from me,' Sasha promises.

14

ANNA

Joel and I go to bed early and sheer exhaustion overcomes me, because I sleep all night, only waking when Ntando knocks on our door.

I force my eyes open and glance at the alarm clock. It's already 5.45 a.m. and the sun has risen. We take hurried showers, get dressed and rush towards the main lodge. Joel is walking in front of me when he comes to a sudden stop.

'Wait!' he whispers, putting an arm out so I can't pass him.

'What is it?' I peer over his shoulder and shudder.

Creeping slowly across the path is a snake, its girth the size of my forearm, about three feet in length.

'I think it's a puff adder,' Joel says taking a step back but at the same time leaning forwards to get a better look.

'Are they dangerous?'

'Yes. Their fangs are so strong they can pierce leather and the venom is highly toxic. If a puff adder attacks a human, and the person goes untreated, they might die due to necrosis after a couple of days. But don't worry, a snake will never hurt you unless it feels threatened.'

That doesn't make me feel any safer. We wait for a couple of minutes as the snake disappears into the undergrowth, and when it's time for me to pass the spot where the snake vanished, I make a run for it. Joel laughs.

With my nerves already frayed, I'm in for a further shock when we enter the lodge. Ntando is standing there in deep conversation with four men, each of them in army fatigues, carrying rifles. They look as if they're about to go into battle. Nancy steps out of a door carrying a steaming mug of coffee. She looks perfectly relaxed, which makes me feel marginally more comfortable.

'Who are the men?' I ask in a whisper.

'They're our anti-poaching militia, employed jointly by our reserve and our neighbours. They're here predominantly to stop rhino horn poachers but I asked them to come over and touch base after the experience you had yesterday. They've already had a debrief with Clayton, who was able to give a good description of the two men.' I notice Clayton then, sitting at the far end of the dining table with Lois seated to his left. He lifts up his mug when he sees me looking at him.

'Can I go out with the men?' Joel asks.

I stare at my fiancé with horror. What is it with Joel and guns? He seems to enjoy all of this whereas it fills me with terror.

'I'm sorry, but it's too much of a risk,' Nancy says. That's a relief. 'These guys are highly trained and we're very dependent on them. We do what we can to look after them. In fact, I've told them to come back for lunch. Unfortunately

Lulama is having the morning off, so although she's left food for you, it'll be up to me to whip up something for the men.'

'I can help you,' I say, spontaneously.

Joel puts an arm around my shoulders. 'Anna is an excellent chef.' I wonder if he's thinking that my culinary skills might be beneficial somehow in his bid for the new job.

'Well, that certainly is a bonus.' Nancy smiles warmly. 'When you come back from your game drive, if you're not too tired, then I'd love the help.'

Our game drive is a subdued affair in comparison to the earlier ones. Perhaps it's because there are only four guests: Clayton, Lois, Joel and myself. Or perhaps it's because we're all remembering the ambush and praying it doesn't happen again. But I also sense a rift between Lois and Clayton. She spends most of the time gazing out of the window and answering Clayton's occasional questions with grunts or monosyllabic answers. I suppose they've had an argument, and if Clayton is anything like he was with me, my sympathies lie with Lois.

Today there are clouds in the sky and the atmosphere is oppressive. It seems the animals sense it too because the only ones we see are two rhinoceros. After the explanation about rhino poaching, I'm relieved that this pair – a mother and child – both have their horns.

'How do the anti-poaching teams get trained?' I ask Ntando.

'A couple were in the army and others get trained on the job. My cousin is one of the militia you met this morning. They're the good guys.'

'It must be a dangerous job,' I say.

Ntando frowns. 'It can be, but no one has been hurt on

this reserve. It is a privilege working in a job like mine or my cousin's.'

'Do you live near here?' I ask. I haven't seen any staff accommodation but I assume there must be some, considering Ntando works such long hours.

'I live on the reserve but my children, they live with my wife and family far from here.'

'You have children?' I exclaim.

His face beams. 'Yes. Two boys.' He removes a worn photograph from his wallet and shows it to me. They must be about six and eight years old.

'How far away is your home?'

'It's a day's drive to get there.'

'How often do you see them?'

'One weekend in every two months.'

'Oh, that's terrible for you,' I say without thinking, because that's obviously not the right thing to say bearing in mind how both Joel and Clayton glower at me.

'I am very happy to have this job; a job which I love and which pays well. I can support all my family, both sets of grandparents, and my sister and her family. It's a good life.'

I smile awkwardly.

The game drive continues to be uneventful. Joel asks Ntando lots of questions but Clayton and Lois barely speak. It seems that Clayton really has changed. Two years ago, if we had an argument, Clayton wouldn't have let it go. He always had to have the last word. Perhaps Lois has got a better measure of him.

On our way back to the lodge we see a herd of buffalo. Ntando stops the vehicle so we can watch them graze.

'Buffalo are one of the most dangerous animals in South Africa,' Clayton states. I turn to look at him and he has a smirk on his face. Lois visibly shivers. 'They're wild and unpredictable and charge at people right at the last minute. That's correct, isn't it, Ntando?'

Ntando nods but he looks a little uneasy. I'm sure he's been told by Nancy to calm us down and it's not helpful for Clayton to unnecessarily ramp up the fear again. 'The reason buffalo are dangerous is that they don't give any warning before they charge. Elephants flay their ears and make a noise, rhinos become obviously aggressive, but the buffalo don't give any warning before charging and they can run at 50 mph. They won't charge the car, though,' Ntando says with a reassuring smile.

BACK AT THE LODGE, we eat our breakfast and to my relief, Clayton and Lois disappear to their tent.

'Are you still up for helping me in the kitchen?' Nancy asks.

'Of course,' I say, even though there's nothing I'd like more than to go back to bed.

It's a commercial kitchen, with stainless steel units, a gas stove and oven and a double sink. A large fridge stands on the shorter wall. I'm surprised at the size of everything considering the lodge only caters for maximum eight guests. I take some carrots and courgettes out of the fridge.

'We grow some of the vegetables ourselves,' Nancy explains, 'But the rest I buy from the local town. A shopping trip takes most of the day, although fresh produce is cheap here. I make a visit into town once a week.'

We work side by side, me chopping up the vegetables and Nancy sautéing and cooking. I'm surprised when she produces several portions of chicken thighs. She must notice my frown because she explains that the plant-based diet is for the guests only; the staff prefer to eat meat.

I'd like to ask her what it's really like living here. Does she not feel discomfort with all of these echoes of colonialism, because I sure do? Where would Joel and I live if we got the job? And would she offer the job to Joel if I'm not part of the package? What would my life be like stuck out here? But I don't feel I can ask any questions. It seems all a bit presumptuous since Joel hasn't as yet been offered anything. So we make inconsequential small talk, where she asks me about my job and I ask her whether she's ever lonely out here alone.

She drops the knife she was holding and stares at me. 'Never,' she says forcefully. 'It's a privilege to live and work out here with these people, and the animals.'

'And you're never scared?'

This time she looks at me as if I'm out of my mind. 'Fear is not real. It is simply an imagined thought as to something that might or might not happen in the future. When those men were pointing guns at you, your fear was from what they might do to you, not what was actually happening in that moment. I left fear behind a long time ago, Anna. I suggest you do too.'

15

ANNA

Joel is sitting on the sofa in the living area and Nancy and I are clearing the table. He jumps up to help us, although Nancy tries to tell him his help isn't necessary. The men have been fed and have left the reserve.

'As a thank you for all your help, I've arranged a special treat for you and Joel tonight,' Nancy says, excitement in her voice. 'You'll be sleeping out under the stars.'

I open and close my mouth because that sounds terrifying. Why would we want to sleep out in the open? Isn't that extremely dangerous? Besides, it's loud enough in our rigid canvas tent; the cacophony outside will make sleep impossible. I remember how she explained that she doesn't feel fear. But just because she has that strength of mind doesn't mean that I do too.

'Don't worry, it's quite safe!' she laughs. 'It's the in thing with many of the leading game reserves. We've set up a deck underneath a tree. It's really romantic, with a mosquito net around you, totally alone in the wilderness. The bed is on a platform so you'll be safe from any animals, and the night sky... Well, the stars are something else. '

'How can it be safe?' I ask.

'Because it's built in such a way that no animals will approach it and of course, you'll have a radio should you need to contact us. It's a totally unique experience; really a once in a lifetime. Although if Joel works here it'll be something you can do again in the future. What do you think?'

'That it sounds absolutely fantastic,' Joel exclaims. He puts his arm around my shoulders. 'Really a dream come true. Thank you, Nancy.'

Nancy nods her head. 'My pleasure.' She walks away.

I'm feeling a bit of resentment at the number of times Joel has said this is a dream come true. 'I'm not sure, Joel,' I say quietly. 'I don't see how it can be safe.'

'Luxury game lodges like this one aren't going to put their guests in danger. Their insurance will cover something like that and they wouldn't be able to do it if it was considered risky.'

I'm quiet because the whole idea fills me with terror. What if a snake slithers down from the branches of the tree and wraps itself around our necks while we're sleeping? Or what if a cheetah finds us? They climb up trees. And then there are those men who ambushed us. What if they find out where we are and evade being spotted by the anti-poaching militia?

'I really want to do this,' Joel says. There's a look of longing in his eyes. It strikes me that when we're in the UK, Joel rarely puts his foot down. If I'm being honest with myself, he invariably gives in to my wishes. He's far from being a pushover but it seems that in our normal lives, my happiness ranks higher than his own. So the fact that he's articulating how much he wants these experiences out here in the bush indicates how important they are to him. 'I really want to do it with you,' Joel says. 'But if you don't want to sleep outside, I'll do it alone. This is a once-in-a-lifetime opportunity for me, darling.'

Another one, I think bitchily. But what can I say? If Joel insists on going alone, then I'll simply stay awake all night worrying about him. I'll be better off staying with him.

'Alright. I'll come too,' I say.

Nancy drives us out to the location of the platform. The sun is beginning to sink, a massive orange ball of fire in the clear dark blue sky. The setting is everything she'd promised. Utterly breathtaking. There is a wooden platform accessed by wooden steps, the platform built into the curves of the tree. A large double bed lies in the centre of the platform and there's just enough space to walk all around it. White mosquito netting wafts gently in the slight breeze, enveloping the bed. There are numerous lanterns with lit candles around the base of the platform and on the platform itself. Clear jars with metal handles are hung from the branches and they hold flickering candles. At the base of the platform, a small table has been laid for two people. It's the most romantic thing I have ever seen; tasteful, low-key and utterly perfect. If only we weren't stuck out in the middle of nowhere surrounded by danger.

'Wow, Nancy. This is incredible,' Joel says. 'I thought I was here for an interview but it's like we're being given the seven-star experience of your guests.'

'That's what I wanted,' she says with a wide smile. 'If you understand the full guest experience, then it makes it more genuine. Tomorrow I'll show you the staff accommodation. It isn't quite as luxurious as our guests' rooms but I want to attract the best people and I believe in looking after my staff. You wouldn't be slumming it if you join our team.'

Joel's face is alight with joy.

'We've prepared some food for you, and there's gin for you, Anna, and beer for you, Joel. When you've finished eating, please put everything away in the freezer boxes so the left-over food doesn't attract animals. Here's a walkie-talkie for you to contact Ntando if you're worried about anything, but hopefully you'll have a wonderful night under the stars. Just one thing. Once you're in bed, when it's totally dark, under no circumstances should you get down from the platform. If you need to go to the toilet, call Ntando. It's not safe for you to be wandering around in the dark.'

'Thank you so much,' Joel says, taking the walkie-talkie from her. We stand there watching Nancy as her Land Rover disappears into the bush, the sound of the engine fading until all we hear are the crickets and the occasional squawk. Joel makes me a gin and tonic and then we sit down to eat our supper as the sun creates streaks of red and orange across the wide African sky. I have to admit that this is extremely romantic and I try to focus on the delicious food rather than worrying whether we're going to be attacked. As darkness creeps in, the candles flicker all around us. We clear away our food and plates and wash our teeth using disposable toothbrushes and water from large thermos flasks. And then Joel leads me up to the deck. I'm wearing pyjamas under my clothes and I shiver as I shrug off my outer clothes, snuggling underneath the thick duvet and finding hot water bottles in the bed. The night sky is astonishing. I've never seen so many stars and galaxies and shooting stars. The noise of the wilderness is disconcerting but Joel holds me tightly and to my surprise, I begin to feel really sleepy. Against all my expectations, I drop off to sleep.

Bang.

I wake up with a start.

What the hell was that?

It comes again. *Bang. Bang.*

It takes me a few moments to recognise the sounds of shooting. And again. *Bang.* It's so close, almost deafening. I reach across the bed for Joel but the bed is empty. I blink to try to see more clearly. Most of the candles have gone out and the bulk of the stars are hidden behind clouds. Whereas when I went to sleep the night was light and I could make out trees and bushes, now there's a heavy shroud of darkness.

'Joel,' I whisper, sitting up in bed.

Another shot rings out. A little further away this time.

'Joel!' I shout a bit louder. Where is he? I'm shaking, terrified. I fumble around for the walkie-talkie, finding it on the floor next to the side of the bed Joel was sleeping in. I press all the buttons, unsure how to get the thing to work. I hear static. 'Hello! Ntando! Are you there? It's an emergency!'

It crackles as if it's connecting but no one answers. What if Ntando and Joel are out there? What if they're both hurt and I'm here all alone? Or perhaps Joel needed the toilet and Ntando is out in the bush with him? The shooting might be the militia scaring poachers away. I swing my legs out of bed, relieved that the lanterns on the steps are still lit, lighting up where to go, but I remember Nancy's words. *Under no circumstances leave the platform.* I press the walkie-talkie's buttons again. 'Please answer!' I say, desperation tinging my voice. But there's nothing. It's as if the batteries are dead. What am I meant to do?

I find my jeans and my mobile phone, which I left in the back pocket. My phone battery is on ten percent. Why was I so stupid not to have charged it? Probably because it doesn't work out here, but at least I can use the torch function. I hold it up in the air, willing the little bars to appear to give me some connection, but there's nothing. No mobile phone coverage. No data coverage. I'm all alone and there's nothing I can do about it. The time on my phone says 1.47 a.m., which means it'll be hours before Ntando or Nancy come to collect us.

I pull on my clothes but get back under the duvet because it's cold now.

'Joel!' I shout. 'Joel! Where are you?'

The heat has faded from the hot water bottles and despite my layer of clothes, I'm freezing. A deep, throaty growl echoes through the night. It sounds close by; too close.

'Joel!' I shout again. 'Joel!'

The night falls silent. It seems to swing from terrifyingly loud noises to equally frightening silence. I start at the sound of a branch cracking.

'Who's there?'

I get no response.

I try to stop myself from catastrophising. What if Ntando called Joel away to help some animal in distress? Perhaps the shots that woke me were to shoo away some predators so that they could rescue a hurt animal? But would they really mount an operation like that in the dark? And why didn't Joel wake me? What I fear the most is that Joel got up to take a pee and he's been attacked. He might be lying injured somewhere, or even worse, dead. I just don't understand why Ntando hasn't responded to me. He has a gun and he's such a lovely man. I feel safe when he's around. I press the buttons on the walkie-talkie repeatedly, but get no response. Try as I might to keep calm, as the minutes creep slowly by, the terror that something truly terrible has happened builds up in my body. I knew we shouldn't have slept out tonight. I had a bad feeling, and now it seems that my intuition was correct.

16

ANNA

I am hyper-alert all night, shivering under the duvet, periodically calling out for Joel and Ntando. I try the walkie-talkie every twenty minutes but it doesn't miraculously gain charge. By the time the thick darkness begins to fade to grey, both my phone and the walkie-talkie are out of battery. As if the weather is mirroring my feelings, the sky is grey, oppressive even. The cacophony from wildlife is almost deafening around dawn and every strange noise makes me jump. I give in to helpless tears at some point because Joel would never just leave me here. Not unless there was a dire emergency. He's the sort of man who calls me if he's going to be late home. Joel is kindness personified.

Shortly before 5 a.m. there's the most terrifying clap of thunder and then the rain starts. It's monsoon-like in its ferocity and within seconds I'm completely soaked. Wetness soaks through the duvet and I shiver violently from fear, cold and dampness. But the rain stops as quickly as it started. It really was a cloud burst. Just a few minutes later, I hear the distant sound of an engine. I stand up and peer into the wilderness and when I see a green Defender appear on the track to the side of the platform, I know I have never felt so much relief. Ntando hops down from the vehicle, giving me a wave. But when he strides closer and sees my face, he frowns.

'I'm so sorry you got wet,' he says. And then he must notice the expression of panic on my face. 'Is everything alright?' he asks.

'No!' My voice is shrill. 'Joel disappeared in the night and there were gun shots and I don't know where he is. And why didn't you answer the walkie-talkie? Why didn't it have enough charge?' I hold it up.

His face falls instantly, his brows furrowing and eyes knotting together. He opens his mouth as if to say something but then clearly thinks the better of it.

'We need to look for him!' My voice is strident, tinged with hysteria, but I don't care because Joel has been out in the bush for at least five hours. 'He could be hurt or kidnapped by a poacher or shot!'

Ntando looks shell-shocked. As nice as the man is, I need to push him into action. 'We need to look for Joel. And where were you last night? I tried calling you over and over. Why didn't you hear me?'

'I'm sorry but I don't know what's happened. I didn't realise... There must be some confusion.'

'You need to call for help. For backup.'

'Yes, yes,' he says, hurrying back to the vehicle where he takes another walkie-talkie and speaks rapidly in a language I don't understand. He runs his fingers through his short hair and hops from foot to foot.

'I'm so sorry I let you down, Anna,' he says. 'I've called

for backup. This is terrible. Really terrible. We'll look for Joel now. Right now.'

And although I am terrified for Joel, a wave of pity comes over me regarding Ntando. He looks so deeply shocked and scared too. I remember how he told me that he supports his extended family and how this job of his is so important. I wonder if he's scared of losing it. I really don't want to get him into trouble, but at the same time, the love of my life is missing and I'll bulldoze whoever I need to to find him.

'Can we drive around? I mean, how far can he have gone?' I ask.

'Of course. We'll look for Joel. I've sent a message to Nancy and I've spoken to my cousin. We'll find him,' Ntando says, but his voice lacks conviction and the bottom of my stomach drops. If something has happened to Joel, I don't think I'll survive it.

I get into the Defender, this time sitting in the front seat next to Ntando. 'Please wait in the car for a few minutes whilst I look for footprints,' he says.

'Is there a gun for me to use?'

'Yes, but you won't have to,' he reassures me. I don't want to be left alone any longer but Ntando is a trained tracker and if anyone can find Joel, I have confidence Ntando will. He heads off into the bush, his gun flung over his shoulder. I'm relieved when he returns just five minutes later but the look on his face tells me that he's found nothing.

'I'm afraid the heavy rain has washed away all tracks. We'll drive around for a bit and if we don't find him, I'll take you back to the lodge and I'll call the other men. We'll find Joel.'

But we don't find him. We stop every so often and Ntando shouts Joel's name. We hear nothing and don't see anything – not even any animals. I suppose we're scaring them away with our shouts. Half an hour later and we're back at the lodge. Nancy is standing in the doorway, holding a walkie-talkie.

'Ntando has told me what happened,' she says, placing her hand on my arm. 'He can't have gone far, Anna, and we will find him.'

'You told me Ntando would answer the walkie-talkie, but it didn't work. I yelled for him all night and no one came.'

Nancy pales. Her lips tighten. 'I don't know what happened, but rest assured I'll find out,' she promises. 'You look exhausted. Can I get some breakfast brought to your tent and perhaps you can get a little sleep whilst we mount a search party?'

'I won't be able to sleep. I'd rather stay here so that I know what's going on.'

She nods. 'Clayton and Lois are having breakfast. Why don't you join them?' She leads me over to the dining table and although Clayton is the last person I want to see, at least I won't be alone. Nancy summons Bhutana and asks her to make me a sugary tea.

'Are you alright?' Lois asks as I sit down next to her. She peers at me and I notice that her forehead doesn't crease. It's the Botox, I assume.

'Joel has gone missing. We slept out in the bush last night and he's just disappeared.'

'Oh my God!' Lois says, blinking rapidly.

'Shit, Anna.' Clayton gets up from the table and walks around to sit next to me. 'He can't have gone far. Nancy's staff are well trained; they'll find him. Would you like a hug?'

I catch Lois glaring at Clayton but she doesn't have to worry. The last thing I want is a hug by my ex. 'Thanks, but no,' I say, shuffling slightly away from Clayton. He doesn't seem to mind and just stands up and walks back to his chair.

'What exactly happened?' Clayton asks.

'I don't know. I was woken by gunshots and Joel had disappeared.'

'I didn't hear any gunshots last night,' Clayton says. 'Did you, Lois?'

'I'd have woken you up if I had.' She scowls.

'We were quite some distance from the lodge,' I explain. I try to stop tears from spilling down my cheeks. It's all feeling too real now.

'Oh, Anna,' Clayton says. 'I'm going to find Nancy and tell her I'll go out and look for Joel. You mustn't worry. I'll help you.'

Lois frowns and I don't blame her. If the shoe were on the other foot, I'm not sure I'd be too keen on my fiancé venturing into the bush.

'I'm not sure –'

'It's non-negotiable. You saw how I was with those men. They've probably returned and taken Joel but I'm not scared of using a gun. You saw how they cowered when I stood up to them.'

'I didn't even know you could shoot,' I murmur. Clayton doesn't say anything and it reminds me again how little I actually know about him. Lois and Clayton finish their breakfast. I haven't managed to eat anything but I have sipped at the sickly sweet tea and it's strangely calming. We all get up from the table.

'Oh, Anna,' Clayton says again, walking towards me with open arms. And even though he creeps me out and I remember all the things he did and said to me, there is something about his familiarity that gives me a modicum of comfort. I let him squeeze me tightly and my tears soak his shirt. But after a few seconds, when he puts his chin on the top of my head, I pull away.

'Sorry,' I mutter to Lois, but she just shrugs.

'It's fine,' she says. Clayton may be the jealous type, but fortunately it seems that Lois isn't.

'I'm going to talk to Nancy and find out how I can help with the search,' Clayton says. The irony of his eagerness to help find Joel isn't lost on me. I wonder if deep down he's quite happy about this turn of events but then I dismiss it. He seems smitten with Lois, almost as if he's a changed man. I think he's being genuine. I follow Clayton as he walks towards a door I hadn't noticed previously, tucked behind the bar area.

'Nancy,' he says, knocking on the door. Nancy appears. She's wearing a hoodie with the Twivali Safari Lodge logo embroidered on it and for the first time since we've arrived, she looks flustered. 'I'd like to help with the search,' Clayton says.

'I'm about to go out.'

'Have you called the police?' I ask, glancing at my watch. It's been seven hours now since I became aware that Joel was missing. I wrap my arms around myself and try not to imagine him lying under a bush, bleeding, being poisoned by a snake or mauled by a lion.

'It's different here,' she says. 'It's not like in Europe where you'd call the police and they'd mount an immediate search. We're too remote out here, which is why we have our own militia. We have to look after ourselves.'

'You mean no authorities are going to help?' Fear makes my voice tremble.

'How can four armed men cover an area this large?'

Clayton asks, articulating my thoughts. 'How big is this reserve? Ten thousand hectares?'

There's a flicker of a scowl on Nancy's face and I suppose she can see her dreams of running a luxury safari going up in smoke. If Joel isn't found safe and sound, Clayton the investor might pull out, and the negative press would ruin her business before it starts.

'The neighbouring ranch has a helicopter. I've put a call into the owner and asked if he will mount an aerial search. He's not there at the moment but hopefully will be back within the next couple of hours.'

'And have you got your men out there looking for Joel?' I ask, my voice cracking.

'Of course. This is an emergency. It doesn't make sense,' Nancy says. 'Rest assured, we'll do everything we possibly can to bring Joel back safe and sound.'

A thought comes to mind. 'This isn't a test, is it? Some weird part of his job interview?'

Clayton scoffs.

'No, of course it isn't,' Nancy says, looking genuinely perturbed. 'Why would I do something like that?'

'What are the chances of surviving if you get lost out there?' I ask in a small voice.

A shadow passes over Nancy's face but she tries to be positive. 'Let's not even go there. I'm going to go out now in the second Defender. Ntando is already out looking and we'll all stay in touch.'

'I'd like to come too,' Clayton says.

'With respect, I'm not sure how that's going to help. I'd much rather you stayed here and looked after Anna.'

'But I can't just stay here doing nothing!' I exclaim. 'I want to look for him too.'

'I'm sorry, Anna, Clayton. You need to stay here. I don't want two or even three missing guests. I understand that you want to feel useful, but under no circumstances must you go beyond the perimeter fence of the lodge; it's not safe. But you could stay up on the deck by the swimming pool and use the binoculars. You might spot him. If you do, use this walkie-talkie.'

She hands me a device that looks identical to the one that didn't work properly last night.

'I'll keep you posted, Anna. And try not to worry too much. If you get peckish ask one of the girls to give you something to eat.'

I watch as Nancy leaves, her Land Rover coughing and spluttering and then throwing up dust as she drives away at speed. She's quite the force of nature; setting up this place in the middle of nowhere, seemingly alone; fearless and competent.

Clayton puts his hand on the small of my back. 'Come on. Let's go onto the terrace and keep a lookout.'

Lois has disappeared, probably having returned to her tent, which means that I'm alone in the main lodge, just with Clayton. How the hell did it come to this?

I perch on the end of one of the sun loungers, holding the binoculars to my eyes, and Clayton sits down next to me. Too close. I edge away.

'I'm so sorry this has happened to you. Joel seems a nice enough man although I thought you'd end up with someone a bit – I don't know – dynamic.'

I bristle but I'm too tired and too sick with worry to come up with a suitable retort.

'You know I forgive you for disappearing like you did. It was a difficult time for both of us but I'll always hold a torch for you, Anna. You deserve the best; true happiness.'

'I've found that with Joel,' I say. I'm scouring the horizon with the binoculars but the light is low and grey and I can't see anything except trees and bushes.

'I just want you to know that I'll always be here for you. Come what may. I'm the one person in the world that will drop everything for you.' He reaches his hand out as if to stroke a strand of hair out of my face but I move away so quickly I almost fall off the end of the lounger.

'I'd rather be alone right now,' I say, as I right myself and stand up. I lean against the wooden barrier.

'Oh Anna, I doubt you could possibly know what you want in a situation like this.'

I turn on him. 'Go and be with your girlfriend, Clayton. Please just leave me alone.'

His face is a picture of hurt. He opens and closes his mouth but I swivel away so my back is to him. After a few seconds, I hear his retreating footsteps and I'm filled with relief. I start silently bargaining with God. *Please bring Joel back safely. I'll move out here with him, no questions asked, if he gets the job. I just want to be with Joel. The true love of my life.*

17

ANNA

As I'm standing scanning the horizon with the binoculars, I wonder about the coincidence that Clayton is here. Could he have planned all of this? He's conniving and controlling. Could he somehow have persuaded Joel to leave me so that he can swoop back in as the hero? But no. That is so far-fetched, and although Clayton has shown his skills at shooting, what does he know about living out in the South African bush? Besides, he's here with Lois, his girlfriend, and the more I think about the two of them, the better suited they seem. She doesn't appear to mind all of his macho and controlling behaviour. In fact I think she handles him well, rolling her eyes at him and not rising to the bait when he says something particularly obnoxious.

I have to sit down again as I feel faint from worry. Joel must be in terrible danger. He would never just disappear. I pray for his safe return yet the kernel of terror inside my stomach is growing minute by minute. And then I see dust rising in the distance. I stand up and lean against the barrier. It's a vehicle headed this way.

'Thank goodness,' I mutter. I can't wait to throw my arms around Joel and tell him that if he ever does anything like that again, I'll divorce him. And maybe we should bring our marriage forward. We don't need a big, fancy wedding; I just want to be married to him now. No delays. It's one of the lodge's Land Rovers, driving quickly, but from this angle I can't tell if it's Nancy or Ntando. I drop the binoculars onto the sun bed and hurry through the building to the entranceway where the vehicles are parked. It's Nancy.

And she's alone.

'What's happened?' I ask, dismay making tears spring to my eyes.

'I'm sorry but we haven't found Joel,' she explains. 'There are a number of vehicles out there looking for him and they'll carry on until they find him. We have excellent trackers here so you mustn't give up hope. I've come back to ring some more people to help in the search.'

'And then what?'

'I'll go back out again.'

'I want to come with you,' I say.

'I don't think that's –'

'It's non-negotiable,' I insist. 'This is my fiancé we're looking for and I can't just stay here doing nothing. Please.'

She hesitates but eventually says yes.

'Meet me here in fifteen minutes,' Nancy says. 'I'll ask Lulama to put some sandwiches and drinks together for us. Bring plenty of clothes. The weather is changing.'

It's true; the grey sky is getting more oppressive and I wonder if it's going to storm. That will make things even worse for Joel if he's out in the bush, hurt.

Nancy drives quickly. Faster than Ntando, and the Defender jumps up and down over the rocks and sandy track, throwing up big plumes of dust behind us. I'm using the binoculars but it's almost impossible to focus on anything with the jagged motion of the vehicle. Crackling comes over the walkie-talkie and Nancy slams her foot on the brake. I jerk forwards. She grabs the walkie-talkie and holds it up to her ear. I can't make out what the person the other end is saying; it sounds garbled. But Nancy just shakes her head and puts it back on the console.

'Nothing of significance,' she says. 'I'm so sorry, Anna.' A brief look flickers over her face and I feel sorry for Nancy, that something like this should happen even before she's officially opened her lodge. I'm impressed by how calm she is, all things considered.

'How long have you owned this place?' I ask as she starts the car up again.

'Two years. It's been a labour of love, restoring it, getting the right staff in place, and now we're on the cusp of opening to the public. I've already got bookings.'

We drive up to a fork in the track and Nancy takes the left hand side and then suddenly the vegetation opens up and it's more prairie-like: long grasses, better visibility.

'There's a river down this way. It's quite far away, but if he got lost then he might have found the river and perhaps is following it. It's the logical thing to do.'

As I've never done any orienteering I have no idea if Nancy's suggestion is a sensible one. And then once again, she slams her foot on the brakes.

'There, to the right,' she says, pointing her hand, her voice a whisper. My heart skips a beat.

There's a loud roar, followed by a terrible screech, and

right in front of us a lioness has her teeth in the neck of a
small impala. They're just metres away and I watch with
horror as the life drains out of the small deer-like animal,
blood dripping from the clutches of the lion. I know that this
is the sight that people wait years to see and pay a fortune
for the privilege, but it sickens me. I let out a small whimper
and look away. It's as if nature is showing me how powerful
she is and that there's nothing we can do to change fate.

'I haven't seen a kill so close up in all the time I've been
here,' Nancy says quietly. 'It's truly wonderful.'

I don't think it is. I think it's sad and distressing to see a
creature die. And even though the lioness is so impressive, I
just want to get out of here. What if those teeth plunged into
Joel? He wouldn't stand a chance. After five minutes or so,
we leave the lioness but I'm not sure that the sound of the
impala's dying moments followed by the crunching and
slurping of the lion eating her prey will ever leave me.

After that, the only wildlife we see is a small herd of
ostriches. We drive around in silence for over an hour, until
eventually Nancy says, 'Would you like to stop for something
to eat and drink?'

I shake my head. I'm not hungry or thirsty. I just want to
step out of this nightmare. And then she gets another call on
the walkie-talkie and this time Nancy frowns, muttering yes
a couple of times. 'Yes, we'll come back now.'

'Have they found him?' I ask eagerly.

'No, unfortunately not. But we have to return to the
lodge.'

'Why?'

'Fezeka, our housekeeper, has found something.'

'Found what?'

'I want to be sure first. Let's just go back.'

'Please, Nancy. What's going on?'

'Probably nothing, but we'll find out soon enough.' Her jaw is set forwards and her eyes narrowed as she turns the Defender and we return the way we came.

Back at the lodge, I follow Nancy as she strides through the main lodge and then around the side onto the path that leads to our tents. A middle-aged black lady is inside our tent, a trolley of clean towels and bed linen just inside the space. Our beds have been made and she's forming a towel into some intricate shape.

'It's here.' She holds up a clear plastic bag. I can't make out what's inside.

'Thank you, Fezeka.' Nancy takes the bag and peers inside it.

'My God,' she mutters. 'Where did you find it?'

'In the mister's shoe. I was moving the shoes to clean in the cupboard and it fell out.'

'Right. Thank you for bringing it to my attention.' She pauses for a moment. 'Have you finished in here, Fezeka?' Nancy asks.

'Yes. I just need to finish shaping the towel.'

'There's no need for that. Please go up to the main lodge and don't say a word to anyone about this.'

'Of course not.' She nods her head deferentially, then pushes her trolley out of the tent.

'What is it?' I ask.

'Inside this plastic bag is rhino horn,' Nancy states.

'What!'

Nancy holds the bag in front of my face and it's full of what looks like coconut shavings.

'Fezeka found this stuffed inside Joel's shoe. Can you explain how it got there?'

'No, of course not! It won't have anything to do with us.'

Nancy's right eyebrow goes upwards.

'What are you suggesting?' I demand.

'I don't know, Anna. It's just very odd that this was found in Joel's shoe.'

I pace around the bed. 'Joel would never do anything like that. He's a conservationist.'

'Look, it's just odd that your fiancé has gone missing and then we find rhino horn stashed in his belongings. Do you know the value of something like this?'

'No, of course not.'

'I reckon that's about half a kilo so it's worth approximately ten thousand dollars.'

I gasp. 'This doesn't make sense, Nancy. Joel is here to interview for his dream job. We've only been here a couple of days. Besides, where would he get rhino horn from? It goes against everything he believes in. Joel is a good guy; he's anti-poaching and he would never ever do anything illegal or immoral.'

Nancy doesn't say anything. Holding the bag, she strides out of the tent and I follow her. We pace back into the main lodge and straight into Clayton. He glances from Nancy to me and back again. 'Any news?'

'No,' Nancy says, her face grim.

'What's that?' Clayton asks, peering at the bag that Nancy is holding.

'Rhino horn shavings.'

'What!' Clayton says, almost exaggerating his reaction. And then it hits me.

Clayton.

Clayton has set up Joel. But how and why?

'Excuse me,' Nancy says, as she disappears into her back

office. I wonder if she's going to call the police now. I don't want them to accuse Joel and me of doing something we haven't done, but perhaps if they come out there'll be more of a search for Joel.

'What's going on?' Clayton asks, putting a hand on my arm. I shrug him off.

'It was found in Joel's shoe, but obviously it's nothing to do with us.'

'They say that rhino horn is an aphrodisiac. That's why it's so valuable. Perhaps that was the real reason Joel wanted to come here. Maybe he's into rhino horn trading.'

'That's ridiculous!' I exclaim. 'Stop slurring my fiancé. He'd never do something like that. Never.'

'Mmm,' Clayton mutters. I'm livid that he's finding this amusing; livid that he's insinuating Joel is a crook.

'Did you plant it?' I ask.

Clayton laughs. 'Where do you think I'd get hold of rhino horn?' He waves at Lois, who is sitting on a white sofa, her legs up, reading a women's magazine. Her toe nails are painted a shocking pink and they match her oversized T-shirt. 'Don't forget that Joel went out with the men when they tagged that rhinoceros. Perhaps he did some dodgy deal then. If you recall, I didn't even go.'

'For heaven's sake, Clayton. My fiancé is missing and you're accusing him of a heinous crime.'

Clayton's shoulders relax. 'I'm sorry, Anna. I didn't mean to upset you. Of course, it's a very tough time for you right now. You're right. Joel is just an ordinary guy, a vet from the home counties. He wouldn't have it in him to poach rhino horn.' He then gazes off into the distance before saying, 'I'm not keeping my side of the bargain, am I?'

'What do you mean?'

'Earlier, I promised I'd look after you, and all I'm doing is upset you further. Can I get you a drink or something to eat?'

'No. I'm fine,' I say. But I'm not. The more I think about it, the more I'm convinced that Clayton is behind everything. Somehow he got himself invited to this lodge knowing that Joel and I would be here. He's probably pretending to be an investor in leisure businesses. And now he's managed to see Joel off somewhere and he's planted rhino horn in our tent. But despite Clayton being controlling and obsessive, I find it hard to believe that he would physically harm someone. I think back to the incident with the ambushers. He could have shot one of them, but he didn't. He only fired warning shots. But why? Clayton has Lois now and they seem content enough in each other's company. Yes, there was that weird thing when he pretended he was dead, but he hasn't tried to contact me over the past two years. Why would he be doing all of this now? Or am I reading too much into things, desperate for answers where there are none?

I walk away from Clayton and pace around the side of the bar, knocking on Nancy's office door.

'Come in,' she says.

I push the door open. It's a small room with a large desk piled high with papers and a laptop in the middle. Nancy is seated, typing something into her laptop.

'Sorry to disturb you but I wanted to mention something about Clayton.'

She glances up at me, frowning.

'You should know that Clayton and I have history. He asked me to marry him a couple of years ago and things were a bit acrimonious at the end.'

'Goodness, that's such a coincidence that you both find yourselves here.'

'Yes, and that's the thing. I don't believe in coincidences. I think that somehow Clayton engineered things so that he was here the same time as me and I reckon he might be behind Joel's disappearance and the planting of the rhino horn in our tent.'

Nancy's eyes widen. 'Goodness, that's quite the accusation.'

'I know, but Clayton has never been rational. I discovered that he had been spying on me, in my home and my car. I had to disappear totally to get rid of him, and now – Well, you can understand why I'm suspicious. I'm sorry, but I really don't trust him.'

18

ANNA

Nancy suggests I have a lie down, and I don't disagree. I'm feeling totally exhausted. It's unsurprising, considering the combination of having only had a couple of hours' sleep last night and the emotional toll that Joel's disappearance is having on my mind and body. I can't think straight. My limbs feel so heavy I can barely drag myself along the path towards our tent. Nancy has promised to wake me if there's any news on Joel. She's bending over backwards to be kind to me and I can sense that she's as desperate as I am for Joel to be found safe and well. I'm not sure she believes me about Clayton's connection to what's happening, though. After all, she only knows the professional Clayton; the smartly dressed man with a big bank balance who is swooping in as a financial saviour. I wonder if she's worried that the promised investment in her game reserve might disappear. I daren't ask how much Clayton has pledged.

As I'm dragging my exhausted feet along the path, wary

as always for venomous snakes and other wildlife, I hear raised voices. I stop and listen. Clayton and Lois are shouting at each other. I consider taking the stone path towards their tent in order to make out their words, but decide against it. I wouldn't want to be caught eavesdropping. Besides, there's nothing suspicious about a couple having a humdinger of an argument. Just because Joel and I rarely disagree, doesn't mean other couples don't. Perhaps Lois is getting annoyed at how concerned Clayton is for me. I carry on walking towards our tent. Once inside, I collapse on the bed fully clothed and I let the tears flow. I reach over to bury my face in Joel's pillow hoping to smell the essence of him but the sheets must have been changed because the only scent is of clean laundry. That makes me cry even harder.

I am so knackered and overwrought that, against all odds, I sleep. I wake up a couple of hours later, my mouth dry and my eyes sore, disorientated as to why I'm in a strange bed and it's light outside. And then I remember. Joel is gone and as Nancy hasn't woken me, there is clearly no further news. I take a quick shower and change into clean clothes. Then I walk briskly back to the main lodge. Just inside the door are two suitcases. One is a large navy case with the logo of a well-known brand I can't place, and the other is a smaller, matching shoulder bag.

Clayton is sitting in the lounge drinking a cup of coffee from a porcelain cup. He only likes to drink out of porcelain so no ordinary mugs for him. He gets up as soon as he sees me.

'Anna, how are you doing?'

'I assume there's been no news?'

'I haven't heard anything.'

'Have new guests arrived?' I ask, nodding my head towards the luggage.

His laugh is strained. 'That's Lois's stuff. She's going home.'

'Without you?' I ask.

'Yes, without me. It's over between us. I never had the connection with Lois that I had with you. We had an argument and she's leaving. Out of my life forever. And you know what, Anna? It feels right.'

'I thought you made a good couple,' I say, as realisation seeps in that with Lois gone, Clayton's infatuation with me may start up all over again. In fact, it just adds to my theory that he's been conniving.

'I tolerated her because we're so far from home, but let's face it, she's not classy like you.'

'So when are you leaving?' I ask.

'I'm going to stay as long as you need me to.'

'But I don't need you,' I say hurriedly. 'It's kind of you but really, you can go too.'

'What sort of friend would I be if I left you alone in the middle of nowhere, in a strange country where you know no one and don't understand the customs, when your boyfriend is missing in the wilderness?'

'My fiancé,' I correct Clayton.

He ignores my correction. 'No, you need me, Anna, whether you realise it or not.'

I feel an edge of hysteria mounting. I want to scream at Clayton to leave me alone but at that moment Nancy appears.

'Any news?' I ask, close to tears again.

'I'm sorry, no. I've organised some food for you as you've

barely eaten today. Lulama will bring it out to you if you'd like to take a seat at the table.'

I glance at my watch. It's 2.30 p.m. and Joel has been missing for over twelve hours. I still don't feel like eating but I know I have to.

'Clayton, would now be a good time to go through some of our financial projections?' Nancy asks. I get what she's doing and I'm grateful. She's drawing him away from me.

Clayton hesitates but then, to my relief, he follows Nancy through to her office.

Lulama is a big-boned lady with a vivacious smile and such a strong accent that I struggle to understand her and then feel embarrassed because I have to continuously ask her to repeat herself.

'You tell me what's your favourite food,' she says, 'and I'll make it for you. We need to keep you strong.'

'Thank you,' I say, even though I'm finding it difficult to make any headway with the delicious platter of vegetarian dishes Lulama has given me. 'Can you make lasagne?' I ask. It's Joel's favourite meal and I want him to have that when he returns. I bite the inside of my cheek and try to cough away the foreboding sensation that's gripping my throat. If he returns.

'Of course, my lovely.' She pats me on the back and I rather wish she'd pull me into a hug. I smile wanly as she leaves me alone and returns to the kitchen, but then I hear her talking to someone behind me. I turn around. It's Ntando. Leaving my food, I get up from the table and hurry over to him.

'Any news?' I ask.

He shakes his head, his face glum. 'I'm sorry, not yet. I'll be going back out again after I've had a bite to eat.'

'Can I come with you?'

He hesitates. I suppose it's not protocol, but what is in these exceptional circumstances?

'You could check with Nancy,' I suggest. 'I told her earlier that I wanted to help with the search.'

'Nancy's gone out.' That's quick. I'm surprised I didn't hear her. I wonder if Clayton has gone with her and hope that he stays out of my way for the rest of the day.

'I'll collect you in twenty minutes,' Ntando says. I can sense his pity and I wish it wasn't there.

After forcing myself to finish at least some of the food that Lulana prepared for me, I'm eager to get going and join Ntando in looking for Joel. The fear is biting away at my insides and choking me. I feel so isolated here. What was only two days ago an idyll is turning into a nightmare. If only I could speak to Mum or Sasha. If only I could go online and check out if people have disappeared and then been found in the African bush, I might feel a bit better. But with no access to the outside world, this place is starting to feel like a prison. If only Katie and Zak were still here. They were well travelled and worldly-wise. They'd know how to help. And then I recall Katie's parting words to me: 'You will take care out here, won't you?' Did she mean anything in particular with that comment or was it just a throwaway comment based upon the ambush we'd all experienced?

Ntando collects me and we walk out to the front of the building to where he's parked his Defender. He hops into the driver's seat and I sit next to him in the front passenger seat. He turns the key in the ignition and it splutters before conking out. Ntando tries again several times over but then he peers at the dashboard and mutters something under his breath.

'What's happened?' I ask.

'It doesn't make sense.'

'What?'

'There's no diesel.'

'Didn't you notice that it needed filling up?' I can't help the exasperation sounding in my voice. Firstly Ntando failed to answer the walkie-talkie and now he's out of diesel. This is negligence.

'Of course I notice. It's my job to make sure that I take it to the filling station at the entrance to the reserve. I had diesel this morning and now I have none.'

'How is that possible? Could you have missed the fact it needed filling up?'

Ntando shakes his head and jumps down from the vehicle. He lifts up the bonnet and fiddles around with something inside, but my view of him is blocked. He shuts the bonnet with a bang and wipes his palms on his trousers.

'I think the diesel has been drained.' I'm sure I see fear in his eyes.

'On purpose or an accident?'

'I don't know, but there's no diesel leak under the car. It doesn't make sense. I'm sorry, Anna, but we can't go anywhere until either Nancy returns with the other vehicle or I get one of my cousins to bring over a jerry can.'

My dismay is reflected on Ntando's face.

Have we been thwarted deliberately or is this just a fluke accident where diesel has leaked from the Land Rover? We walk back into the lodge.

'Will you stay with me?' I ask Ntando.

He frowns. What I can't tell him is that I feel safer with him, a total stranger, than I do with Clayton, my ex. If Clayton has made Joel disappear, if he's planted rhino horn shavings in our tent, if he's drained the Land Rover of diesel, then I hate to think what he'll do next. All I'm sure about is Joel must be in terrible danger if he isn't already dead, and I'm not safe either.

19

ANNA

The day is becoming increasingly oppressive, the sky leaden and the squawks of the wildlife much quieter than yesterday. Ntando and I walk to the terrace. I take the binoculars from the coffee table in the lounge and Ntando uses his own. We stand side by side scanning the horizon. After about fifteen minutes, when my arms are beginning to ache, I see something.

'Look, over there!' I exclaim. 'At two o'clock.

Ntando points his binoculars to where I was pointing and lets out a sigh. 'It's a couple of zebra,' he says.

I wonder if I'm hallucinating now; so desperate I am to find Joel, my mind is playing tricks on me.

'I'm going to get a drink. Would you like something?' I ask Ntando.

'Some water would be great but it should be me getting it for you.'

'You're more experienced at looking through the binoculars,' I say.

I walk back inside where the air is a little cooler thanks

to the big rotating fans in the ceiling. At the bar, I help myself to two large glasses of bottled water.

'Hello.'

Clayton appears from nowhere and startles me.

'How are you doing?' he asks.

'Fine,' I say curtly, although of course, the opposite is true.

'I've missed you so much, Anna,' he says stepping towards me, his arms outstretched.

'Leave me alone!' I say tightly, edging away from him.

'I'm just so happy I can be here for you in your time of need.'

I feel like physically slapping Clayton. How dare he talk to me like this when my mind is focused on Joel? 'I don't want anything to do with you,' I mutter.

'You're only saying that because you're worried,' he says. 'My feelings for you have never changed.'

I wonder now whether he dumped Lois in the hope of getting me back. If so, he's very mistaken.

'I don't want anything to do with you,' I say more firmly this time. Ntando is just outside and I'm sure he'd hear me if I yelled. 'Please leave me alone.'

A nerve twitches in his jaw and he opens his mouth as if he's going to say something, but clearly changes his mind. His face softens. 'I get it, Anna. This is a very hard time for you. I'll leave you alone as you request but please know that I'm here for you regardless.'

As I'm walking back through the lounge, holding the two glasses of water, I think about my beloved Joel. How excited he was for this trip, and even more excited at the prospect of getting a job out here. Has Clayton put paid to all of that? Would he really have the nous? It makes my blood boil, never knowing when he'll next be overstepping the mark. Lois is lucky to be out of a relationship with him. I think back to the evening Joel came home announcing he'd been contacted by a headhunter who invited him to apply for a veterinary job in South Africa. How did that headhunter find Joel? How did he even know that Joel was open to a new job? As far as I knew, he wasn't actively looking for a new post. Was there something fishy about it? Could Clayton have somehow engineered this job interview? It seems very unlikely but I will never trust the man. How can I, after I discovered he'd put spyware on my phone and was bugging my home and tracking my car?

After another twenty minutes or so, during which time Ntando never once lays down his binoculars, I hear Nancy's voice. Thank goodness she's back. She'll be able to sort out diesel for Ntando's vehicle and perhaps she has news.

I leave the terrace and walk inside. When she sees me, she steps away from Bhutana.

'No news,' she says, pre-empting my question. 'But I have been into the local village and one of the men there is driving into the nearest large town. He'll go to the police station to report Joel missing. The police will mount a proper search including notifying traffic cops and ports and airports.'

'Thank you,' I say, feeling so relieved. At least now fully trained teams of people will be out looking for Joel. Clayton isn't anywhere to be seen, but I don't want to risk being overheard. 'Could I have a quick word with you in private?' I ask.

'Of course,' she says, leading me back into her office.

'I'm really uncomfortable around Clayton,' I admit.

Nancy frowns. 'I'm sorry to hear that.'

'The more weird things happen, the more convinced I am that he has something to do with Joel's disappearance.'

'Yes, you mentioned that earlier. It's just he's only an investor and he doesn't know his way around the bush. I think it's much more likely that Joel got lost in the dark and is now...'

She doesn't finish her sentence but I can tell from the pitying look on her face that she's trying to find words to say that he's been killed by an elephant or a lion.

'Clayton has told me how much he's missed me. It's totally inappropriate to be saying something like that when my fiancé is missing. It's as if he's been waiting for this moment so he can step in as the good guy when I'm down on my luck.'

'Yes, that is an odd thing to say,' Nancy agrees. 'I'm sorry to hear he's been behaving like that. I'll see if I can have a word with him.' She bites the side of her lip as if she's contemplating something. 'Would you feel safer if I move you from your tent to a small lodge next to my home? It's just a single room and bathroom but it's where my personal guests stay. My friends and family. And it's literally adjacent to my lodge. If you shout, I'd hear.'

'Yes, I would appreciate that. Thank you very much.'

'I'll ask Bhutana to help you move your belongings.'

'And by the way,' I add. 'Ntando's car was drained of diesel. I hope he won't get into trouble about it. It meant we couldn't go out to search again this afternoon.'

'What?' Nancy exclaims.

'I'm sure he'll explain.'

The room next to Nancy's beautiful lodge is essentially a wooden shed. It houses a small double bed, wardrobes that look like they've come from Ikea, and a simple bathroom with a shower and toilet. Although the soft furnishings are the same as elsewhere in the property, it's simple in comparison to the beautifully styled tent. There is a musty scent, as if the place hasn't been aired in a while, and the air is hot and heavy. I swing open the windows although the humid air outside doesn't do much to help. In contrast, the exterior of Nancy's home, the lodge next door, replicates the main lodge. I'd love to see inside, but it doesn't seem appropriate to ask. Besides, I've got more important things on my mind: namely to spearhead the search for Joel and to avoid Clayton. Unfortunately this hut I'm in doesn't have views – just dense bushes, whereas from our tent, I could see for miles and watch any helicopters seeking Joel. So far I haven't heard any aircraft and I wonder when the air search will start. Perhaps I should have stayed in the tent.

I'm startled by a loud bang of thunder, which is followed almost immediately by a monsoon-like downpour of rain. This is just what we don't want. Bad weather hampering the search. It feels like everything and everyone is conspiring against me and Joel, even the weather.

20

ANNA

Unless you've experienced someone you love disappearing, I don't think you can fully comprehend how fear takes over. I've never been one for catastrophising (except perhaps when it comes to flying) but like most people, I've wondered how I might cope in the face of an emergency. However well you prepare yourself, the reality is different. Every molecule of my body is longing for Joel; fear grips my heart, which either beats too fast and drums in my ears, or feels as if it's being crushed and unable to function properly. I'm finding it hard to breathe too, as if the air is being choked out of my lungs. It's not helped by the weather, which is now truly horrendous. It's a bit like a prophetic fallacy, the weather mirroring my fear. If Joel is out there, he must be utterly terrified. What if he's lying injured on the ground? The rain is so heavy it must have turned the earth into a muddy puddle.

I can't stay by myself in this hut any longer, so I pull on my anorak, put up the hood, and brave the weather. At least I hope the snakes will be taking refuge somewhere away from the path. Even though it's nearer from this hut to the main lodge, I'm soaked through by the time I walk into the lounge. Nancy must have seen me walk in, because she hurries over to me.

'How are you doing?'

A feeling of hysteria rises up my throat. How does she think I am? And why isn't she out there looking for Joel?

'You have a satellite phone, don't you?' I ask, making an assumption.

'Yes,' she says, hesitantly.

'I want to call the British embassy. See if they can help in any way. And I'd like to call Joel's parents. They need to know what's happening.'

'Is that a good idea? I mean, why worry them unnecessarily? Perhaps wait until tomorrow.'

'I'd still like to call the embassy. And I'd like to talk to my mum. Is that possible?'

'Of course,' she says. 'Give me a couple of minutes and I'll bring it out.'

I pace the lounge and then pour myself a small brandy from the honesty bar. I want to numb the pain but at the same time, I need to stay alert. It tastes too sweet, but in a weird, masochistic way, I relish the burning in the back of my throat.

Nancy reappears. 'I'm so sorry, Anna, but the satellite phone isn't working. I think it's been blown out by this storm. It's happened before.'

'What does that mean?'

'That we'll have to wait to be reconnected. Once this bad weather passes through, it'll likely work again.'

'So we have no contact with the outside world, nothing at all?'

Nancy looks pained as she nods at me. 'Terrible timing, I know.'

I wonder. Could this be another setup by Clayton? Could he have made his way into the office when Nancy wasn't looking and somehow played with the equipment? He's certainly technically able.

'Clayton –' I say, but then when Nancy gives me a look as if I'm crazy, I change my mind. I can't blame everything on him. Even Clayton can't control the weather.

'I know this adds to the concern, Anna, but please rest assured that there are teams of people out there looking for Joel. All the neighbouring game reserves know that he's missing. As soon as the weather clears, our neighbours will be receiving new guests by plane. They'll ask the pilot to search for him from the air. And the police are on the case too.'

'But are people out there now, in this weather?'

'Yes. Our militia are driving around, and Ntando too. The rain will make it harder to find him, of course, but it won't stop them from looking.'

'Can you drive me to the nearest town?'

Nancy looks doubtful. 'It won't be possible tonight. With this torrential rain, the track will be impassable. But I'll take you tomorrow, as soon as the sun comes out again and the tracks dry out. Conditions change very quickly here.'

That doesn't fit exactly with her promise that she has teams of people looking for Joel despite the weather, but I suspect she's just trying to put my mind at rest. It's probably too dangerous to be out in these conditions. But then I think of Joel and just pray that he's found shelter somewhere. He's physically fit and a positive thinker so I know he'll be fighting.

'I'm so sorry this has happened to you. And to Joel. I was going to offer him the job. I think he'd be perfect.'

I choke back a sob.

'If you don't mind me saying, I think you could do with an early night. You look absolutely exhausted. Lulama has made you a warming vegetable stew. There are only the three of us here now, so why don't we eat and then you can go to bed.'

'Alright,' I say, because there is no alternative. I follow Nancy out of the office and into the lounge where Clayton is sitting on a sofa, his bare feet up on the coffee table, drinking a large glass of red wine, the bottle half empty. I'm surprised he doesn't remove his feet when Nancy walks in.

'Any news?' he asks.

I shake my head.

It's an awkward meal. Whenever I look down at my plate I feel Clayton's eyes on my face. The sensation is real because I catch him staring at me when I glance up. If Nancy notices the tension between us, she doesn't say anything. She tries very hard to make conversation, to act normally in an abnormal situation.

'How did you and Joel meet?' Nancy asks.

'Walking the dog in the park.' But I don't want to talk about Joel, especially in front of Clayton. It chokes me up and reminds me how much I'm missing him, so instead I turn the questions to her. 'What led you to Twivali Safari Reserve? Was it in your family?'

Nancy laughs. 'No. The safari was my idea, my dream. I was brought up in Johannesburg but I knew I wanted to get out of the city as soon as I could. I worked in hospitality for a while. My marriage broke down and shortly afterwards I inherited some money. I reckoned it was time for a complete life change. I had the freedom and the finance so I started looking around for reserves for sale. When I found Twivali it was love at first sight.'

'Did you have to do a lot of renovations?' I ask, thinking that she's very brave to do this all alone.

'A fair bit. I wanted to put my own stamp on the place, particularly because it wasn't very well run before. At that point I realised I needed more funds than I'd anticipated, which is where Clayton comes in.'

Clayton nods but doesn't say anything.

'I hope this is a great success for you,' I say, although I can't help thinking again as to how her dream might be soured if Joel doesn't return unscathed. From a selfish perspective, I'm glad that Nancy is invested in finding Joel.

Our conversation dries up once more. I pick at the delicious food but the other two finish their plates. When Bhutana clears our dishes away, Clayton gets up from the table.

'I'm going to have an early night so I can get up at the crack of dawn to help with the search. Assuming Joel hasn't been found by then, of course.'

'Thank you,' Nancy says. I can't bring myself to thank Clayton too.

'Can we see if the satellite phone is working?' I ask Nancy.

'Of course.'

I follow her back into her office. She tries it again but shakes her head sadly. 'I'm afraid the weather will have to properly clear up before it resets itself.'

I don't know anything about satellite phones but I feel sick at the thought that we have no contact with the outside world.

'I've got a bit of work to do and I want to check in with the team as to how the search is going. Are you alright to walk yourself back to your room?'

'Is it safe?'

'Yes. It's so much nearer to the main lodge here than the tents are, and no animal will venture this close to us. Just take an umbrella and help yourself to a lantern. They're by the main door. If there's any news, I'll wake you.'

'Thank you,' I say, but I doubt I'll sleep.

The rain is still torrential, and despite using a big umbrella and running as quickly as I can, I'm drenched when I swing open the door to my wooden hut. Inside the lights are low. I shake the umbrella before leaving it propped up against the exterior wall, then peel off my anorak, hanging it on a hook just inside the door. I stride into the room. The bed has been made up again in my absence and there's a bunch of fresh flowers on top of the chest of drawers. Both Joel's and my suitcases are placed on a luggage stand.

I take a long, hot shower and then feel guilty for using so much water. Dressed in my pyjamas I walk to the door intending to lock it. But there is no lock; not even a hook and latch. That's strange and it makes me feel uncomfortable. On the other hand, I suppose Nancy's personal guests have no need to lock their door. Or perhaps it's just an oversight. I consider pushing the chest of drawers in front of the door but decide against it. If there's some news in the night and Nancy needs to wake me, she'll have to come in.

I get into bed and shiver, despite it not being cold. The rain is battering on the roof but at least this hut feels sturdier than the tent, and even though the door doesn't lock, I feel safer here, being nearer to Nancy. I read on my kindle for a bit but the words don't sink in, so I switch off the light and try to sleep. But all I can think about is Joel. Is he hurt? Is he being kept captive somewhere? If so, why haven't we received a ransom request yet? Or perhaps we have. Perhaps the kidnappers have contacted Joel's lovely parents but we wouldn't know about it because we have no access to the outside world. I try not to think about the worst. My fiancé bleeding out and being ravaged by a wild animal. Or being shot and dying in pain and all alone. I toss and turn and lose track of time.

And then there's a knock on the door and before I can ask who is it, it creaks as it swings open. I sit up in bed, my heart racing as I wait for Nancy to give me news. *Please let it be good. Please.* I switch on the bedside lamp.

'What the hell are you doing in here?' I ask, staring at Clayton in horror. I pull up the duvet so it covers me up to my shoulders. He's wearing a waterproof jacket, which he takes off and places over the back of the chair, drops of water falling onto the floor. 'I want you to leave,' I say, panic in my voice.

'Don't be like that,' Clayton says, edging towards me. 'I have to talk to you. To tell you my truth.'

His truth? What the hell does he mean? Is he going to admit what I've feared? That he is behind all the horrors of the past twenty-four hours?

'Stay away from me,' I say, my knuckles white as I grip the duvet.

'I'm not going to hurt you, Anna,' Clayton says. He pulls the chair out and turns it around, then sits down so he's facing me, leaning away from his wet jacket. 'The opposite, in fact. I love you, Anna.'

'I don't love you,' I say. 'I want you to go. Now.'

'I've dreamed of this moment for the past two years.'

'My fiancé is missing. He might be dead or injured and you think it's okay to barge into my room in the middle of the night and declare your love for me! You're deluded, Clayton, and you need to leave. Now!' I shout.

His face falls.

'Did you plan all of this? Have you done something to Joel, because if you have, I'll kill you.' I don't know where the words come from because I've never been prone to violence, and of course I'm bluffing. Or maybe I'm not. I feel such fury in my veins, I really could hurt him.

'Anna, Anna. Relax. I would never do anything like that.'

'So how did you know I'd be on this safari? How did you plan all of this?'

'Oh, my darling. It was written in the stars. If you want something that much you can make it a reality. It's called manifestation. Getting back together with you has been my greatest desire for the past two years. And at long last it's materialised. I know I came across as the macho man in the past, the provider, and so desperate to protect you from anything that might bring you harm, but I did a lot of thinking after you disappeared. I realise that I might have been over-protective, trying to wrap you up in cotton wool. My intentions were good but I realise now you're an independent woman and that a lifelong partnership is one of equals. You'll be impressed that I took some courses, did some couples' counselling and gained a lot of insight. I am a better man today than I was two years ago. Much better.'

I can't believe what Clayton is saying. He is utterly delusional. Good luck to him if he thinks he's a changed man. Perhaps he is. But I want absolutely nothing to do with him. I'm engaged to be married to Joel, the love of my life.

Clayton stands up and peers at me. 'You're not saying anything.'

Because I'm gobsmacked. I can't decide if I feel pity for Clayton, if he's just creepy, or if I'm scared of him. A mixture of all three, probably.

'I'd like you to leave my room.'

He tilts his head to one side and looks sad. 'Just one little hug?' he asks.

'Please get out before I scream.'

He backs away then, his hands held out in front of him. 'No need for that, Anna. I understand it's still a difficult time for you. Please think about what I've said and we can talk again tomorrow. In the meantime, sleep well, my love.'

I am still trembling long after he has left the hut, the door closed behind him. When I think my legs are strong enough to hold me, I get out of bed and walk to the chest of drawers, dragging it across the room so that it's directly in front of the door. After double-checking that both the window in the main room and the small, opaque window in the bathroom are firmly closed, I get back into bed and try to sleep. I must drift off eventually because when I wake up, sunlight is streaming into the room.

There's a knock on the door.

21

ANNA

'Who is it?' I ask.

'Good morning. It's just Bhutana. Nancy asked me to bring you breakfast in bed.'

'Thank you,' I say through the closed door. 'Has there been any news?'

There's a beat of silence before she says, 'No. I'm sorry. I don't think so. Shall I leave the tray outside your door or bring it in? It's just not a good idea to leave it for too long because of the wildlife.'

'Just one moment, please.' I drag the chest of drawers away from the door and then open it. Bhutana must have heard me but she doesn't say anything. She just puts the tray on the end of the bed.

'Do you need anything else?'

I glance at the tray piled high with freshly squeezed orange juice, a pot of tea, fruit salad, pastries and a boiled egg. 'Thank you. This is lovely.'

She gives me a sad smile and leaves.

My appetite hasn't returned and I don't think it will until

Joel is found, but I do my best to nibble at the food. I then take a shower and get dressed. When I eventually open the door to the hut and step outside, I jump.

Clayton is sitting on a rock just in front of the door.

'What are you doing here?' I ask through gritted teeth.

'I wanted to apologise for coming into your room uninvited last night. It just breaks my heart to see you so unhappy. With hindsight, it was a conversation to be had in the daytime. I realise I smothered you in our relationship but I've truly learned from that, and now I can give you love and freedom.'

'You don't get it, Clayton!' My voice has an edge of hysteria to it. 'I'm in love with Joel. We're getting married. There is no you and me, so you'd better get over it.' This man is totally delusional. How can he talk to me like this when my fiancé is missing?

'But Anna, Joel isn't around anymore, and I am, so it's my job to look after you.'

'I don't need looking after!' I yell. 'Just go away and leave me alone.'

He steps forwards and puts his hands on my shoulders. I step backwards but I'm right up against the door with nowhere to go. I tense as I watch his face go from white to flushed. He tenses up and I think he's going to hit me, but no. He releases his grip, steps backwards with a hangdog look on his face.

'I'd do anything for you, Anna.'

'Is everything alright?' Nancy asks, appearing just a few steps away at the top of the path.

'No!' I say at the same time that Clayton says yes.

'I'll see you later,' Clayton mutters, edging past Nancy and striding towards the main lodge.

'You need to keep that man away from me. He came into my room uninvited last night and he's totally creeping me out.' The more I think about it, the more convinced I am that Clayton planted the rhino horn to make Joel look culpable. For what reason, I don't yet know. Perhaps just to make Joel look bad in my eyes, but that has backfired totally because I know Joel would never do something as horrendous as rhino horn poaching.

'Oh dear,' Nancy says, frowning. 'I thought he was just being kind towards you.'

'Kindness that I don't want. I think he's behind everything. He planted that rhino horn and perhaps he's got rid of Joel.'

'Clayton?' Nancy looks at me in disbelief. 'You're under a great deal of stress at the moment and it's understandable that you're looking for answers. I wanted to let you know that although we have no news at the moment, a plane will be going out this morning.'

I glance up at the sky and indeed it's a perfect cerulean blue, the sun's warmth is heating up the rain puddles from last night, creating little patches of rising mist, and the birds are singing loudly.

'I need to get out of the reserve,' I say. 'Can you take me into the nearest town, where there's a police station, please.'

'Yes, of course. We can do that this afternoon as I want to oversee the search parties this morning. Hopefully by then we won't need to go into town. I'm very hopeful that Joel will be found soon.'

I pray she's right.

A few minutes later, I see Nancy leave in one of the Defenders. The place seems so quiet and I'm at a loss for what to do. I wish I could go out there too and help in the hunt for Joel, but what do I know about the bush? But I'm compelled to do something. I can't sit around here just hoping; that's not in my nature. I've no idea where Clayton is, but hopefully he's gone out with some of the men. But the staff will still be here: Lulama the cook, Fezeka the house-keeper, and Bhutana the general helper. Perhaps they've heard something or seen Clayton acting suspiciously.

The main lodge is very quiet. I walk behind the bar and knock on the door to Nancy's office. I know she's not there but perhaps a member of staff is inside. There's no answer. I try to open the door but it's locked. I then walk through the swinging door between the dining room and into the kitchen. It's perfectly tidy, with nothing on the work surfaces except a pair of oven gloves and a neatly folded tea towel.

'Hello!' I shout.

There's no answer.

To the left of the fridge is another door. I open it and it leads me outside, to the rear of the lodge where visitors never go. Up ahead are two tents and a makeshift building constructed from corrugated iron. I glance inside. It houses a toilet and a simple shower. Is this the staff accommodation? If so, it's awfully basic and a world away from the luxury guests are treated to. I can't imagine that Nancy would expect Joel and me to stay in something as spartan as that.

'Hello!' I say again, but it's obvious no one is here. Cautiously, I unzip one of the tents. Inside are two single mattresses and a couple of open crates that have been crafted into storage units. Piles of neatly folded clothes are inside. Pinned to the side of the tents next to each of the mattresses are photos, mainly of smiling children. I recog-nise both Bhutana and Fezeka, as they hold toddlers on their knees. I'm shocked that Nancy isn't providing them with better accommodation. It must get so hot inside these tents.

But more to the point, where is everyone? Bhutana was here this morning and I assume the others were too. Could they be cleaning the guest tents? I hurry back through the main lodge and down the path towards the guest tents.

'Is anyone around?' I shout. The only answer I get is from some strange chirruping-type animal. A frog perhaps.

As I hurry back to the lodge, fear snakes down my throat. Why am I the only person here? Surely Nancy would have told me if she'd organised for all the staff to leave. And what if a wild animal barges through? What am I meant to do then? I rush out onto the terrace in front of the beautifully styled living room, grabbing the pair of binoculars that have been left on the coffee table.

Suddenly I hear the spluttering of a car engine. Where is it coming from? And then a green Defender comes into view and as I train my eyes on it, I see that all the staff are inside. Ntando is driving, Lulama sitting in the front passenger seat, with Bhutana and Fezeka sitting behind them. Where are they going? Why didn't they tell me there were leaving? And is it safe to leave me here alone?

After a minute or so of sheer panic where I'm frozen to the spot on the veranda, I give myself a stern talking to. I'm being ridiculous. Everyone is out looking for Joel; everyone except me. And I'm the one person who should be doing the most. I need to take advantage of this solitude and search the grounds around the lodge and use the binoculars to scour the horizon. I'm high up here and I'll be able to see if an animal is coming – or a human, for that matter. And so long as I keep my eyes on the ground in front of me, I will be safe from snakes too. I'm not sure I fully believe any of that but I absolutely have to do something.

I walk out of the front of the lodge, the binocular strap around my neck, to where the two Defenders are normally parked. The road is gravelled here and it sweeps around the front in a loop, then climbs up a gentle hill. The bushes are neatly manicured, interspersed with cacti. There must be a gardener to keep this looking so neat, but I haven't seen anyone gardening since we arrived. I walk up to the top of the drive where there's a cattle grid but I don't dare walk beyond it. I remember what Ntando and Nancy told us – don't venture beyond the perimeter of the lodge. There's a wire fence which I hadn't noticed before, mainly because it's hidden in bushes and trees, and I assume it delineates the perimeter of the lodge and outbuildings.

Despite it being only 10 a.m., it's hot outside and all residue from yesterday's storm has vanished, exactly as Nancy predicted. I follow a discrete path which leads back past the staff quarters, past my hut and then to Nancy's lodge. It feels like snooping but at this point I don't care. I walk up to the window next to the front door and peer inside. The interior is smaller than it appears from the exterior and there's an open-plan living room with a kitchen on the far wall. I knock on the door, although I'm not surprised that there's no answer. The front door is locked, so I carry on walking around the edge of the wooden building. There are two steps that lead up onto a terrace. I open the squeaking gate and walk onto the wooden veranda. Here there are four sun loungers and a small barbecue, but it's the view that captures my attention. It's a different angle to the landscape from the main lodge or the guest tents, but equally mesmerising. There's a hill to the right, and to the left the glimmering pale blue water of a small lake – another watering hole. My heart misses a beat as I see movement to the edge of the lake. Lifting the binoculars to my eyes, I see an elephant emerge from the bushes and wade into the small pool of water. It lifts its trunk high into the air and then curves it down into the water. A few seconds later it spurts water back over its body. If only Joel were standing by my side watching this wonderful sight. After several long minutes, the elephant wanders back the way it came. I train the binoculars away from the watering hole but then I catch the briefest glimpse of something red. Is it a bird? They have brightly coloured birds here, don't they? I hurry down from the terrace and in amongst the shrubs in front of Nancy's lodge. Weaving between prickly bushes, hopping quickly in the hope that my heavy footsteps will scare away any snakes, I edge forwards until I'm at the perimeter wire. Standing on tiptoes, I bring the binoculars to my eyes and try to find that splodge of red again. I wonder if it was a bird that's now flown away, but no. I find it. I play with the focus of the lenses until the image sharpens. And then I gasp.

It's a red shoe. What the hell is a red shoe doing abandoned over there?

For a second, my legs feel weak and nausea rises up my throat. Could that be Joel? But no. Joel doesn't own any red shoes. I peer again and reckon it looks like a woman's shoe. *What the hell.*

I know I'm not meant to go beyond the perimeter fence but I need to know what a shoe is doing abandoned in the bush. With some difficulty, I clamber over the wire and gingerly make my way towards the red shoe. I'm about five metres away when I come to a halt. I think I'm going to throw up.

There's a body.

And it's not just *a* body.

It's Lois.

She is lying on the dusty earth, her arms outstretched above her head, her unseeing eyes looking straight upwards towards the bright sun. Her pale yellow sundress is torn and there are reddish stains – blood, I assume. I stumble backwards, scratching my arms on prickly bushes.

I can't help myself. I scream, my voice piercing the stillness.

I don't care if I get torn to smithereens by the vegetation; I just have to get out of here, back to the safety of the lodge. Anywhere I can barricade myself in. I'm unseeing as I scramble back the way I came, hauling myself under the perimeter wire, scratching my legs and arms as I weave up the bank to the safety of the paths. I don't even pay attention to the dust that rises up behind the wheels of an approaching vehicle.

'Anna, what's going on?' Nancy says as she jumps down from her Defender. 'What's happened to you?'

'It's not me. It's Lois. She's dead!' I let out a sob. 'We need to get out of here. I think Clayton killed Lois – and next, he'll be coming for me.'

22

NANCY - THEN

Before I came into money, I would take the day flight for the eleven-hour journey from Johannesburg to London. But this time I was booked into business class and took the night flight, indulging in a slap-up dinner with champagne, followed by a surprisingly comfortable sleep on my narrow flat bed. It's been too long since I've returned to London, and I'm looking forward to the hustle of the city and plenty of indulgent shopping trips.

After collecting my large but fairly empty suitcase, I make my way through security into the arrivals hall. It's heaving with people and for a moment I feel a little claustrophobic, as if everyone else is inhaling the stale air, leaving insufficient for me.

And then there are strong arms around me and a kiss is placed on the top of my head.

'It's so good to see you!' Clayton says as he releases me from his strong grip.

I step backwards to give him the once over. He looks terrible. Skinny, unshaven, almost grey in the face and a whisper of the confident man that visited me eighteen months ago in South Africa.

'God, Clayton. What's happened to you?'

'I'm alright,' he says, with little conviction.

'You don't look it,' I say, shoving my big suitcase towards him. 'Well, I'm here now so your big sis can take over.'

'I'm so happy to see you,' Clayton says, giving me a shoulder bump. 'Come on. Let's find the car and I'll take you home.'

Clayton and I look nothing like each other, even though we're siblings. Sometimes I wonder whether it's because we had such different upbringings but in reality, he takes after our father's side of the family and I'm more like Mother. Or at least, that's what the photos suggest. Clayton has classic dark good looks, with his curling black hair and startling blue eyes. I, on the other hand, am blonde, and with the help of my hairdresser become a little blonder every year. I hope that our looks are the only thing we've inherited from our parents, but I fear not.

'How was the flight?' Clayton makes easy work of pulling my suitcase.

'Fine. I recommend business class.'

'You're preaching to the converted.' He laughs, but it sounds a little forced. I still find it strange that my sibling speaks with the poshest of English accents, whereas I will never be able to ditch the flatter South African accent. But unlike Clayton, I speak Afrikaans, and if I had to make my way around the Netherlands, I'm pretty sure I'd understand most things. He may have had the more expensive education but I feel better educated.

Clayton and I were separated when we were six and eight. He was shipped off to boarding school in England, whereas my schooling wasn't deemed so important, so I was sent to a girls' day school in Johannesburg. I can't imagine how terrified he must have been, when aged just six he was escorted onto an airplane knowing no one, and then brought up by stern matrons and brutal housemasters. At least that's how I imagine it was. Clayton refuses to discuss it. Of course, it explains a lot, for both of us.

'How's Theo?' Clayton asks brightly.

'We're getting divorced.'

He stops suddenly, which isn't helpful as we're striding along a moving walkway with people right behind us.

'Oh no. What happened?'

'Come on,' I say, pulling Clayton forwards by his sleeve. 'I don't want to talk about him.'

When we've paid for the parking ticket, and Clayton is reversing his smart, black sportscar out of the parking lot, he asks me again. 'How come you didn't tell me things were bad with Theo?'

'Please, Clayton,' I say. 'I don't want to talk about it. You're my family. You're the only important person in my life, which is why I've done this mercy hop over to London to sort you out. We've got lots of talking and strategizing to do.'

Clayton grimaces.

In my unprofessional opinion, I believe my brother is on the verge of a breakdown. During our childhoods we barely knew each other, but when I hit my early twenties, I decided that the bright lights of London were more likely to bring me all the things I desired: wealth, influence, love and a family. Even the big cities of South Africa – no offence to them – Johannesburg, Cape Town and Durban seemed provincial in comparison to the cosmopolitan, fast-living home town of my brother. I emigrated. With nowhere to live and no contacts, I gravitated towards Clayton, who seemed as eager to be close to me as I was to him. Two years younger than me, he appeared so much more mature, swanning about town on a motorcycle; assured, good-looking and with contacts in high places. I was proud to be his older sister. He found me a job working in a travel agency, because back then I had few skills other than my knowledge of Africa. We lived together and life was good. We both dated, a lot, but were there for each other as every relationship petered out or proved to be a disappointment. With hindsight, Clayton was my perfect man and I was his perfect woman. We had each other, so the only reason we had to date was for sex.

Although I earned a modest income in my job, Clayton worked in finance and he was soon raking in huge sums. We had our inheritance and our trust funds, but mine was beginning to run out and Clayton had no need to draw upon his. Life was good, until it wasn't. It's like I woke up one morning and realised that my heart lay in Africa. I missed the big skies and warm weather and the jovial people. Yet I was torn. How could I leave my darling brother? He depended upon me so much. It was me who made sure he had something to eat when he returned home late after closing a deal; it was me who selected the girls I thought he should date; who made sure that his diary included play and work. Yet I was the one with the ticking clock. I wanted a family and I certainly didn't want to bring up children in London. And then our uncle died and, much to our surprise, left all his money to Clayton and me. Clayton said he had no need of it – his salary and banking bonuses were so large – and he gave me his portion, telling me to live my dream. I wonder if he would have been so generous if he hadn't just met Anna. She was the only girlfriend I was never introduced to; never vetted. Indeed, I didn't even know of her existence until it was too late. But for me, the time had come to go home. I had money, the security of knowing that my beloved brother would be there for me should I ever need him, and with those security blankets I began the long search to find a game reserve. A reserve just for me. A reserve and a husband.

But now the tables have turned. Clayton is in a mess and it's time for me to support him again. We make idle chit-chat as he drives confidently to central London and parks the car in his underground garage. He's quiet now as we take the lift up to the seventh floor.

'Welcome home,' he says, with little enthusiasm, as he stands back to let me into his flat.

'Jeez,' I mutter. The place is a tip. What has happened to my neat-freak brother? There are dirty pizza boxes on the coffee table, empty wine bottles on the kitchen counter, and a pile of unwashed glasses in the sink. There's a stale smell, of old food and cigarette smoke. Since when did Clayton smoke? I remember how whenever I got up from an armchair or sofa, he would automatically plump up the cushions left behind, and how he lined all his tins up in the cupboards just so. How has he gone from being OCD to this? It doesn't make sense.

'I've made up the spare room for you,' he says.

'What's happened to your housekeeper? Didn't she used to do all of that stuff for you?'

'I fired her.'

'Why, Clayton?'

He sinks onto the sofa and puts his head in his hands. 'I'm in debt. It's a mess, Nancy. I took my eye off the ball at work and I lost the firm millions.'

I can't help but inhale loudly.

'Really? What happened?'

'You don't need to know the detail, but I'm on gardening leave without pay whilst they investigate. I'm finished in the city. No one will employ me now.'

'But what about all the money you had stashed away?'

'Spent it.'

'On what?' I ask.

'I started gambling a bit. I was good at online poker to begin with but now... Now, I never win.'

This man is a shadow of his former self and it's a shock to me. But I'm a fixer and this time it's my turn to make things better.

'First things first,' I say. 'I'm hungry. What have you got in the fridge?' I open it. There are two mouldy lemons, a bottle of vodka, three bottles of white wine and several beers. I peel a few notes out of my wallet and hand them to Clayton. 'Whilst I'm unpacking and tidying this place up, I want you to go to the nearest supermarket and buy some food. Vegetables, fruit, meat. Healthy stuff, okay?'

He nods contritely.

A couple of hours later, I've tidied up the flat, put on a load of washing, changed the linen on my bed as it looks unappetising, and have whipped us up a Spanish omelette. We eat in silence. Afterwards, I make us both a cup of coffee and tell Clayton to join me on the sofa.

'Give me your laptop,' I say.

'Why?'

'Just do it.' He passes it to me.

'What are the gambling websites you use?'

He reels off a few names.

'One at a time. Give me the passwords.'

Clayton looks stricken but I know the only way to cure my brother is to go cold turkey. He does as I ask and on one site after the other, I delete his accounts. 'I'm keeping the laptop and your phone for the duration of my stay,' I announce.

This makes him angry. 'For God's sake, Nancy. You're not my keeper.'

'Actually, I am. You're a mess and I'm the only person in the world who's going to rescue you.'

'Anna,' he murmurs.

'Do you think Anna would be interested in you in the state you're in? She was attracted to the successful, debonair Clayton, not the pathetic wreck you are now.'

He opens and then closes his mouth.

'So my diagnosis is, you're depressed. You can either go to your doctor and get medication or you and I can come up with a plan to make you better. What do you choose?' My brother may be miserable but I still see that flicker of pride and how he could never accept a diagnosis of depression from a health professional. Clayton loathes doctors; perceives them as the fix for the weak. Doesn't believe in mental illness, despite the hard evidence of our mother. All I can say is it's just as well he's never been seriously ill.

'I'd like you to help me,' he says, unable to meet my eyes.

'Good choice. How long have you been in this mess?'

'I suppose I started spiralling after Anna's mistake.'

'Mistake?'

'She left. Disappeared. But obviously it was a mistake. She's the love of my life, Nancy, and I can't live without her. She's been influenced by her hideous best friend, Sasha, who never liked me. I think she was jealous of me. And now Anna has gone. Poof. Just vanished.'

'Oh, my poor brother,' I say, flinging my arms around him. 'What do you mean she's vanished?'

'She came off social media, changed her phone number, left her job. I can't find her. She could be anywhere in the world. The one place I know she's not is her old flat and where she used to work.'

'Alright, so first off we need to find Anna. Once we find her, then you can take steps to get her back but so long as she's vanished, I don't see how you're going to get well.'

'I agree,' he says. His voice sounds choked.

'So this is what we do. We pretend that you're dead. If she thinks you're dead, then she will have no reason to stay hidden from you. You say she's vanished off social media, so I assume she used to be on it.'

'Yes. She was on Facebook and Instagram, but she deleted both her accounts.'

'Are you positive she is hiding from you?'

He nods sadly. 'I tried calling Sasha, who told me to stay away and that Anna never wanted to see me again. I even went to see Anna's mother, but the woman threatened to call the police. It's not like I was going to hurt her! I contacted her work and they refused to give out details. I even stalked her laboratories for weeks, but she wasn't working there any longer. I contacted the police and reported her as a missing person but got nowhere because I wasn't next of kin. Sometimes I think it would be easier if she was dead, because then I would be able to grieve properly.' A tear falls down his cheek. The old Clayton would never cry. Never. My brother is totally broken.

'How much does Anna know about me, our family?'

'Nothing. I never told her about you, Nancy.'

That stings. Why wouldn't he tell Anna about me? I

realise I was on the other side of the world, but still. 'I don't understand,' I say, hurt evident in my voice.

'I can't explain why,' Clayton says, his head back in his hands. 'I think I wanted to have her all to myself. I didn't want to share her with anyone, not even you. I'm sorry. That was obviously a mistake.'

We're both quiet for a moment.

'It might work to our favour,' I say. 'Have you still got the phone number of Anna's friend, Sasha?'

'Yes. But she blocked me. I think the number still works because I tried it from a phone box.'

'Do you know her full name?'

'Yes, Sasha Whetherby.'

'Great. I'll find her. So I will call Sasha Whetherby and tell her that you died. That you took your own life whilst travelling in Australia. She will of course tell Anna, and hopefully Anna will come out of social-media hiding. We'll find her, but you will need to be patient. Whilst we're waiting, you can come back to South Africa with me and help on the game reserve.'

He grabs my hands and brings them to his lips. 'Thank you, darling Nancy,' he says. 'Thank you.'

I pull my hands away because I really don't want my brother's slobbery lips all over them. 'I'd do anything for you, Clayton. You know that, don't you? You and me, we're all we've got.'

He nods.

A few days later and we're both in business class on our way back to Johannesburg. It was easy for me to find Sasha Whetherby. I rang her at her work – a solicitor's firm in the city. I gave her the tragic news about my recently deceased brother and lapped up the shock in her voice. I asked her to pass the news on to any of Clayton's old friends and said that there had been a private family funeral and due to the circumstances of his death, no public notices. Nothing for anyone to do.

Now we just have to sit back and wait.

23

ANNA

'Dead?' Nancy exclaims. 'You say Lois is dead?' She pales and grips the door of the Defender.

'You need to call the police!' I say, panic in my voice. 'And we need to get out of here. Now. Clayton is behind all of this.'

Nancy doesn't move, barely blinks, and I suspect she's in shock. This must be her worst nightmare, to have one guest dead and another missing.

'Are you sure she's dead?' she asks slowly.

'I've never seen a dead person before but yes, I'm sure.' My voice cracks. I turn away from Nancy and I vomit into a bush. This is too horrific.

'I need to go and check,' Nancy says.

I take deep breaths and wipe my mouth with a tissue. 'No! It's too dangerous.'

Nancy passes me a bottle of water that she takes from the door of the vehicle.

'She's dead, Nancy. And where is Clayton now? He might

come back any moment and I'll be next. You too, perhaps. He's totally deranged! Do you even know where he is?'

She shakes her head.

'Can you call the police?' I ask.

'It's best if we drive to the local town. That gets us away from here and we can notify the police in person. They're more likely to respond that way.'

I don't wait for her to suggest I get in the car. I jump up into the passenger seat. Nancy is a bit slower than me but I'm sure it's shock. I hope she'll be all right to drive. With a shaking hand, she starts the car.

'What if we run into Clayton? Is he with Ntando?' I ask.

But then I recall seeing Ntando drive away with all of the staff, so where is Clayton? Could he be with the militia or even the men who ambushed us?

'I'm not sure, but don't worry, I'll take the back roads. We won't run into anyone.'

'You've got a gun, haven't you?' I ask.

'Yes, of course,' Nancy says, 'but I have no intention to use it.'

She drives fast, her white knuckles gripping the steering wheel, leaning forwards. The tension is evident from the strained muscles in her neck.

'You're right,' she says eventually. 'There have been strange things going on and I discounted Clayton. But perhaps I was wrong. Perhaps I just didn't want to see it. If Clayton still has a soft spot for you, he could have got rid of Joel, and then killed Lois.'

'And tried to frame Joel for rhino horn poaching,' I add. 'I've thought he was weird for a long time but I didn't think he was deranged. Do you really think he has killed Joel?' I let out a sob.

'Try not to worry too much,' Nancy says. 'We will find Joel and Clayton will be caught.'

The car bounces along the unmade path for about twenty minutes and then, to my relief, we turn onto a tarmac road. It's long and straight, and a wire fence runs the full length of the road. I chew at the skin around my nails, making them bleed, but at least the physical pain keeps some of the emotional pain at bay.

'Is that the perimeter of your game reserve?' I ask.

'Yes. We have a lot of land.'

We continue driving for perhaps another fifteen minutes and then arrive at a T-junction. There are signs to towns I've never heard of in both directions. I wish we had arrived by car rather than plane, as I might have a better sense of my bearings, but frankly, I've no idea where we are.

'Which town are we going to?' I ask.

'Heldorp,' Nancy says. 'There's a police station there.'

I didn't notice any sign to Heldorp, but then again, I wasn't paying much notice. We drive through a small village which is little more than some concrete huts with washing hanging on long lines. I don't see any electricity poles and the place looks run down and basic. A world away from the luxury of Twivali Safari Reserve. The scenery is more barren here, with few trees and shrubs, just low-lying scrub, and heat rises in a shimmer in the distance. Then Nancy takes another turning to the right and a long wire fence comes back into view.

'How long until we get there?' I ask.

'Another forty minutes or so.' She glances at her watch. 'Nothing is nearby around here.'

Nancy makes a sudden and unexpected turn off the road

and we're back bouncing along an unmade track, passing alongside a riverbed.

'Isn't there a main road to the town?' I ask, as a flicker of nerves pings in my stomach.

'No,' she says, without looking at me. Her knuckles tighten further and the tension is back in her neck.

'What's going on, Nancy?' I ask, gripping the door handle.

'You'll see.'

I have a sudden urge to get the hell out of here. I try to open the door but we're bouncing at speed and she's locked them.

'What the hell are you doing?' Nancy yells at me. 'You'll get yourself killed.'

'I want to get out of here.'

'Don't be an idiot. If I drop you off here in the middle of nowhere, you'll be killed by an animal in an instant. How would you ever find your way back?'

She's right and I remove my hand from the door handle.

And then the track starts to look familiar and my fears become very real. She slows right down as we arrive at the wrought iron entrance gate with the shiny sign that says:

Twivali Safari Lodge Private Game Reserve.

And standing next to the sign, his hand on the top of it and a big, sickening grin on his face, is Clayton.

'Why have you brought me back here?' I ask in a tremulous whisper.

'Because my brother is in love with you. He's a wonderful man and deserves happiness, which is what the two of you are going to find together.'

If I wasn't already sitting down, I would collapse. Clayton is Nancy's brother. They're in this together and she has brought me right back to the proverbial lion's den. I know in this horrific instant that I am their prisoner. That there is no escape for me. That I am at the mercy of a pair of lunatics. She stops the car. I try to open the door again but the central locking is still on. I could try to jump out of the window, but what then?

It's as if Nancy can tell what is going through my mind. She puts a hand on my arm. 'If you run, you will die. You will never get out of the reserve alive. It's impossible.' And I know she's right. 'I'm sorry, Anna, but you are not going to leave. You're too upset to realise this now, but Joel isn't the man you thought he was and Clayton is the man for you. He always has been and always will be. We understand that it'll take a while for you to come to terms with Joel's disappearance but when you do, you'll realise that we've saved you.'

'You're crazy!' I yell.

'Please, Anna. No raised voices. We don't want to scare the animals.'

I feel like hitting her but now isn't the right time. She's in control of the car which is inching slowly forwards onto the gravelled road towards the entrance of the lodge. I glance over my shoulder and see Clayton ambling down the path towards us.

'Did you kill Joel?'

Nancy sighs. 'People get lost in the bush all the time, but you'll be fine because you have Clayton to protect you.' She pauses for a while as she brings the vehicle to a halt and turns the engine off. 'Joel chose to leave.'

I open my mouth to dispute what is clearly the most

nonsensical statement I've ever heard, but then decide to say nothing. I'm not safe. I need to keep my concerns to myself.

'Did Clayton kill Lois?' I ask in a whisper. I'm not sure I want to know the answer.

'Forget about Lois. You're safe here with us. You're the only person who matters. Come along. Let's go and join Clayton and pop open a bottle of champagne.'

I stare at her as she releases the central locking and jumps down from the driver's seat, clutching the car keys in her hand. She's totally deluded and I'm stuck here with this crazy couple.

'Are you coming?' Nancy asks, her head tilted to one side, the generous host in appearance once again. But now I know she's the consummate actor.

I get out of the car and force my legs one in front of the other. It feels like I'm walking into a jail, one I have no idea how to escape from. This beautiful lodge with all of its five star luxury is simply a facade.

'Welcome!' Clayton says, as if I haven't just seen him this morning. 'It's time to celebrate.' He pops open a bottle of champagne and pours me a large glass. I take it from him but my hand is shaking so much, drips fall onto the wooden floor. I put it down on the table.

'I know this will be a surprise, Anna,' Clayton says, his face beaming. I can't believe that I once found this man attractive. What delusion does that handsome face hide! 'But both Nancy and I hope it's a happy surprise. We own this game reserve and life here is wonderful, but there was just one thing missing. You. We've thought it all through. You're a wonderful chef so you can run the kitchen at the lodge – just until we have children, of course. And then I wouldn't want you working anymore. But what a glorious place it'll be to raise a family. We can open the reserve up to guests if we decide, or just enjoy it ourselves. The world is truly our oyster.'

I glance at Nancy, but her face is relaxed and content. Is that what Nancy wants? This is utterly ridiculous. Have they killed Joel? My beloved Joel with whom I was meant to be spending the rest of my life? I need to know.

'What have you done to Joel?'

'Forget about him,' Clayton snaps.

'It's alright. It's understandable that Anna is concerned for Joel. It'll take time, Clayton. Patience is a virtue.' Nancy smiles.

What the hell!

'Is Joel dead?' I ask, my voice barely audible. *Please don't have killed him*, I beg silently. Maybe I can save him if he's here somewhere, still alive.

Clayton strides over to me and reaches for my hands. I try to pull them away but Nancy throws me a look that I haven't seen before and it scares me. I let Clayton hold my hands. 'Anna, darling Anna. Please forget Joel. I swear we haven't hurt him; he's just chosen to go away. He had a change of heart and realised that you and I are a much better match.'

I know that's ridiculous. Joel loves me. He's an ordinary, caring, humble man who is meant to be my husband. They don't know Joel. He would never just disappear. Never. I'm terrified that Clayton has killed him, as he's obviously killed Lois. Just discarding her body over the fence, waiting for animals to devour her carcass so nothing is left behind.

'Look, Anna. We don't want to hurt you. We want you to be on our team, to be part of our family. Clayton loves you and I love whomever Clayton loves.'

'I didn't even know you had a sister,' I say.

Clayton looks towards the floor, bashful even. 'My mistake,' he says eventually. 'I wanted to keep you all for myself and at the time we were together, Nancy had just returned back here, to South Africa. I would have introduced you at our wedding.'

'But I don't love you!' I exclaim. 'I'll never love you.'

'You did once,' Nancy says, her voice frustratingly calm. 'You accepted his proposal of marriage.'

I think back to that hideous evening when I was so mortified to be proposed to in front of that massive audience in the Palladium theatre. I couldn't have said no. I compare it to Joel's proposal. It was a beautiful sunny Saturday and we made a picnic and drove down to the River Arun. We lay on the grassy bank and watched the butterflies and dragonflies, the sun warm on our faces, and we ate big chunks of cheese and freshly baked bread. After a couple of glasses of wine, I felt drowsy and closed my eyes. I had never felt so content. Joel leaned over and gave me a kiss. I opened my eyes and he was sitting up beside me.

'Anna, I love you so much. Will you marry me?' he asked. He had fashioned a little daisy chain, which he slipped onto my finger even though I didn't say yes. It was the perfect marriage proposal. Low key. Intimate. Just the two of us. Exactly as I would have dreamed of as a little girl.

'I love you too,' I said, holding his hands. 'But it's too soon. We've only known each other three months. Ask me again in another three months' time.' It wasn't until much later that I admitted to Joel that I'd briefly been engaged before. That I had felt bamboozled into the engagement and that I hadn't loved my previous boyfriend, not how I loved him. Joel was true to his word and he proposed again three months later. This time he had a proper ring, a small solitaire diamond, but he also gave me a necklace with daisies on it. It became our symbol of love.

So Nancy is wrong. I never loved Clayton. I was impressed by him; I enjoyed his company. But love? No.

Now what? How long will they keep me here? How am I going to escape their clutches? How will I find out the truth about Joel?

'I don't mean to scare you,' Nancy says, which of course immediately sends my blood pressure through the roof, 'but you mustn't try to run away. It's really dangerous out there. The animals will get you like they got Lois.'

.

24

NANCY

We let Anna go back to her room. I hope that we've successfully persuaded her to stay with us, but if she tries to escape, then so be it. If the animals don't get her, I will. I've done it before and if I have to, I'll do it again. Not that I want to, because that will surely break Clayton's heart, and the whole purpose of this exercise is to heal it.

Those months when I returned to South Africa and Clayton stayed in England were miserable months for me. I missed my brother much more than I anticipated I would. I assumed it was the result of the distance. We were thousands of miles apart; of course it wouldn't be the same. In hindsight, I realise that he had no need of me during that time. He was obsessed with Anna and she took my place as his emotional crutch. When Anna left him I was happy. Yes, that makes me sound like a bitch, but I got my brother back, albeit at a physical distance. Once again, I became the most important person in his life, and I had Theo. I never loved Theo, but he served a purpose. But Clayton spiralled downwards into depression and I became truly concerned for his wellbeing. Things improved when he came back to South Africa with me. He settled well into the wilderness lifestyle, much to my surprise. But it took much longer than I anticipated to draw Anna out of the darkness. By the time she came back onto social media and I realised that she was engaged to be married to another man, I knew our plans had to change. Clayton was getting restless. He threatened to go off travelling to find himself. He talked about going to India to be guided by gurus and then perhaps going back into banking in Australia. This was not what I wanted. I could see that I was going to lose my brother all over again and I could not let that happen.

I had a number of ploys to get Anna out to the game reserve: her winning a competition perhaps. But when I discovered that her fiancé was a vet, and a vet for large animals, and even better than that, he had spent six months in Africa as a student and still hankered after that lifestyle, it was as if fate had dealt us the perfect hand. It was easy then, finding a headhunter to act as my go-between, inviting Joel out here for an interview. And the irony is, he would have been a perfect vet for us here on the reserve. He had exactly the right calm demeanour and his assistance in darting the rhino was invaluable. Sadly, we had other plans for him and he was just a pawn in our game plan to bring Anna home to Clayton.

My brother is not as clear headed in strategizing as I am. That surprises me, as he was clearly successful in his investment advisory role, but he is weaker than me and gets led astray by matters of the heart. So I only shared the bare bones of my plan. Once I got Anna here on the reserve, I knew there would be three possible outcomes.

Firstly, Anna and Clayton would get back together again with little intervention from me. They would realise that they were meant for each other and Joel would disappear off the scene, broken-hearted but departing voluntarily. I knew this option was unlikely, as Anna clearly thought she was in love with Joel.

The second plan was to set things up to show that Joel was an idiot, positioning Clayton as the hero so that Anna could fall back in love with him. That required a little forward planning but was easy enough to pull off. I went into the local township and recruited two men to act as ambushers. They needed the money and took little persuasion. I gave them guns and told them that they needed to act as kidnappers, focusing in on Anna. I explained to them, and to Ntando, that this was all part of the interview process for Joel. I wanted to see how Joel reacted in the face of an emergency. Not well, as it turns out. He froze, as I anticipated he would. What provincial British vet would have the experience and wherewithal to face down being held up at gunpoint? Everyone played their parts beautifully, and although I know it created a temporary rift between Anna and Joel, sadly, it was insufficient to break their bond. I then planted the rhino horn. Of course that was a long shot and Anna didn't fall for the suggestion that her Joel is a crook.

So then it was onto the third option: getting rid of Joel. And here we are, the plan executed perfectly. Now all Clayton needs to do is woo Anna. Of course, I had to get rid of the staff. I couldn't have them hanging around helping Anna escape. I told them that there were teething problems and that Clayton and I needed to sort them out before the official opening. They weren't happy with being told to go away on unpaid leave, but what did they expect?

Full pay for doing nothing? I'm not that much of an idiot. At least they know they've got guaranteed jobs when they return, which is far better than the majority of people who live out here, scraping by on practically nothing.

Clayton pours me another glass of champagne. He's quite giddy and it's sweet to see.

'Thank you so much, sis,' he says, clinking his glass against mine.

'It's over to you now,' I say. 'And the most important thing is, don't come on too strongly. You need to woo Anna subtly, otherwise you'll scare her off.'

'What did you do to Lois?' he asks.

'I had to get rid of her for you. No choice, I'm afraid. Lois was threatening to tell Anna that she was the hired girlfriend. She had the audacity to try to blackmail me. She wanted ten grand to keep her mouth shut so, naturally, I had to make sure that her mouth will stay shut forever.'

'Shame,' Clayton says. 'I thought she was doing a reasonable job pretending to be my girlfriend. Does anyone know she's here? Has she got family?'

'Worry not.' I placed an advert in a few British local newspapers, seeking an actress for a one-off assignment in South Africa. I was inundated with enquiries. I chose Lois because she seemed vacuous. She was pretty enough but had cheapened herself with unnecessary cosmetic surgical procedures, and she seemed unscrupulous in what she'd do for money. She was even prepared to sleep with Clayton for an additional two hundred quid a go. Quite the little whore. I got her to sign a non-disclosure agreement, so she was forbidden to tell anyone where she was going. I just hope she abided by it. Things went wrong a couple of days ago. She pieced together exactly what we were up to and started questioning whether Joel had really just *got lost* in the bush. I knew we had trouble on our hands, but when she tried to blackmail me, that was a step much too far. It's not like I enjoy killing people, but it's dog eat dog out here and I'll do whatever is needed to protect Clayton and myself. The two of us had such miserable childhoods, we deserve happiness. The environment we're living in makes it so much easier to dispose of people. I wonder whether subconsciously that was why I chose to live here. The animals will clear up all of my dirty work. I'm pretty sure that if Anna was stupid enough to look for Lois' body again, the only fragments left behind will be ripped clothing and those bright red shoes. The lions, hyaenas and vultures will take care of the rest.

25

ANNA

I have never been so terrified in the whole of my life. I am stuck in the middle of nowhere with two crazy siblings who have gone to extraordinary lengths to bring me here and isolate me from the rest of the world. My heart is broken because it's obvious they've killed Joel in the way they killed poor Lois, just chucking their bodies out into the bush, ready to be devoured by animals. I didn't know such evil existed. I try to think back as to whether there were any warning signs. But no. This was such an exciting trip for both Joel and me, I could never have guessed that it was all a trap to ensnare me.

How the hell am I going to get out of this place? I know I can't just walk out. That would be sure death, as I've no idea where I am and any one of those beautiful animals could kill me. I know there's a satellite phone because Nancy showed it to me, and now I'm sure that it wasn't broken. That was just a ploy to stop me from contacting the outside world. If I can get access to it, then I could call the police – not that I know the emergency numbers here. But I could call Mum and she could notify the British embassy and the police. But what if I can't get access to it? There are guns here. Perhaps I could shoot Nancy and Clayton, but even though I doubt they'd hesitate to kill me, I'm not sure if I would be able to take aim and pull the trigger. I've never even held a gun. So what else can I do?

I pace up and down the hut, feeling totally claustrophobic. There will be an opportunity at some point. I just have to be ready to grab it. If I can think straight, that is, because right now my brain feels muffled and my heart is thumping so rapidly I wonder if I'm going to have a heart attack. I suppose the best thing to do is to go along with their absurd plan. If I'm compliant I'll be less likely to be hurt. Perhaps I can lull them into a false security where they think I'm going along with their craziness and then an opportunity to escape might present itself.

I step over to the wardrobe and lift my handbag off the floor. I reach inside to take out my phone, but it's gone, along with Joel and my passports. Of course they've taken both. That means I can't even look at photos of Joel. I let out a frustrated scream and burst into tears. What have these terrible people done to me? What is it about me that Clayton is so obsessed with? I lie on the bed and sob into my pillow.

After a few minutes, I feel exhausted. Self-pity isn't going to solve my situation, and I realise the only way out is to give them what they want and bide my time. I take a hot shower and stand underneath it for ages, dreaming of that little plane landing on that makeshift airstrip and me running out to it to discover Joel is already seated inside and the plane lifts off into the sky as Clayton and Anna come running. It seems ridiculous that just a few days ago I was terrified of flying. There are many more, far greater fears that are my reality today.

As I'm getting dressed, there's a knock on my door. I freeze.

'Anna, it's only me.' It's Nancy's voice. 'Dinner will be ready in ten minutes. Come to the pool area.'

Do I have a choice? I could stay in my room but then, what will they do to me? What would happen if I go on a hunger strike? I don't suppose they'd care. As I pull on a jumper and grab a scarf, I decide to go with my original plan. Lull them into believing I'm going along with their craziness and hope they let their guard down.

I stride towards the main lodge, my teeth gritted together, my shoulders back. I am not going to be cowered by these siblings. There's the heady, smoky scent of a barbecue, the sweetness of wood, charcoal and meat. I'm drawn towards it and, despite everything, my stomach gurgles. As I round the corner, I see Clayton leaning over a circular fire pit that he's turned into a barbecue. Next to it is a table for two covered with a white linen tablecloth, silver cutlery and sparkling glasses. On the ground there are candles in lanterns, and more of them attached to posts. Gentle jazz is playing from hidden speakers, creating a scene of romance straight out of a novel. It causes me to come to a standstill.

'Anna!' Clayton exclaims as he looks up and sees me. 'I'm making your favourite meal. Steak cooked medium rare on the fire, marinated in herbs, baked potatoes, and Nancy is just collecting the salad. I've opened a lovely bottle of pinot noir grown just outside Franshoek. South African wines are some of the best.'

I hesitate.

'Come, come,' he says, beckoning me with a wide smile, as if this was the most ordinary of situations.

Every nerve ending in my body is screaming *beware* but I know I need to put on the greatest act of my life. I walk towards Clayton, forcing a smile onto my face.

'This looks lovely,' I say.

'I wanted our first dinner to be as romantic as possible. Take a seat,' he says, gesturing towards the table with a pair of large tongs.

I sit down, my hands underneath my thighs to stop them from trembling. The cicadas are out in full force and the African sky is vast and dark, the stars just beginning to come out. I shiver.

'You sit down too, Clayton,' Nancy says, as she strides towards us holding a large bowl. 'Let me be the server tonight.'

Clayton grins, puts down the cooking implements and walks over to the table. He takes the bottle of wine and pours a soupçon into his wine glass. He then swills the wine around, sniffs it and takes a sip. How pretentious, considering it's just us, but I know I need to go along with the charade. Besides, I need a drink to calm my nerves.

He pours me a large glass, tops up his own and offers some to Nancy.

'No, keep that for yourselves. It's a special bottle. I've got some white wine in the fridge, which I'll help myself to shortly. How do you like your steak cooked, Anna?' she asks, her voice saccharine sweet.

'Medium rare,' Clayton answers for me. He sits down opposite me and stares into my eyes. As hard as I try, I can't hold his gaze so I look away towards Nancy, who is leaning over the fire, her face lit up in an orange glow. So much for this safari lodge serving only plant-based food.

'Coming right up.' She brings me a plate with a large steak and a baked potato with a crispy skin, and places it in front of me. She then returns with a big bowl of salad, which actually looks delicious, including fruits, nuts, avocado, plump mini tomatoes and salad leaves. 'Please help yourself.'

'Aren't you going to join us?' I ask Nancy, because despite my fear of the woman, I'm even more terrified to be left alone with Clayton.

'Absolutely not. This is your special evening. We made a braai especially for you. Clayton said it's your favourite meal.' She blows us a kiss and disappears inside the lodge.

I have nothing to say to Clayton but he doesn't seem to notice and he witters away about how happy he is that I'm here with him, and that the last two years have been hell without me. I zone out because I'm more terrified about what will be expected of me after the meal. I nibble at the steak, which is delicious, even if I wish it wasn't, and when Clayton has polished off all the food on his plate, he shouts, 'Nancy, we're done!'

A couple of minutes later, Nancy comes bustling out of the lodge carrying two small glass dishes. She clears our plates and puts them down in front of us.

'Chocolate and orange mousse. Another of your favourites, I gather.'

'Yes, thank you,' I say meekly. 'It's very kind of you to go out of your way.' I dig my nails into the palms of my hands and try to look at Nancy as I'm speaking. It's hard as she repulses me and my words are lies.

'Would you like some more wine? A brandy or cognac perhaps?'

'No, nothing more,' I say. We've polished off the bottle of red and I don't want to be too drunk; just enough to take the edge of the horror of this situation, but not so much that I feel any loss of control.

'It's been a long day. Time for bed, I think,' Clayton says, glancing at his watch. He stands up, walks over to me and helps pull the chair back as I get to my feet.

I turn and head in the direction of my wooden hut but Clayton puts out his hand and grabs my forearm. 'Not that way. Please come with me, Anna.'

'I'd rather not –'

He interrupts me, turning me so that I'm facing him. 'We're back together again, Anna. I want you to share my bed, to hold you, to feel your skin against mine,' he says in what he clearly thinks is a husky, sexy voice.

I try to suppress a shiver. 'No, I don't think –'

'It's the only way I can keep you safe. The only way.' He lets his words linger and his eyes are firmly fixed on mine. I have no doubt that this is a thinly veiled threat. I either do what he wants or I come to some danger.

I don't say another word. He steers me into the lodge. We walk through the big open-plan living and dining room that once I thought was the height of African luxury and out the other side towards the main door. 'Hold on,' he says as he opens a cupboard and extracts a shotgun. I struggle to stop myself from whimpering.

'Don't worry, Anna. As Ntando isn't here, I need to make sure that there aren't any dangerous animals around. I'll keep you safe, darling.' He slings the shotgun over his left arm and puts his right arm around my shoulders so I'm forced to walk with him side by side. His fingers press into the flesh of my upper arm, burning.

'My belongings –'

'Are all inside my tent now. Nancy transferred everything over whilst we were eating our dinner.'

So that's how it's going to be. We're going to masquerade as a loving couple and I suppose I'm going to have to prostitute myself to him. Will I be able to do that? Will I be able to pretend that it's Joel who is making love to me? The prospect sends deep shivers through my veins. But what if I reject him? Will he dispose of me in the way he's disposed of Joel and Lois?

We walk into the tent that Clayton was previously sharing with Lois and I see that all of my belongings have indeed been transferred over. My clothes are hanging on the rail and my wash bag sits next to the sink. It abhors me to think that Nancy has been rifling through my things.

'Please, use the bathroom first,' he says.

I grab a pair of pyjamas and a sweater and walk into the bathroom. The design of this tent is a little different to ours, with the bath behind the bed. Even so, there's no real privacy here as the shower and sink are behind a three-quarters-high wall. Only the toilet is in a separate room, but even it doesn't have a lock. I feel so vulnerable. I undress and put on my pyjamas as quickly as I can, hurriedly wash my face and use the toilet, then emerge with a jumper over the top, covering myself as much as possible.

Clayton is bare chested, tanned, with well-defined muscles. If the circumstances were any different, I would accept that he is good looking. He smiles at me coyly and then strides to the bathroom. I slide underneath the duvet and listen to the water pouring from the shower. Despite the thick, luxurious bedding, I can't get warm and I'm still shiv-ering as he returns to the bed. He's wearing boxer shorts now, which to my relief he keeps on.

He wriggles towards me and makes a clumsy attempt to hold me in his arms. I'm rigid with fear and revulsion, and my breathing is shallow and erratic.

'Darling,' he says, stroking my hair. 'I'm not going to hurt you. I'm not going to force myself on you. I'd never do anything like that. I love you, Anna, and we'll take this slowly. You can relax now.'

Just telling me that I can relax doesn't make any differ-ence. His words are just that: words. We lay there entwined for long minutes, until my body eases a little and I dare to hope that Clayton might be telling the truth. I wonder even if he's awake, his breathing is so regular.

'Did you kill Lois?' I whisper.

'What?' His body jerks slightly, as if I've just pulled him from the initial stages of slumber.

'Did you kill Lois?'

There's a long pause. 'It wasn't me,' he says quietly. 'I swear it wasn't.'

'Was it Nancy then?'

Another lengthy pause and he pulls away from me. 'It's not like we're bad people, Anna. But Lois was blackmailing us. We paid her to do a job yet she was threatening to expose us and demanding a large sum of money. She could have ruined everything between you and me. We were backed into a corner.'

And there it is. The admission of guilt. I suppose he's trying to blame Nancy and she'll blame Clayton. It doesn't make any difference to me. I am a prisoner of murderers. And poor Lois. What did she die for? A little greed and opportunism on her behalf, and the delusional belief of a crazy brother and sister. I feel like Lois's life was snuffed out because of me and I'm not sure I'll ever be able to get over that. And Joel, too. Assuming I'll ever get out of this place, how will I live with the fact that two people died because of me?

26

NANCY

When they arrive for breakfast, I realise I haven't seen Clayton look so happy in years. There is a bounce to his step and a lightness to his voice, a smile that seems glued to his face. My plan has worked and that makes me feel joyous too. The only person with a long face is Anna. She has dark rings under her eyes and she appears sleep deprived. Perhaps she and Clayton were making love well into the night.

When I first conceived the plan, Clayton asked me if I was sacrificing my happiness for his. Didn't I want a family of my own? Why would I want to live vicariously through my brother and sister-in-law? But it isn't like that at all. My contentment is so tightly bound up with Clayton's that it is impossible to unravel the two. It goes back to our childhood, the missing years and my illness. And no, I don't want pity.

On the face of it, our childhood should have been idyllic. Our mother, Elspeth, was a young British socialite, brought up by nannies and home tutors, whose mother died when she was just two. Her father, a member of the House of Lords (who rarely attended by all accounts) had no idea what to do with his daughter, and it seems she was almost feral in her teens. When she was thrust into high society at eighteen, it was a terrible shock. Whether she was addicted to drugs before she met our father, I don't suppose we'll ever know. Perhaps not. I like to think not. She was swept off her feet by our debonair father, Vincent Klerk. A South African, he was, according to the one photo we have of him, devastatingly good looking, much like Clayton. Unusually for an Afrikaner, he was dark. Only his pale blue eyes suggested his Dutch colonial ancestry. Our mother told us that they met at a society dance when he was visiting London for work. She was just twenty-two years old. Within a week, they were engaged. Five weeks later, much to the dismay of her father, they were wed at Chelsea Registry Office, in time for her to return to South Africa with Vincent. They settled in a wealthy Johannesburg suburb, with stunning mauve Jacaranda trees in their garden and a bevy of staff. I was born within a year and Clayton just two years later. By then, there were deep fissures in their relationship. Vincent found his young wife flighty and silly. She'd never worked; never had to. That was probably her downfall, because she was bored. Johannesburg wasn't London. There were dangers she never had to consider when she flitted between Mayfair and their country retreat in Dorset. By the time I was four, our father had vanished. According to Mother, he left for work one morning and never returned. He communicated via solicitors' letters and paid her a monthly stipend to employ the staff and keep her and us in the manner to which we'd become accustomed. On top of that, Mother came into a trust fund when her father died. She was a very wealthy woman.

Unfortunately, naivety, wealth and boredom are a dangerous mix. My memories of her are scarce. I remember she held a party one evening. She was dressed in a pale pink taffeta dress, her hair pinned up, and she looked stunning. Our house was decorated with flowers and servers were on hand for drinks and canapés. She must have been drunk and probably high even before the guests arrived. There was a great commotion, an embarrassment. I don't know what happened, but the guests left rapidly. Mother had a big red wine stain down her beautiful dress and she was laughing maniacally. I was ushered to bed by a maid, so I'm not sure what happened next. I do remember her screams. They happened a lot and they were absolutely terrifying.

We had a nanny called Beatrice. She was the centre of our lives; a warm, cuddly black lady who braided my hair and read me bedtime stories. Once, when I awoke from a nightmare, I called out for Mummy and Beatrice came hurrying into my bedroom. She swept me into her arms and rocked me until I was calm. I knew deep down that she wasn't my Mummy but she acted like it. Our real Mummy was either drunk or high pretty much all the time. Perhaps my childhood memory is wrong, but she was certainly manic. We went through a lot of staff, but fortunately Beatrice remained.

That was until I was eight and Clayton was six. She was fired. Clayton was sent to boarding school in England. I was sent to live with my austere uncle and aunt the other side of Johannesburg. I never questioned why. I doubt any sort of social services were involved. Perhaps our errant father organised it. I was dreadfully homesick for Beatrice. Heartbroken that I no longer saw my beloved little brother. My aunt was stern and lacking empathy. Much like my mother, I was left to fend for myself.

It's all too easy to blame my current issues on my childhood. Of course, I have a deep fear of abandonment and I don't need therapy to understand that about myself. It's why I cling so desperately to my brother, the only person in the world who truly understands me, who will be there for me come what may. But I also have two medical conditions.

I cannot have children. It is utterly devastating and has taken me years to come to terms with. What's worse is it's of my own making. I got pregnant at sixteen and went to some butcher to terminate the pregnancy. Who could I have turned to? The father I didn't know? The drug-addicted mother who was dying? The austere aunt who didn't believe in sex before marriage or her husband who could barely bring himself to look at me? Despite plenty of money, I had no adult role models, no one to turn to. So I found a back-street abortion clinic. The doctor – a Wilhelm Blomkamp, who most probably wasn't even medically qualified – terminated my pregnancy with such efficacy as to ensure I would never become pregnant again. I tracked down Wilhelm Blomkamp a few years ago. He was retired and didn't use the pre-nominal title of doctor. He died. That gave me a modicum of comfort.

And that is why I am so eager for Clayton to have children. His offspring will be my offspring. We will share DNA, and I will be the mother to them that my mother failed to be to me. They will be blessed because they will have two mothers. Their birth mother, Anna, and me, their adopted mother.

There is another reason why it might be a good thing that I won't be a natural mother (although it pains me deeply to admit it). I have tremendous mood swings. I veer from ecstatic highs to dark lows. In the early days of my relationship with Theo, I had psychotherapy. I didn't want to subject my husband to my mood swings and so I took medication. I've taken it on and off over the years, but it dulls my brain and I don't like the side effects. I just know that if I can create a stable family, then I will be all right. We'll all be all right.

I have the morning nicely planned out. After Anna finishes her breakfast, I suggest that Clayton nips into town to buy the list of provisions I've made. Of course, it's hardly a nip. He'll be gone for at least four hours. I want Anna to realise that she's integral to the success of all of our lives here.

'I was wondering if I could share our plans for Twivali with you?' I ask her, my head tilted to one side, my voice soft.

She looks surprised, but she needn't be. So long as she remains compliant, Anna is now a valued member of our team.

'Clayton and I have plans for us and for the lodge. Financially, we don't need to run it as a guest facility but it seems a shame not to share the wonder of the game reserve with other people, don't you think?'

She stares at me.

'Come through to the office. I want to show you the paperwork.' I pat her arm and she tenses. Poor Anna. She really needs to relax.

I open the office door and bring another chair around to my side of the desk. I pull a large lever-arch file from the shelf behind me and take out two copies of our business plan.

'Perhaps you'd like to read this in your own time. It's how I intend to run the game reserve. We can charge big bucks and keep it ultra-exclusive. Clayton has explained to me that you're a food scientist and a fabulous chef. We thought you could be in charge of the kitchen. Develop the menus, creating a tasting menu perhaps. Make the visit to Twivali a culinary experience.'

'I'm not a chef,' Anna says quietly.

'You're being too modest.' I grin at her but she doesn't smile back. 'And then I want to show you this. The plans for the house that we're going to build for you and Clayton and your future children.' I spread out the detailed plans on the desk, smoothing down the large sheet of paper. 'Four bedrooms, three bathrooms, a state of the art kitchen – because no doubt you'll want to test your menus in your home – and at the back a small building for your children's nanny.'

Anna freezes. 'Children?' she murmurs.

'You do want children, don't you?' I ask. I'll be absolutely devastated if Anna can't have kids. I know that Clayton is desperate for children.

'I haven't really thought about it,' she says in a whisper.

I don't believe her. I just think she's in overwhelm, which is fair enough.

'Would you prefer that the nanny quarters be integral to the house, perhaps?'

'I don't want a nanny for my children,' she says, surprisingly firmly.

'Fair enough. You'll have me, anyway. What do you think of the house?'

'It looks lovely.'

I lean back in my chair and grin. 'It will be. The perfect home for you all. I know this is a lot to absorb, especially as you no doubt envisaged your future in England, but life here in the African bush will be so much better. Your children will experience freedom. They'll have unconditional love from the three of us and such a healthy lifestyle. My quality of life was far better than Clayton's, who was packed off to school in England. South Africa is a glorious country and we have our own little piece of heaven right here.'

Still Anna doesn't say anything, which is beginning to annoy me. She would never have the money to live an existence like ours. I'm tempted to tell her how I bought this lodge especially to create the perfect life for her and Clayton. My goodness, my brother scared me. He told me that he had no purpose without Anna in his life. That at best he might go off traveling but at worst he'd take his own life. And I know Clayton. He wouldn't take the easy way out like our mother did – an overdose where she slipped into unconsciousness. No. Clayton would put a gun to his head. The thought makes me want to vomit.

But I hold my tongue. Clayton and I have had months, years, to plan this. It's a brand-new concept for Anna. I know I need to be patient.

'How would you like to spend the day?' I ask her, smiling.

'I'd like to know what you did to Joel.'

Anger sears through my veins and I stand up suddenly, knocking my chair over. She starts, recoiling in on herself.

'Anna,' I say, leaning so close to her she'll be able to feel my breath on her cheeks. 'You're my sister now. This is the beginning of our fabulous new life. Don't let Clayton and me down. You do know what will happen if you do something stupid, don't you?'

She trembles as she nods her head.

'In which case, why don't you sit at the dining table and write down a few meal ideas.' I hand her a fresh pad of paper and a pen engraved with the words, *Twivali Safari Reserve*. 'You've got free rein.'

She stands up. 'Can I get access to the internet for research?'

Does she really think I'm that stupid? My shoulders sink with disappointment. I thought she understood.

'Of course you can't. We don't have it,' I lie. I pause for effect and speak in a low voice. 'Don't go doing anything silly, will you?'

She stares at me, her eyes wide and fearful, and in this moment, I relax. Anna is malleable. She understands exactly what I mean.

27

ANNA

One day into my captivity and I'm not sure how much longer I can keep up the pretence of going along with Nancy and Clayton's craziness. The situation is so much worse than I could ever have imagined. Nancy is a psycho. One moment she's sweetness and light, the next she's threatening me. Do they really think that I'm going to stay here for the rest of my life, have babies, bring up a family? As soon as I need to see a doctor, I'll tell him or her that I've been captured, being held against my will. I'll tell them about Joel and Lois and then... My thoughts peter out as I imagine such a conversation. They'll think I'm mad, won't they? I can just imagine Nancy coming with me and saying in a hushed voice to the doctor, *Anna has a few psychological issues, paranoid episodes. She's on medication but often forgets to take it. Perhaps you need to give her something stronger.*

I'm sure a missing person's file will be opened on Joel and me in the UK, but will it be international? Surely, yes. I told Mum that we were coming to South Africa for Joel's job interview but I didn't give her the name of the reserve. I was trying to protect her because I knew that she'd be heart-broken to think we might emigrate. That was so stupid of me. But what about those other guests, Katie and Zak? If Joel and I hit the news, then they'll put two and two together. That thought brings me my first nugget of hope since Joel went missing.

I stare at the blank pad of paper on the table in front of me. I don't for one second buy the idea that they're going to open the reserve up to the public. They can't take the risk that I'll say something to guests, so why is Nancy even mooting the idea? Does she really think that I'll fall back in love with Clayton and will stay here out of my own free will? Does she think that somehow they can break me? They're delusional, and that's what makes my situation so terribly scary. I can't predict what they're going to do. Well, perhaps I can predict Clayton. I know that he'll become increasingly controlling of me. But Nancy? She's off the scale of crazy.

'How are you getting on?' Nancy strides out of the office.

I scribble some nonsense on the paper just so it looks like I'm doing something.

'Do you fancy a coffee? I'm going to make myself one.'

How can she act as if this situation is completely normal? I don't answer immediately and annoyance flashes across her face. *Pretend, Anna,* I say to myself. *Pretend.*

'Thank you, Nancy. That would be lovely. White with no sugar, please.'

'Coming right up.'

'Would you prefer only vegetarian dishes or can I include meat dishes too?' I hurriedly write down a recipe for a lemon chicken dish, one of the few recipes my frozen brain can recall.

'Put down everything and we can distil them at a later stage.'

My writing is almost illegible as my hand shakes uncontrollably. But I quickly fill up the page with barely remembered recipes that are most probably missing the key ingredients. Just because I like cooking, just because I'm a food scientist, doesn't mean that I know recipes off by heart or have any skill in creating them myself.

By the time Clayton returns, I realise that my only hope of getting out of this place is by manipulating him. He's in love with me (although it's definitely infatuation and not real love) and at least I have a basic understanding of how he ticks. Nancy is anathema. I'm going to act in the way that he wants me to act. To lull him into a false sense of security. And this is going to be the greatest acting role of my life.

My first opportunity to speak to him alone is when I'm helping him unpack the groceries he's brought back from town. Nancy is having a swim. I offered to cook supper tonight but she declined, saying she doesn't trust me yet. Who knows what I'll put in their food? She's right, of course. It would be relatively easy for me to poison them with some dangerous plants found out here; crushed-up oleander, elephants' ear or arum lily perhaps, which would at least make them incapacitated for a while, during which I could make a bid for freedom.

'The produce is amazing,' I say, as I put an array of fresh vegetables in the big commercial fridge. 'So much better than we can get in the UK. I can see how it's easier to live a healthy lifestyle out here.'

Clayton beams at me. 'What did you think of the plans for our new house?' he asks.

'Amazing!' I exclaim, dropping a courgette to clap my

hands together. 'It's really living the dream, isn't it? But I have got some reservations.'

His face falls. 'What?'

'Don't worry,' I say, placing a hand on his forearm. 'I need a bit of time to think things through.'

When we've finished putting everything away, I say, 'I'd love to go out on another game drive. Could you take me?'

'Not today,' he says abruptly.

I realise that I've become too compliant too quickly. Clayton isn't stupid. He probably thinks I'll try to wrestle the gun out of his hands and turn it on him. I probably would try that, although it's a super-risky manoeuvre.

I keep myself to myself for the rest of the day, reading a book in the living area (although I don't absorb a single word) and helping Nancy prepare supper for the three of us. It's when Clayton and I are alone, back in his bedroom lying in bed, that I start to sow the seeds of my plan.

I take his hand and run a finger across his palm. It sickens me, but this is something I have to do for my survival. He's still suspicious of me and I know that the only way to erase those suspicions is to give myself to him.

'I love you, Clayton,' I say huskily. 'The problem is I can't live here. This is your sister's place and I'm sorry to say this, but she scares me. I can't be around her long term. I know this is going to hurt you and she's your flesh and blood, and I can see the tremendous bond the two of you have, but I don't see how we can have a happy marriage with Nancy breathing down our necks. Remember what Princess Diana said: there are three people in this marriage? It doesn't work.'

'What are you suggesting?' he asks.

'We need to move to London. Just you and me.'

He tenses and I can tell that he thinks this is a trick.

'No,' he says, but I take a deep breath, roll towards him and place my lips over his. I cannot believe that I'm doing this, that I'm selling my body to save my life, but I know this is the only way that Clayton will believe me. I run my hands over his taut chest and I try so hard to pretend that I'm with Joel, that it is my beloved Joel who has flipped me onto my back, who is running his lips down my torso, who is making love to me. I remind myself again and again that I'm doing this to survive.

It's painful but at least it's all over quickly, as it often used to be with Clayton. And despite my body screaming to get away, I cuddle up to him.

'Thank you so much for rescuing me,' I murmur, my breath hot on his ear. 'You know me better than I know myself. I hadn't realised how much I missed you,' I say.

'And I missed you, my darling. So much.'

'I never had this sort of connection with Joel.'

'Do you really mean that?'

I can sense he's still suspicious of me, that this softening of myself towards Clayton, garnering his trust in me that I won't do something stupid, will take time. But it seems that the one thing I have a lot of here, is time. I just need to be patient.

As Clayton sleeps, I cry silent tears. How much I miss Joel and Mum, Nick and Sasha; my ordinary life that I desperately crave. I pray that Joel didn't suffer too much, that one day we can find some of his remains and have the memorial service that he deserves. And then exhaustion creeps up on me and I sleep a troubled, restless sleep.

'Good morning, darling.' Clayton wakes me up by kissing me and placing a hand between my legs. I try to relax into him. I let him make love to me again but I'm too tense and it hurts so much that I want to scream with pain, not that Clayton seems to notice.

'I can't live without you,' he whispers. 'I love you so much.'

'And I can't live without you, either,' I reply. 'But darling, Clayton. Not here. I can't live with your sister. She's crazy, the way she goes around killing everyone.'

'She's done it to protect me,' Clayton says, as if that makes it all right.

'I know. And I know that she must always have a role in your life. But I want to make our life together in London, not here.'

'How do I know you won't tell the police that Nancy killed Joel and Lois?'

'I would never do that!' I exclaim, my voice heavy with indigence. 'That would be betraying you. I understand why she did what she did, but I can't be constantly looking over my shoulder, wondering what she's going to do next. Do you understand?'

Clayton nods and to reinforce my message, I run my fingernails down his body, gently playing with him, even though all I'd love to do is squeeze so hard, he would yelp out in agony.

'We need to go to London. Maybe not immediately, but within the next couple of weeks. What do you say?'

'I love you, Anna. If you want us to go to London, then so be it.'

'But we mustn't tell Nancy. Not yet, at least.'

An hour later, Clayton and I are nursing coffees in the lounge. To my relief, Nancy is nowhere to be seen.

'I'm not sure about moving back to London,' Clayton says.

'Shush.' He's such a fool.

And it's too late.

'What did you say?' I swivel around when I hear Nancy's voice, my heart sinking. 'What are you two talking about?' She narrows her eyes at us.

I nudge my foot against Clayton's but he doesn't take any notice. 'Anna wants us to move back to London.' I elbow him but he still ignores me.

'London?' Nancy spits out the word.

'Anna wants us to return to the UK and pick up where we left off,' Clayton says, leaning back as he rests his head in his clasped hands. I recall Joel calling him a ridiculous buffoon, and how right he was. Or is Clayton just playing me?

'And you, Anna. Is that what you really want?' Nancy speaks through gritted teeth.

'I mean, I really do appreciate everything you're doing for us here. And plan on doing in the future – such as building us a house...' I let my words peter out. Nancy's eyes narrow.

'I don't think Anna is really cut out for life in the bush but as you know, I'll go wherever makes my love happy.' I wish Clayton would just shut up. I would like to clamp my hand across his mouth but instead I'm motionless. I daren't look at Nancy, so I keep my eyes on Clayton, whose face is one of bliss. And still he carries on. 'You're welcome to come and visit us in London whenever you like, my darling sister. Our home is your home.'

Nancy stands up then and hurls her cup of coffee across the room. Clayton looks as startled as I am.

'No!' she yells. 'No! You're both staying here with me. This is your home. Our home. What the hell, Clayton? We planned everything out, and as soon as you're back in her knickers you let her take control! You know that you need *me*! She isn't enough!'

I hold my breath. Is Nancy going to come for me? Attack me? I have to defuse this situation immediately.

I stand up too. 'Oh my goodness, Nancy. I'm so sorry. I can't thank you enough for everything you've done for me and for Clayton. We had no idea that this would upset you so much. That's the last thing Clayton and I want to do, isn't it, darling?' I turn to look at him briefly and his mouth is hanging open. 'Forget London. We'll stay here, make a life with you exactly as you had envisioned. Please forgive us.'

'Clayton?' she asks, her eyes narrowed.

'Anna is right. We'll stay here.'

I hold my breath. Have I saved the situation or is she going to explode? Thanks to Clayton's careless words, I've just made a very big strategic mistake. This is way too soon to tell Nancy about our plans.

'Your home is here, on the reserve,' Nancy says, spitting out her words.

'You're right,' I say. 'I apologise deeply.'

'I apologise too,' Clayton adds.

It's obvious who wears the trousers around here.

Later that afternoon, I have some time alone with Clayton.

'I'm scared of Nancy,' I admit. Perhaps the first truth I've told him. 'I know we said we'd stay here but I just can't, Clayton. Do you understand? Can you rescue me?'

'Oh, darling,' he says, gripping my tightly. 'I've always wanted to be your hero.'

I'm about to make the biggest gamble and hope that his loyalties lie first to me and second to his sister. This could quite literally be the difference between my life and death. I know it would be better to be patient, to drip-feed him my thoughts, but I don't think I can survive another few days out here.

'We're going to have to leave together, without Nancy knowing,' I say. The words almost choke in my mouth, my heart pounding with fear as I wait for his reaction. 'It's for the best, and in time, when we have children in England and she comes to visit, she'll see that it's the right decision for us all.'

'What are you proposing?' Clayton asks.

I set out my plan.

28

NANCY

After everything I've done for Clayton and Anna, how dare they suggest they want to return to London! I am absolutely livid. My brother is so weak, just bending in whatever direction Anna suggests. I grab the keys to one of the Defenders, take one of the rifles out of the cupboard and hurry to the car. I spin the wheels as I drive away, dust rising up behind me in a cloud of red-brown.

This whole plan was all about the three of us creating a happy family. I will not be left here alone. Absolutely not. I would rather kill Clayton and Anna than see them return to England. I drive aimlessly, hoping to see some wildlife. Despite everything, I love the animals. Yes, I'll shoot if I find an animal in distress but I never kill for the sake of killing. Those trophy hunters disgust me, the way they think money can buy them the right to kill. Taking a life, whether it's an impala or a human, must only be done out of necessity. I don't see any animals in distress; in fact I only see a few springbok, guinea fowl and ostrich. After an hour or so, I'm sufficiently calm to return to the lodge.

Clayton and Anna are sitting with their heads close together, conspiratorial, and it's having the opposite effect on me than I imagined. I don't trust her.

'Clayton, a word,' I say, my hands on my hips.

Anna smiles at me, but I see straight through it. She's conniving but she's met her match. I smile back at her, although I'm pretty sure my smile is more of a grimace.

Clayton gets up. 'In the office,' I say curtly. He follows me inside and I lock the door behind us.

'What the hell were you thinking?' I ask.

'Anna wanted –'

'This isn't about what Anna wants. It's about what you and I want. What's best for our family. I'm so hurt, Clayton. Broken, in fact.'

His face falls. 'I'm sorry, Nancy. I thought you'd be happy for me. I thought you wanted me and Anna to be together come what may.' My weak brother can't bring himself to meet my eyes.

'Can't you see that Anna is manipulating you? The second you touch down at Heathrow, she'll turn you in to the police. How can you be so naive?'

'I think you're wrong, Nancy. We've reconnected. Properly reconnected, if you get what I'm saying.' He winks at me.

'For heaven's sake, Clayton. Stop being led by your dick. Of course she's going to give you her body. That's how she's buying your trust. It's what women throughout the ages have done. Sold their bodies to get what they want. It's disgusting but a fact. Surely you can see that. Besides, what are you going to live off in London? I've paid off all your debts but remember you left under a cloud. It's not like you can hop back into a job in banking.' I run my fingers through my hair. I need to make my brother see sense. 'I'll pay for everything if you stay here. Absolutely everything for the rest of your lives. You'll want for nothing, Clayton.'

He sighs. 'This isn't about money. I can't take any more from you; you've given me enough. No, Anna and I need to stand on our own two feet. We have a great future together.'

'You're not listening to me!' My voice has gone up an octave. 'I've risked so much for you. I got rid of Lois to save you, to save your relationship.'

'But I didn't ask you to do that, Nancy. You chose to do that. We could have dealt with Lois another way.'

'There was no other way.' My voice is icy now and I can feel I'm about to erupt. Never have I felt violent towards Clayton, but right now... And then I see it oh-so-clearly. Clayton will always put Anna before me. His supposed love for her is led by lust and I can never – would never want to – compete against that. My brother is lost to me because of Anna. I miscalculated the whole of this plan. There is only one solution to stop Clayton from leaving. I will have to kill Anna.

I sink back into my chair as the realisation sinks in. Clayton turns, undoes the lock to the door and leaves the office. Silence and sadness sit heavily on me.

I wait until darkness falls. Clayton and Anna are in the kitchen, making supper together. I am on the outside looking in, a place I will always be. For the next hour, I pretend. I pretend that we didn't have any conversations about them leaving. I pretend that I am happy that their relationship is back on, that their future lies together. I pretend not to notice that Anna is also giving the acting performance of her life. I see how she swallows hard before letting Clayton kiss her; how, when she thinks no one is looking, she gazes into the far distance, no doubt plotting how she can make her escape from my brother. And my heart bleeds for him. He will never get true happiness with Anna. It's all a lie.

I suggest we take our drinks outside to enjoy the beautiful night. We each sit on chaises longues wrapped with cashmere blankets, our heads back, gazing at the stars.

'Clayton, why don't you go and get the telescope. I'm sure Anna would love to look at the galaxies.'

'Good idea,' he says, getting up from his lounger.

'It's in my lodge,' I say. Actually, it isn't. But I want to buy some time alone with Anna.

I wait until his footsteps fade away.

'I know you want to leave but that's not possible,' I say, my voice a monotone.

There's a long pause before she replies. 'What are you going to do? Kill me like you killed Joel and Lois?'

'If you try to leave, with or without Clayton, I'll shoot you in exactly the same way I shot Joel.'

'But why?' Anna whispers. 'Why are you doing this? I don't understand.'

I swing my legs off the sun lounger to face Anna. She does the same. Our knees are nearly touching now. 'Because I deserve a family. I can't have children of my own so you and Clayton and your children were meant to be my family. But now I know for sure that I can't trust you. You don't love Clayton, do you? All you're doing is coming up with feeble ways to escape, to lure him to England so you can turn him in. What do you think will happen? That Interpol will swoop in and arrest me here? That Clayton will just let you go? You underestimate us, Anna.'

The light is low and I can't make out her expression but the candlelight makes her eyes glisten. I reach under my blanket and wrap my fingers around the cold metal. It feels reassuring in my hand.

'Clayton will be heartbroken but I will care for him just like I did last time.' I pull the pistol out and point it directly at Anna's forehead, right between those glistening eyes. I draw my finger back.

There's a click.

My world goes black.

29

ANNA

I ready myself for the end. There's a click that sounds so loud in the silence of the night. Even the cicadas have fallen silent. My last thought is that at least I'll be with Joel.

And then there's a deafening single shot. The sound is violent, so painful. Is this it? Am I dead?

But it's not me who is crumpling to the ground. Nancy falls, dropping her pistol with a loud clatter, her limbs falling like a rag doll's. My eyes try to focus and it takes me several long seconds to see Clayton standing in the doorway, his arm still raised, a rifle pointing to the exact place where his sister just stood.

'Clayton!' I scream, my voice piercing the night. Am I next? Is he going to kill me next? I try to dart backwards but I catch my foot on the end of the sun lounger and I stumble awkwardly.

'Anna,' he says. His voice is trembling. 'I saved you. My Anna. I killed my sister for you. My only blood relative. But I've got you, haven't I?'

'Lower the gun, Clayton,' I say, drawing upon strength I didn't know I had. I lever myself up and walk towards him. 'Lower the gun.'

And he does.

I stand stock-still for a moment with about two metres between us. I've just watched Clayton kill his sister at point-blank range. He killed her to save me. My God, these two are as demented as each other. But I'm alive. At least I'm alive. How the hell am I going to get out of here?

We stare at each other. He is standing directly under-neath an exterior light attached to the wall and I see that his eyes are watering, that he's about to break.

'You saved me,' I whisper. If I thought it was hard to act before, now every survival instinct I have in me tells me that I have to run straight towards my enemy, not retreat. And so I do. I throw myself into his arms and he sobs into my hair.

'We'll start our new lives right now, Anna. We're free, darling. It all starts now.'

'Yes,' I shush him. It's like he hasn't registered that he's just killed his sister. All he seems to be aware of is me. Clinging so hard.

'Let's get out of here and catch the next flight to London, just as we planned,' I suggest.

He's silent for a moment.

'Are you alright?' I ask, although I immediately realise that's a stupid question. He's just killed his sister.

'We'll stay here,' he says eventually.

'What?' All hope drains from me and it feels like my legs are going to give way.

'I've changed my mind. We'll have a better life here in South Africa. This will be our family home now and we'll be rich. I'll be inheriting Nancy's wealth. It's ironic how much better she was at conserving her inheritance than me. We'll be happy here, Anna, just you and I.' He steps away from me and holds out his hand. I take it, even though it abhors me.

'Let's go to bed.'

But what about Nancy? I want to scream, but the words stay silent in my head. I can't bring myself to look at her, collapsed in a heap on the ground. Clayton is so calm. He turns and smiles at a me. *How is that even possible?* He's just killed his sister. Doesn't he realise what he's done? Is he in such shock that he's in complete denial?

He leaves the rifle on a sun lounger and we walk in silence to his tent. The first time without any gun to protect us from stray animals. Yet I realise the animals are not the danger here. Clayton is, and with every step, the terror mounts. I am alone in the middle of a ten-thousand-hectare reserve with a man who is completely insane; a man who is an excellent shot and who has just killed his sister.

We reach the tent and he puts the light on, shutting the door behind us. 'I did it for you,' he whispers, more to himself I think than to me. 'I would do anything for you, Anna.' He pulls his clothes off and gets into bed, without using the bathroom.

'Come,' he says, holding out his arms.

I remove my trousers and shirt, but keep on my under-wear. I shiver as I get under the duvet.

'Hold me, Anna,' he says. I'm rigid, barely able to breathe as I lie in his arms. But he's very still too. After a while, I realise that he simply needs the comfort of my body against his, that sex is definitely not on his mind, and I'm able to relax. Just a little. I wait patiently, trying to keep my mind clear. And then his breathing becomes slow and steady, his limbs loosen their grip on me and I shift away from him in bed. I lie there for many more long minutes, knowing that now is my only chance of survival.

Very slowly and as quietly as I can, I blink several times, my eyes adjusting to the low light. I reach for my trousers and top, which I dropped on the ground next to the bed, and slowly get dressed, all the time stopping, straining my ears to listen to Clayton's regular breathing. I tiptoe around the bed to where Clayton dropped his clothes onto a chair. Picking up his trousers, I find the pocket and my fingers close around a bunch of keys. I pray these are the ones I need. I walk as slowly and silently as possible to the door, every nerve ending on high alert. Every time the floor creaks, my breath catches. I stand stock-still, my hand on the door handle. Very gently, I turn it. It squeaks. I pause. Nothing. And then I'm outside.

The air is cold and I shiver. A light on a sensor comes on and I hope it doesn't wake Clayton. I realise that I'm out here alone, with no gun and no one to protect me. But am I safer out here or in the tent with Clayton? I'm not sure.

I hurry now, grateful for the low-level lighting, grateful for the bright moon that glows white on the path, the keys clenched in my right hand, metal digging into my palm. The door to the main lodge is open, just as we left it, so I hurry inside. The lights are still on and I glance down at the keys in my hand.

They're not car keys.

There are three metal keys. Two look like door keys, the third is small. A key to a safe perhaps. I saw how Clayton put the car keys in the wall safe in their office. How he blocked my view to the safe with his broad back. And I know that the

only way I will get out of here is by car. The office door is
locked but the second of the two keys opens it. I switch the
light on and walk straight to the safe. I'm sure that he
punched in the numbers 2105. Is that Nancy's birthday
perhaps, or another date that means something to the two of
them? I try it.

Nothing happens.

I let out a little yelp. No. This safe cannot thwart me. Did
I see the code properly?

I look at the little key, but the safe has no keyhole so it
can't be for the wall safe. I try 2105. Nothing. 2106. Nothing. I
try every number from 2101 to 2109. Nothing. Then I try 2205
and the lock gives and snaps open. My breathing is so loud
now it's almost deafening me. I swing the door wide and
inside lie several envelopes, several passports – including my
own, I presume – and a set of car keys. I haven't got time to
be checking anything, so I just grab the keys and the passports. I sprint out of the office, through the front lobby and
out to where the two Defenders are parked.

My hands are shaking as I try to insert the key into the
driver's door. It works and the door clicks. A light comes on
as I open it so I haul myself up into the seat. I've never driven
one of these vehicles and in fact I can't remember the last
time I drove a shift car. Will I remember? I shove the key in
the ignition and turn it. The engine is so loud. Almost deafening. Surely it'll wake Clayton even though he's the other
side of the building from me? There's a splutter and the
engine stalls. I try again, this time remembering to put my
foot on the clutch. The engine catches and I shove the gear
stick forwards, then I fumble for the lights. I'm going to need
the headlights, otherwise I might drive straight into a herd of
elephants. I swallow hard. I must keep it together. This is my

only chance. I release the handbrake, put my foot on the accelerator and slowly lift my left foot off the clutch. The car jerks forwards. This is it. I have to get out of here.

I'm concentrating so hard, peering at the track ahead as I drive through the gates and out onto the track. I have absolutely no idea which way to go and just pray that eventually I'll end up on the main road, the one that Nancy drove on just yesterday. I shove the gear stick into second and then third gear and I'm racing along the track now. I let out a whoosh of breath but just a couple of minutes later a light shines in my eyes. Glancing in the rear mirror I can see headlights coming closer and closer. No! Clayton must have taken the other Defender and is chasing me. How the hell am I going to get away from him when he knows these tracks like the back of his hand and I haven't got the slightest clue where I'm going? I go faster now, the engine shrieking, every bone in my body jerking and bouncing as I continue along the track. But he's still catching up on me. The lights are getting brighter and brighter.

Bang. Was that a shot?

It comes again. *Bang. Bang.* Is he shooting at me?

I swerve the vehicle from side to side and yes, the shots are so close. Is he aiming for me or for the tyres? I keep on going, round a corner.

But straight in front of me is another set of headlights. How is this possible? Did Clayton call for backup? I slam my foot on the brake and come to a sudden stop wedged between two vehicles. I could get out and make a run for it, but I saw how Clayton took aim and killed his sister. I have no doubt that he'd do the same to me. So I sit in the driver's seat trembling from head to toe, waiting.

Someone jumps out of the vehicle in front and runs towards me. To my utter relief I see that it's Ntando.

'Clayton is behind me,' I yell. 'He's got a gun and he's going to kill me – and you too, probably.'

Ntando ducks down in front of my Defender and pulls out a walkie-talkie, speaking rapidly into it in a language I don't understand. Then he stands up and walks to my door, glancing behind me at Clayton, who is approaching my vehicle, a rifle slung over his shoulder. At least he's not pointing it at me.

'Get out of the car,' Ntando says. I grab the car keys and hop down. The relief that Ntando is here to protect me is overwhelming. 'Put your arms above your head,' he instructs.

'What?' I look at him in shock. I've got this all wrong. Ntando is working for Clayton. Of course he is. Clayton is his boss. Ntando told me how his extended family is reliant on his job, so naturally, he's going to follow Clayton's orders. My heart sinks.

'Please, Miss Anna, put your arms above your head.'

This time I do as he tells me. With one of his hands placed gently on my shoulder, he steers me towards Clayton.

'No, don't take me back to him!' I cry. 'He's crazy. He's trying to kill me just like he killed Joel and Lois, and now he's killed his own sister, Nancy.'

I can sense the hesitation in Ntando's step, but it's no good. Clayton is right in front of us.

'Thanks,' he says to Ntando as I'm passed from one man to the other. 'She's off her trolley, this one. Don't listen to a word she's saying. Now come along, Anna. Time for your medication and bed, methinks.'

Clayton's grip on my shoulder digs into my flesh. 'Walk

or you'll make me do something I regret,' he hisses. He steers me towards his Land Rover. 'Get in.' He pushes me as I haul myself up and then I feel hard, cold metal in the centre of my back. 'If you ruin everything, Anna, I'll shoot. I'll kill you first and then myself.'

I watch as Ntando walks back to his vehicle, my beacon of hope disintegrating.

Clayton gets into the driver's seat and turns to me, his hand outstretched. 'Give me the car keys.'

I hesitate. 'Give them to me!' His voice is hard and I know that I have no choice but to comply. I want to wail and scream at the injustice of it all but I don't. I hand him the keys, my hope of escape totally dashed.

He starts up the vehicle and puts it into reverse, backing up a few metres before doing a three-point turn and heading back the way we came.

'I am furious with you,' Clayton says. 'You've manipulated me, thought you were so much cleverer, didn't you? I've gone out of my way for you. In fact I did everything for you.' He turns to look at me briefly and jabs a finger in my direction. I cower against the passenger door. 'Our entire relationship, I did everything for you. I proposed in public when I would have preferred for that moment to be intimate. I bought you a house, a car, but then you ran away, and now you're doing exactly the same thing all over again. I killed my sister for you, that's how far I went.'

He pauses for a moment and I relive the moment Nancy collapsed to the ground. I wonder what he proposes to do with her body and a shiver reverberates through me.

'I'm not going to be the mister nice guy any longer.' He spits the words out. 'You're going to have to be punished now.' He's quiet for a couple of long minutes and I dread to think what plan he's devising.

'I love you, Anna, but you're a headstrong woman and it's obvious I'm going to have to break your will. You need to come around to my way of thinking, otherwise our relationship is never going to work. I'm going to use the sjambok on you.'

'The what?' I ask, then I wonder if I actually want to know.

'A sjambok is a leather whip made from adult hippopotamus hide. Nancy owns an antique one. It belonged to our father.'

'You're going to use a whip on me?' I ask with horror.

'I'm not going to enjoy it, Anna,' he says, as if this is a perfectly normal conversation. 'I'm not a sadist, but what's right is right. I can't have my wife behaving like this, running away in the middle of the night, involving the staff, putting yourself and everyone else in danger. It's not on.'

I want to scream, *but I'm not your wife and I never will be*, but I'm too scared to talk. I grip the door handle and wonder if I should throw myself out of the moving vehicle. I glance backwards and see the headlights of Ntando's Defender behind us. No. There's no point in even trying. I assume the doors are locked, but even if they're not and I throw myself out, Ntando will kill or capture me.

Despair settles in my stomach. How am I ever going to get out of here? How will I withstand what Clayton is suggesting? Or will I eventually succumb to Stockholm Syndrome, falling in love with my captor despite everything?

We pull into the gates and Clayton parks the Land Rover at the front of the building. I glance behind me but can't see the lights from Ntando's vehicle. Perhaps he's driving more slowly.

'Get out and don't try anything stupid,' Clayton says. 'I do not want to use the gun on you.'

I slip down from the Defender but my legs are so weak I fall. Clayton runs around to my side of the vehicle and helps me up to my feet.

'Are you hurt?' he asks.

'No,' I say, although I can feel blood trickling down from my knee. How bizarre that Clayton is worried about me being hurt when he's planning on whipping me. I don't suppose I'll ever understand him.

'Lean on me,' he says, putting his arm around my shoulders. He repulses me and I wish I could run a mile but instead I walk with him into the lodge. The lights are still on, glaringly bright considering it's the middle of the night. He manoeuvres me into the small office where he opens a drawer and takes out some plastic ties.

'Hold out your hands,' he orders.

'No.'

He slaps me. A hard slap with the flat of his palm that makes my head reverberate and my cheek sting. 'Don't make me do this, Anna,' he says with a growl.

I hold out my hands and he wraps a plastic tie around my wrists.

'Now come with me.' He guides me out of the office and into the lounge.

'Sit down.' He gestures to the sofa. I do as he says and, with remarkable speed, Clayton is kneeling in front of me and tying my ankles together. I try to kick out at him.

'Stop that, woman. If you hurt me, I won't just use the sjambok on your backside. You'll make me use it on your hands and the back of your legs and it'll really hurt you, Anna. Don't force me to do that.'

Force him! I consider spitting in his face but I know that once again I'm going to have to bide my time. I tried to get away too quickly and this is my penance.

'Stand up.' He puts a hand under my armpit and hauls me to my feet. It's hard to stay balanced, but he helps me walk in tiny little steps to the middle of the room. Then he drags a chair over and positions me so my forearms are leaning on the back of the chair, so that I'm facing the main entrance.

'Stay here whilst I get the sjambok from Nancy's lodge.'

He disappears. I try to move but my feet are bound too tightly and there's nowhere I can go. I tug my wrists apart but all it does is tear at my skin. I try to kick out but just manage to topple the chair over, landing heavily on my shoulder, waves of pain ricocheting through me. I lie there, futile on the floor, waiting for what seems like an interminable time.

'You silly, silly girl,' Clayton says, hauling me back up. He's holding a whip. He gets me into position, my forearms leaning on the back of the chair. 'You asked what a sjambok is,' he says. Then he flicks his wrist and the sjambok whistles through the air, hitting the floor with a high-pitched slam.

'I'll make this as quick as I can,' Clayton says, as if that makes it all okay.

I can sense him getting into position, raising the sjambok high into the air.

'Stop!'

I jerk my head upwards and standing in the doorway is Ntando, a rifle pointed directly at Clayton.

'Don't hurt her!' Ntando says.

I want to cry with relief, but I can see Clayton's rifle on the sofa out the corner of my eye. He's just two or three steps away from it and I know he's a good shot. This could turn into a gun battle. He drops the sjambok, grabs his rifle and walks towards Ntando.

'Come on, man. I know you're not going to shoot. You need the work here, don't you? Let's be sensible. If you drop the gun, I'll let you keep your job. You're a good ranger so we'll pretend this hasn't happened.'

I watch, my eyes wide, my jaw open as Clayton takes another step towards Ntando. Clayton lifts his gun up.

Bang.

Ntando was the first to pull the trigger.

Clayton drops to the floor.

'Oh my God, my God,' Ntando says, rushing to Clayton's side. He kneels on the ground next to him and feels for his pulse. 'I've killed him.'

'Thank you,' I cry. 'Thank you.'

It takes long moments for Ntando to remember that I'm here, tied up. He is visibly shaking as he steps backwards from Clayton's body and strides towards me. Removing a pocketknife from his trousers, he cuts through the plastic ties and releases both my wrists and ankles.

'You've saved my life,' I say and then I throw my arms around him. We stand there rocking together for a couple of minutes, my tears soaking through his sweater.

There is the sound of an engine, then footsteps and voices. 'Ntando! What's happened?'

Three men race into the lounge. They talk to each other but I don't understand a word.

'What are they saying?' I ask.

'Congratulating me for saving you from this bastard,'

Ntando says. But there's a look of sadness on his face. 'I wish
I hadn't killed him. I've never killed before.'

'You saved me,' I whisper.

'He was a bad man, wasn't he?' Ntando says.

'Yes, and very troubled. Just like his sister.'

30

ANNA

Ntando walks around to the other side of the bar and finds a bottle of brandy. He pours the brown liquid into five glasses, one for each of the men and an extra-large measure for me.

'How come you were out driving in the night?' I ask. 'Did Clayton ask you to stop me?'

'No. I had a bad feeling about what was going on here. Earlier this evening I had drinks with some of the rangers from the adjacent lodge. I asked them how many teams were out looking for Joel and they stared at me, not knowing what I was talking about. Turns out that neither Nancy not Clayton had contacted anyone. No one except the staff here knew Joel was missing. Yet Nancy had promised she'd alerted all the neighbours. Then earlier, she sent me and the rest of the staff away. Said we should have a couple of weeks off whilst they were sorting things here. None of this made sense. I went to bed this evening but you know, my gut instincts are good. Being a trained ranger helps with that. I couldn't sleep, so I got up, drove out into the reserve. I hadn't expected to find Clayton chasing you.'

'I will be grateful to you for the rest of my life,' I say. My hands are still shaking too much for me to bring the glass to my lips. 'Clayton killed Nancy this evening.'

Ntando shakes his head with dismay. He mutters a few incomprehensible words to the other men.

'What did you say?' I ask.

'That we will have to call the police. That we'll all have to stay here until they arrive.'

'How will you call them?' I ask, remembering communication with the outside world is impossible here.

'I'll use the satellite phone in the office, but first you'd better show me where Nancy's body is.'

The thought of looking at either Clayton or Nancy makes me want to throw up and I race to the open door, bending over, my hands pressing into my chest. But the cool night air calms me and my stomach settles. Ntando appears by my side.

'Are you alright?'

'Not really,' I say.

'This is a terrible situation, but you need to show me where Nancy is before I call the police.'

I nod. It's best I get this over and done with. We walk back through the lounge and out of the door that leads onto the wooden veranda. I have to force myself to put one foot in front of the other. We walk to where Nancy, Clayton and I had been sitting, watching the stars. It feels both like a couple of minutes ago and years ago.

'Here,' I say.

But even as I utter the words, I realise my mistake. There is nobody here.

'It was here,' I say, confusion in my voice. 'She fell just by the sun loungers.'

Ntando steps forwards and produces a small torch, shining it at the wooden floor. There are dark stains and smears all the way along the wooden planks, all the way to the edge of the veranda and down the steps.

'She's gone,' I say, needlessly.

'We must stay away otherwise we'll be contaminating the evidence,' Ntando says.

'Oh my God!' My hand rushes to my mouth as I realise what happened. 'Clayton must have dragged her away, thrown her body out into the bushes like they did with Lois. He must have done it whilst he was getting the sjambok. How could he have done that to his own sister?' I exclaim. My stomach convulses again.

'You need to come inside,' Ntando says, gently leading me back into the lounge.

The three other men leave, but after calling the police, Ntando stays by my side for the rest of the night. I can't stay in the lounge because the thought of being so close to Clayton's body sickens me. So we go to the tent where I had been staying with Clayton. Ntando stays outside whilst I have a shower and then he sits in the armchair whilst I huddle fully clothed in the bed. We don't talk and at some point I drift in and out of uneasy sleep.

When the sky begins to lighten, I'm awoken by voices.

'The police are here,' Ntando says.

The rest of the morning is a whirlwind of activity. Police arrive in four-by-fours. A helicopter takes to the skies and whirs above the lodge and around the reserve. Drones also hover, controlled by the militia. I lose count of how many people there are out there, but it's scores of men. Both Ntando and I are interviewed for what seems like hours, repeating again and again the sequence of horrific events.

And then, around midday, there are loud shouts.

'They've found him!' Ntando comes rushing towards me. 'They've found Joel and he's alive!'

'What?' I exclaim and promptly burst into tears. 'How's that possible?'

'He was found in a watch tower. He's severely injured and dehydrated but he's alive. The helicopter is taking him to the nearest hospital.'

'Can you take me there?'

'Of course.'

We check with the policeman in charge and to my relief he agrees that Ntando can drive me to the nearest hospital. It's hardly near at four hours away, and I don't know how I'm going to be able to wait that long. I grab a few of my belongings and off we go.

The drive is interminable. I'm desperate to know if Joel is all right, whether he's still alive, whether he has suffered any lasting damage. To know exactly what happened. Eventually we arrive at a run-down town with low buildings and throngs of people jostling along the streets. The hospital is on the far side of the town. Two brick buildings are wedged together, and as soon as Ntando pulls up to the front door, I'm out of his vehicle, racing inside.

'I'm looking for my fiancé, Joel Reynolds. The Englishman brought here by helicopter.'

'Yes, yes,' the woman at reception says. 'I'll take you through.'

She waddles so slowly I'm just desperate for her to hurry. We walk along two long corridors and then she opens a door on the right-hand side. 'In here,' she says, holding the door back.

I stare at the bed. It's empty. No! This can't be possible.

'Where is he?' I ask, but the woman is striding away, much faster than when she walked here. 'Excuse me, but where is he?' I shout at her retreating back.

A nurse appears, dressed in a white tunic and black slacks. 'Joel Reynolds. Where is he?' There's sheer panic in my voice.

'No need to worry,' the nurse says, patting my arm. 'He's going to be just fine. He's having another X-ray to make sure that there are no remains of the bullet.'

Tears flow down my cheeks and I lean back against the wall as I allow the relief to settle in my body. 'He's really going to be okay?' I ask again.

Her smile is radiant. 'Absolutely fine. He's had the wound cleaned and stitched up. He's on a drip of fluids and antibiotics but he'll be out of here in a day or two.'

'Thank you,' I say.

Half an hour later, I am kneeling on the floor next to Joel's bed, my arms around his neck. I can't believe that he's here, that's he's alive, that's he's going to be all right. Traumatised, I suppose we both are, but all right.

'What happened?' I ask eventually, once we've stopped laughing and crying.

'When we were sleeping on the platform, Nancy woke me and said that a baby rhino was in distress and she'd called a few rangers to go and help. She asked if I'd like to join her. I was thrilled and excited at the prospect. You were sleeping so soundly, and she told me I'd be back within the hour so there was no need to wake you. Didn't you hear me leave? I was surprised, because you're such a light sleeper.'

'No, I didn't hear anything until the gun shots.'

'I wonder if she put some sleeping pills in your supper,' Joel muses. He's probably right.

'Anyway, I got in her Land Rover. She drove a short distance and then told me to get out of the car. It never crossed my mind that it was a trap. She then stood up in the vehicle and shot me. It all happened so quickly. I was totally stunned and I think I was unconscious for a few seconds. When I came around she was standing there, a horrific grin on her face.

'The animals will get you!' she shouted, and then she fired another shot, but it missed. She obviously wasn't hanging around to find out if I was dead or alive. She put her foot on the accelerator and she was gone. I was left crawling on the ground, in total shock.' I squeeze his hand. 'Why the hell did she do it? I've spent the last three days trying to understand what I did to upset her, why she wanted me of all people dead?'

'Nancy is Clayton's brother. The whole thing is my fault. Clayton was still in love with me and it was some crazy ruse to get you out of the picture so I could be with Clayton forevermore.'

'What?' Joel asks, his face creased with confusion.

'I'll tell you more later, but what happened to you next? How did you survive?'

'I thought I was going to die, that the lions would get me, but I forced myself to keep moving. My leg was agony but I knew that if I stayed in one place, I was doomed. I crawled along for hours and then I found this deserted watch tower. Honestly, darling, I don't know how I got myself up there, but I suppose my will to live was so great. I made a tourniquet from my shirt to stem the bleeding and I lay there for however long it's been since I was shot. I fell in and out of consciousness but all the time I focused on you and our future together and I forced myself to stay alive. Have they arrested Nancy?'

I shake my head. 'She's dead. Clayton shot her and then it seems he chucked her body into the bush, and Clayton is dead too. Ntando saved me.'

A nurse bustles into the room. 'I know you two have a lot of catching up to do, but Joel needs to sleep now. He's been through a lot.'

I place a kiss on his forehead. 'Sleep tight, darling.'

I sit beside him for a few minutes, watching as he closes his eyes and drifts off into a deep sleep, and then there's another gentle knock on the door. It's Ntando. I get up and join him in the corridor.

'The police want to interview you and me. They've asked us to attend the police station.'

I freeze. I've heard that the South African police can be corrupt and at times brutal, but Ntando seems relaxed. 'Should I be worried?' I ask him. After all, we were both interviewed extensively this morning before they let us leave for the hospital.

'No. It's procedure.'

We make our way to the police station, which is just a few blocks from the hospital. I'm interviewed by a policeman and woman but they are surprisingly sympathetic. I suspect they have no desire for the British police to get involved, for the embassy to step in, to make this an international story. But my main concern isn't for me, it's for Ntando. After all, it was him who shot and killed Clayton. I make sure that they know that he killed in self-defence, that Ntando was only trying to save me. That Clayton had a gun pointed at Ntando and he'd tied me up with the intention of whipping me. The police officers look shocked but after about an hour they let me go.

I have to wait for another fifty minutes before Ntando is released. The poor man looks exhausted.

'What's happened?' I ask, praying he hasn't been charged with anything.

'It's fine. I've not been charged but I can't leave the country.' He laughs then. 'As if I have the money to go abroad. I won't even have a job now.'

I feel really sorry for this good man and ponder how Joel and I might be able to help him.

31

ANNA – FIVE WEEKS LATER

We left South Africa four days later. I had no desire to go back to the lodge, so Ntando very kindly collected all of our belongings. The British consulate did get involved in the end and they were amazing. They changed our flights and organised a car to take us to Durban airport so I didn't need to take another flight in a small airplane. We even got upgraded to club class. I'm not sure who organised that.

On the flight home, Joel turned to me and said, 'I don't want to wait to get married. Can we do it soon?'

I smiled. 'Yes. I think that's an excellent idea.'

Mum, Nick my stepdad, Sasha and Joel's parents are bending over backwards to help with our wedding plans. Our story hit the papers and we were offered big money for an exclusive with one of the tabloids. We turned it down. But when the lovely boutique hotel where we're going to have our wedding reception learned who we are and what we'd been through, they gave us a massive discount on the hire of the rooms and the meal. People have been so kind to us.

It's now five weeks since we left South Africa and one week until our marriage. We didn't want to wait a moment longer than we had to, and it's not as if we want a big wedding. It's going to be intimate and beautiful. My wedding dress is off-the-shelf, but it's perfect, an ivory-coloured sheath dress with spaghetti straps. Simple and elegant. Sasha is my bridesmaid and she's got free rein to wear whatever she wants. It'll probably be something brightly coloured and highly inappropriate for a bridesmaid dress, but that's just one of the reasons I love her.

Joel has returned to work and is delighted to be tending to benign cows and sheep, while I've decided to look for another job, although I haven't told my boss yet. Right now, Joel is upstairs, taking a shower after a messy day on a farm, and I'm preparing supper. The phone rings; it's an international number.

'Hello,' I answer warily.

'Is this Anna Evans?'

'Yes.'

'This is Lieutenant Colonel Jacobs from the South African police. I have some information for you.'

I hear the shower being turned off upstairs.

'Please, can you hold on a moment whilst I get Joel.'

'Certainly,' he says.

I run upstairs and whisper to Joel, who sits on the side of the bed, a towel around his waist.

'Thank you. We're listening.' I put the phone on loud-speaker.

'We have found human bones.'

'Nancy?' I ask.

'No. They're male bones. We will be carrying out dental

check records but we think it might be the remains of Theo Theakston.'

'Theo Theakston?' I ask, frowning at Joel.

'Nancy's husband. Although she was telling people that they were divorced, in fact Mr Theakston had gone missing. We believe she killed him.'

'And Lois or Nancy's remains?' Joel asks.

'We found the red shoes and some fabric remains belonging to Lois but the only remains of Nancy Theakston is a single white trainer, smeared with her blood, which we believe she was wearing at the time of her death. You must understand that we have a very large area to search and animals... well, there probably won't be anything left –'

'We understand,' Joel says, grimacing.

'Thank you very much for letting us know,' I add.

'There's more,' Lieutenant Colonel Jacobs says. 'We found evidence that Clayton Klerk was involved in rhinoceros horn poaching, but no charges will be brought against Ntando Smith. He is a free man.'

'That's such a relief,' I say.

'Thank you for telling us,' Joel adds.

'We appreciate your cooperation with this case. Goodbye.'

I let the phone tumble onto the bed.

'It's all over,' Joel says as he flings his arms around me.

I stay silent as he hugs me tightly, because will it ever be truly over?

'We should talk to Ntando, find out how he is,' Joel suggests.

We have been in regular contact with Ntando. Initially, we wanted to send him some money to thank him for saving my life, but he was insistent he didn't want that. I was worried we had insulted him by offering. However, instead of buying us wedding gifts, we are asking all of our friends and family to make a donation to the local school where Ntando's children study. I'm hoping that we will be able to buy the children books, computers, a new roof for the main building, and perhaps raise enough money for the salaries of a couple more teachers. That might be wishful thinking, but I'm going to carry on raising money for the school for as long as it takes.

Joel picks up the phone and calls Ntando, pressing the loudspeaker button.

'We just heard from Lieutenant Colonel Jacobs,' Joel says. 'Congratulations.'

'Yes, it's a relief. It means I can start the new job I've been offered. I'm going to be a senior ranger on another game reserve. It's nearer to my home and I'll be getting more money.'

'We're thrilled for you,' Joel says. 'Lieutenant Colonel Jacobs mentioned something about Clayton being involved in rhino horn poaching. Do you know anything about that?'

I'm not sure I even want to know. With the murders, I'd totally forgotten about the rhino horn found in Joel's shoe. Frankly, I would rather never think of Clayton again.

'Yes, it seems he was in a great deal of debt,' Ntando explains. 'My second cousin is a detective and they're still investigating his financial affairs. When Clayton came to South Africa he had no money and Nancy paid for everything. But it seems that Clayton wanted his own money, so he turned to rhino horn poaching.'

'I'm not surprised,' I mutter.

'You know,' Ntando sighs. 'Despite all the terrible things

Nancy did, she was a keen animal conservationist, yet her good work was being undone by her brother.'

Ntando is clearly a more forgiving person than me, because I can never associate Nancy with goodness. As far as I'm concerned, she was evil through and through.

It's the next morning and Sasha, Mum and I are having a spa day in lieu of a hen party. Mum is treating us and I can't wait for a day where all I'm going to do is chill. I don't sleep as well as I used to and my nerves are constantly on edge. Joel has suggested therapy and I think I might do that once we're married.

I'm putting on a jacket when the postman delivers our letters. I flick through them. There are several that feel like cards. We've been getting a few of those from friends and relatives congratulating us on our upcoming marriage. I open them. The first is from a distant cousin, the second from a friend of Joel's. The third is a postcard with the picture of Twivali Safari Lodge on the front. On the rear are typed words, all in capitals:

CONGRATULATIONS ON YOUR WEDDING!

I think I'm going to faint. Who sent this? Have the staff returned? Could this card be from Bhutana or Lulama? Or is it from Nancy? The police only found one trainer. Could she have survived? Will I ever be able to truly relax until her bones have been found?

With trembling hands, I open the last envelope. It's A4-sized and out tumbles a magazine. Clipped to the front is a note.

*Dear Anna, we were so shocked to hear what happened
after we left. I thought you'd like to read the article I
wrote. All the best, Katie x*

I flick through the magazine to page 22. There are two
stunning photographs taken by Zak. The first is of a lion, its
head thrown back, mouth open wide. The second is of the
interior of the lodge, along with the far-reaching views
beyond. I shiver. I don't want to read Katie's article. I don't
need to see pictures to recall every last detail of the lodge.
The horrors of our stay are in my head during every waking
and sleeping moment. I stride into the kitchen, press down
the pedal of the rubbish bin and drop both the magazine
and postcard inside. I hope Katie will understand.

Perhaps I will never sleep easily, not until I'm sure that
Nancy is really dead. After all, they conned me once before,
pretending that Clayton was dead. Nancy knew how well
that ruse worked, so maybe she's doing it all over again.

'No,' I tell myself sternly. 'I cannot let my imagination
play cruel tricks on me.'

The doorbell rings. I hurry to the front door and swing it
open. It's Mum.

'You look like you've seen a ghost,' she says, frowning.

'No.' I plaster a smile on my face. 'Just thinking about
what a wonderful day we're going to have.' Strangely,
Nancy's words echo in my head. *Fear is not real. It is simply an
imagined thought as to something that might or might not happen
in the future.*

A LETTER FROM MIRANDA

Thank you very much for reading The Lodge. I set this book in South Africa, which is a country I love and have been lucky enough to visit multiple times. It's a land blessed with breath-taking scenery, extraordinary wildlife and some of the loveliest, most friendly people in the world. I have never felt unsafe on my travels but there is no disputing that South Africa has troubles, including a water shortage and load-shedding (number of hours that electricity is switched off for everybody), and the disparity between the haves and have nots is deeply distressing.

Staying on a game reserve such as the imaginary *Twivali Private Safari Reserve* and spotting the big five is my idea of the perfect holiday. I've visited a handful, and for my family and myself, it is where lifelong memories have been made. Nothing beats stumbling across a family of lions or a baby elephant frolicking in the mud.

Most game reserves put conservation at the heart of what they do. I wanted to highlight the terrible rhinoceros horn poaching that threatens the extinction of these magnificent beasts. There are a number of charities supporting the conservation of rhinos and these include www.rhinos.org and www.savetherhino.org. I am sponsoring a baby white rhino called Shamara who is being cared for at www.therhinoorphanage.org. Please check her out along with her orphan siblings.

I couldn't have written this book without the help of my friend Sarah Campbell-Watts. She knows everything about the intricate workings of African game reserves and kindly agreed to be my first reader. Thank you so much, Sarah! Any mistakes are totally my own. A massive thank you and love to my cousin Chris Silverston, who is the reason I've been able to visit South Africa so many times.

I feel bad portraying game reserves in a negative light, so please remember that this book is a work of fiction! If you get the opportunity to visit one, go for it. I guarantee you'll have one of the best holidays of your life and you'll be supporting the vital tourism industry in South Africa. Drop me a line if you'd like to know where I've stayed.

Once again, everyone at Inkubator Books has been amazing. I have phenomenal support from Brian Lynch, Garret Ryan, Jan Smith, Line Langebek, Stephen Ryan, Claire Milto, Alice Latchford, Elizabeth Bayliss, Ella Medler and the rest of the team. Thank you for everything you do.

I owe so much to the book blogging community who take the time to review my psychological thrillers, share my cover reveals and talk about my books on social media. I would like to name every single book blogger but I worry I might inadvertently leave someone out! You know who you are, and I thank you from the bottom of my heart for sharing your thoughts on my books. Thank you in particular to Carrie Shields (@carriereadsthem_all), Dawn Angels (Psychological Thriller Authors and Readers Unite Facebook Group) and Zooloos Book Tours.

And finally and most importantly, thank you, my lovely reader. I pinch myself every day that I'm a full-time writer and it could never have happened if you didn't choose to read my thrillers. Reviews on Amazon and Goodreads help other people discover my novels, so if you could spend a moment writing an honest review, even if it's just one word, I would be massively grateful.

My warmest wishes,

Miranda

www.mirandarijks.com

ALSO BY MIRANDA RIJKS

<u>Psychological Thrillers</u>

THE VISITORS

I WANT YOU GONE

DESERVE TO DIE

YOU ARE MINE

ROSES ARE RED

THE ARRANGEMENT

THE INFLUENCER

WHAT SHE KNEW

THE ONLY CHILD

THE NEW NEIGHBOUR

THE SECOND WIFE

THE INSOMNIAC

FORGET ME NOT

THE CONCIERGE

THE OTHER MOTHER

THE LODGE

<u>The Dr Pippa Durrant Mystery Series</u>

FATAL FORTUNE

(Book 1)

FATAL FLOWERS

(Book 2)

FATAL FINALE

(Book 3)

Printed in Great Britain
by Amazon

26098101R00158